He hadn't meant to start her tears flowing,

truly had no idea for which reason she cried—she had several. Faced with her tears, he could do nothing but take her in his arms until the sobs subsided.

Longing, deep and intense, washed through him like an ocean wave, threatening to pull him under. He could not succumb. Judith was far too upset, too vulnerable. Even knowing it, he wanted to kiss her tears away, take her to another place where no pain existed, only ecstasy. Duty battled with desire. His wish to comfort argued with his selfish need.

"I truly hate your chain mail," she said. "You keep yourself encased in cold metal."

"Right now you should be thankful for it. 'Tis all that keeps you safe from me."

"What if I do not wish to be safe from you…?"

Dear Reader,

What a perfect time to celebrate history—the eve of a new century. This month we're featuring four terrific romances with awe-inspiring heroes and heroines from days gone by that you'll want to take with you into the *next* century!

Corwin of Lenvil, a protective Saxon knight, is one of those characters. He's the handsome hero in Shari Anton's exciting new medieval novel, *By Queen's Grace,* which is the sequel to *By King's Decree.* Corwin infiltrates a rebel camp in order to rescue a kidnapped royal maiden who long ago broke his heart. There's passion and danger at every turn as the lovely Judith begins to trust in—and fall in love with—Corwin.

In *The Lady and the Outlaw* by DeLoras Scott, the unforgettable, English-bred Antoinette Huntington has a romantic run-in with a rugged outlaw on a train headed to Arizona Territory. In Suzanne Barclay's new medieval tale, *The Champion,* knight Simon of Blackstone will leave you breathless when he returns from the Crusades to right past wrongs. In doing so, he rekindles a love that was lost but not forgotten....

Wolf Heart is the fascinating, timeless hero from *Shawnee Bride* by Elizabeth Lane. He's a white Shawnee warrior who rescues a young woman from certain death, yet must make her his captive. Can the deep love that grows between them transcend the cultural barriers?

Enjoy! And come back again next month for four more choices of the best in historical romance.

Happy holidays,

Tracy Farrell
Senior Editor

BY QUEEN'S GRACE

SHARI ANTON

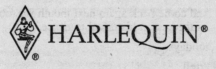

HARLEQUIN®

TORONTO • NEW YORK • LONDON
AMSTERDAM • PARIS • SYDNEY • HAMBURG
STOCKHOLM • ATHENS • TOKYO • MILAN • MADRID
PRAGUE • WARSAW • BUDAPEST • AUCKLAND

ISBN 0-373-29093-4

BY QUEEN'S GRACE

Copyright © 1999 by Sharon Antoniewicz

Visit us at www.romance.net

Printed in U.S.A.

Please address questions and book requests to:
Harlequin Reader Service
U.S.: 3010 Walden Ave., P.O. Box 1325, Buffalo, NY 14269
Canadian: P.O. Box 609, Fort Erie, Ont. L2A 5X3

To the members of
Wisconsin Romance Writers of America.

Your encouragement and continued support
are greatly appreciated.

With special thanks to Carrie Bebris, Susie Just and
Leslie Parker, whose opinions and comments I value.

Chapter One

England, 1109

The heron never knew what hit it.

Poised against the bright blue sky, a peregrine falcon stooped and attacked with swift and fatal accuracy, saving its screech at a successful kill until its prey hung limply from sharp talons. From the meadow below, Corwin of Lenvil watched the young huntress's skill with awe, though not with surprise. Ardith had trained the falcon, and no one in England rivaled his twin sister's talent with hunting birds.

The game bearers rushed off to fetch the heron, pursuing the dogs that marked where the bird had fallen. The falconer whirled the lure to call the peregrine. Corwin shifted in his saddle to fetch a piece of meat, the falcon's reward, from his leather pouch.

"I am nearly out of bait, Gerard. Do you think it safe for us to return to the castle yet?" he teased his brother-by-marriage and hunting partner.

Gerard, Norman baron of the vast fief of Wilmont, tossed back his mane of long blond hair and laughed. The falcon perched on Gerard's thick leather glove flapped her wings in protest of the sharp sound, straining the belled jesses that secured the bird to her master's arm. The highly trained palfrey on which Gerard sat, however, moved not a muscle.

"Safe? Nay," Gerard said. "I shudder to think of what Ardith has planned in retribution for not being allowed to hunt with us. Would that I could stay away until nightfall."

A tempting thought. Corwin couldn't think of anywhere he'd rather be than out hunting with Gerard, especially when they hunted with falcons—a bird a man of Corwin's rank had no right to fly. Few Saxons in Norman-ruled England enjoyed the privileges he did, and at times like this Corwin thanked the fates that his overlord had possessed the good sense to fall in love with and marry his twin sister.

Corwin held the tidbit of meat in his gloved fingers, raised his hand high in the air and whistled thrice, inviting the falcon back to her former perch. "I shall do you a great favor, my lord," he offered. "If I praise this bird to the very heavens, 'twill sweeten Ardith's mood so greatly she may forgive you your folly."

"How good of you, Corwin," Gerard said wryly.

"My pleasure, my lord."

Corwin snatched away the meat an instant before the falcon landed, leading with widespread talons. He tensed his arm to accept her weight, swiftly secured the jesses, then gave her the prize she expected. For so fierce a hunter, she took the meat from his fingers gently—a mark of Ardith's training.

"You might do well to remember that Ardith is none too pleased with you, either," Gerard chided. "She is not happy that you leave on the morrow after so short a visit. Since your father's death, you do not come often enough or stay long enough for her liking."

Since his father's death several months ago, Corwin's

life had changed, not all for the better. He was now the lord of Lenvil, a prosperous manor that had been in his family for generations. While he enjoyed the running of it, he also chafed, at times, at the loss of the luxury to come and go as he pleased.

"Ardith knows I now have Lenvil to oversee, and I have duties to perform in your service. Besides, she will have Bronwyn here with her until after her babe is born. Our sister will surely be more of a comfort to her than I could be."

"She understands why you leave, yet it sits hard with her. Mayhap, after the babe is born, you can return to Wilmont for a fortnight or so."

Corwin heard the command with Gerard's suggestion, and decided he would be happy to comply *after* Ardith gave birth. Until then, he wanted to be as far away from his twin as possible.

The twin link he and Ardith shared could be both a blessing and a curse. It allowed them to feel each other's pain, and had saved both of their lives over the course of the years. The link had weakened as they became adults, and distance proved a buffer. Still, when Ardith had given birth to her first child, he'd *known,* even though he'd been at Lenvil, a full day's ride away from Wilmont. This time, he would be in the far south of England, hundreds of leagues away.

"You have only to send for me and I will come."

Gerard nodded slightly, then turned toward the game bearer who approached him.

"My lord, all but one sack are full," the game bearer announced. "Should one of us return to Wilmont for more?"

Gerard smiled at Corwin. "What say you, Corwin? How long do we wish to delay our return?"

"I say we had best fill the last sack or Ardith will accuse us of being sluggards." He sighed. "Then I suppose we should go back. I still have several things to do before I leave on the morn."

Twice more they unleashed their falcons. Gerard's took down another heron. Corwin claimed the better prize of a swan. He hated to see the hunt end, but knew it must. Along with Gerard, Corwin hooded his falcon and turned his palfrey toward Wilmont.

The gates stood open, as was usual during daylight hours, allowing the hunting party to pass through without hindrance into the bailey. Game bearers headed for the kitchen; stable lads rushed forward to take charge of the horses. Tenants, merchants and servants bustled about the bailey, going about their work or errands.

As Corwin dismounted, he glanced toward the stables, and the four wagons waiting nearby. One had been packed with tents and provisions for his week-long journey; the others would be loaded with planks, shingles and nails.

On the morn, along with six mounted guards and the wagons' drivers, he would leave for Cotswold, a manor in southern England near Romsey. In Romsey, he would hire the carpenters necessary to make the improvements Gerard had in mind for the estate. That Gerard had asked him to captain the entourage to Cotswold was a favor to Corwin, giving him an excuse to be far from Wilmont for several weeks. The added responsibility of hiring the carpenters and directing their labors was a mark of Gerard's trust—a trust Corwin had earned several times over, both as a friend and knight. A trust he'd tested sorely only once, for Ardith's sake.

"'Twould seem the loading is nearly completed," Gerard commented.

"I will inspect them after I see to the falcon," he said,

hoping the wagons passed his inspection. He wanted nothing to go wrong on this journey, not so much as a shifted plank to unbalance a wagon and tip it off the road.

Corwin followed Gerard and the hunting hounds up the outside stairs that led to the stone keep's second floor, then through the oak doors that opened into the great hall.

The servants had begun to prepare for the noon meal. Trestle tables were being set up in rows down the length of the hall. Soon serving wenches would bring out the bread trenchers upon which to place food and cups to hold ale. Only those who ate at the high table—the lord's family and guests—would eat off of clay plates and drink wine from goblets. Corwin considered himself honored to take his meals here as family.

Indeed, he felt as at home at Wilmont as at Lenvil. As a boy, he'd spent many months each year at the home of his overlord—had learned to read and write, to skillfully wield a sword and lance, and had become fast friends with Gerard and his brothers.

In Gerard's wake, Corwin crossed the hall, kicking up the scent of rosemary from the recently changed rushes. At the far end of the hall, beyond the dais, he unwrapped the jesses from his arm and reluctantly returned the falcon to her perch among her fellow hunters.

Corwin ran a finger down the falcon's softly feathered chest, feeling the taut power in the beautiful, deadly predator. He wanted her as any man who appreciates fine hunting birds would want her.

At Lenvil, Corwin kept several hawks, good hunters all, his favorites being a lovely goshawk and a daring little kestrel. This peregrine would be a pleasure to own, a joy to fly whenever he pleased. Though he'd become a landed knight, a warrior whose skills rivaled nearly all but Gerard's, a man whose education far surpassed that of most Normans, he wasn't of noble birth.

An unfair restriction, in his opinion, but one King Henry refused to consider changing. Indeed, the king was most adamant about enforcing the Forest Laws. Poachers weren't tolerated in the king's woodlands. Bringing down a deer could mean a hunter's death. Henry grudgingly allowed his nobles to hunt smaller game. Gerard, thankfully, allowed his landed knights to hunt within the boundaries of their holdings—but held to the restrictions on hunting birds.

Once more Corwin stroked the falcon's chest, knowing that dwelling on the unfairness of the law served no purpose. There were simply some things he couldn't have, rights he would never obtain, all because he'd been born to the wrong family.

Gerard interrupted Corwin's musings. "While you inspect the wagons, I will go up and see how Ardith fares."

"I fare just fine." Her voice came from the bottom of the stairway that led up to the family chambers.

For Corwin, looking at his well-loved sister was almost like looking into a silvered glass. Though his hair was colored a more earthy shade of brown than hers, they shared the same azure-blue eyes. In a generously cut gown of deep blue, having left off her veil and circlet to allow her plaited hair to swing behind her, Ardith waddled toward him.

"Since the two of you went off hunting and left me here on my own," she said in a disgruntled tone, "I put the time to use by writing a note to Judith. Corwin, would you do me the favor of delivering it?"

Corwin hoped his shock didn't show as he took the note from Ardith's hand, wanting to say her nay but unable to come up with a good excuse to deny her request. She wouldn't understand his reluctance to stop at Romsey Abbey. Or to see her friend Judith.

Only once had Corwin crossed Gerard. Ardith had been desperate to see a midwife-nun at Romsey Abbey and, even while knowing Gerard would be livid, Corwin had taken her. Gerard *had* been angry, had blustered and handed down assorted punishments. Still, Corwin felt no remorse and would do it all over again if the need arose.

Unfortunately, at Romsey Abbey he'd also met Judith Canmore, a royal heiress, a niece of both Queen Matilda of England and King Alexander of Scotland. Someday she would leave the cloister to marry, but until then served as companion to Matilda whenever the queen made one of her frequent retreats to Romsey. Judith had been kind to Ardith and the two had become friends. Judith's favor, however, didn't extend to him.

Well, he didn't have to put the letter into Judith's hand, just give it to whoever answered his knock on the abbey's door.

"'Twould be my pleasure," Corwin finally answered, forcing a smile.

Ardith answered his smile with a beaming grin. "When you return, you will have to tell me if Judith has changed. By now, I imagine she has grown into a beautiful young woman."

Three years had passed since their meeting, and Judith probably had blossomed from a winsome girl to a beautiful woman, but Corwin was loathe to set eyes on her. The last thing he wanted to do was admire Judith's soft, dove-gray eyes and shiny, sable-brown hair. Wonder what curves hid beneath her concealing robe. Long to taste the adorable bow of her lips, only to have her turn up her pert royal nose at him—again.

'Twas one of the few times his lack of rank had been tossed in his face so forcefully, and it wasn't an experience he cared to relive.

Judith rolled up the sleeves of her black robe, preparing to scrub the pots the nuns had used to cook the noon meal. Her punishment could have been worse, but she knew Abbess Christina chose this particular chore knowing how much Judith disliked it.

The other nuns had finished their after-meal tasks and left the kitchen. All but Sister Mary Margaret, who watched over Judith to ensure a thorough cleansing of the pots.

"Truly, Sister, you need not stay," Judith said, smiling at the frown on the nun's age-wrinkled, kindly face. "I can manage on my own."

"And have the abbess learn that I shirked my duty? I think not. She will have *me* scrubbing those pots. What did you do this time?"

Judith slid the first of many pots into the tub of water and began scrubbing, recalling the heated disagreement that had ended with Judith nearly in tears and the abbess red in the face. "I refused the abbess's entreaty to take the veil."

"You have done so before without drawing punishment."

True, but she'd never before been so vehement, or used disrespectful language. "Aye, well, I fear I refused a bit too pointedly and loudly this time."

"If the queen were here—"

"But she is not, so cannot intercede for me. So, I scrub pots."

Queen Matilda had been called back to London from her latest retreat at Romsey Abbey, to rule the kingdom while King Henry went off to see to some business or another in Normandy. As always, after one of Matilda's prolonged visits to the abbey, the abbess again tried to convince Judith to take the veil. Again Judith refused.

Sister Mary Margaret pulled up a stool and eased her short, plump body down on it. "You could do worse than to take the veil, you know. A woman of your rank could move high in the Church.''

For seven years Judith had lived among the nuns at Romsey Abbey and been content for the most part. These days, however, when she knelt down to pray—which happened often in a nun's day—she prayed for deliverance from another seven years. She shuddered at the thought. Madness would overtake her long before then.

Lately, contentment had been elusive. More often her discontent flared over the simplest things, like the black color of her robe or the lack of a particular seasoning in the stew.

'Twas time to make another appeal to her family, remind them she'd long ago reached marriageable age. Prod them into rescuing her from her ordeal. Not to her parents—they would bow to any royal edict. Uncle Alexander would only caution patience, if he took note of her plea at all.

Best to seek aid from Aunt Matilda, who might listen, who would best understand her wish to be free of Christina's heavy-handed persuasion to take the veil. Except it could be months before Matilda returned.

"I have no wish to rise high in the Church," Judith said, putting the clean pot aside and grabbing the next dirty one. "Christina wants me to take her place as abbess, just as she once tried to convince Matilda to do the same, before Henry came to Matilda's rescue."

A rare, small smile graced the nun's face. "I remember their disputes well. I have since thought that if Matilda had listened to the abbess and accepted, she might have spared herself much heartache."

Heartache, aye. King Henry wasn't the most attentive or faithful of husbands. Sweet heaven, the man had at least a dozen bastards scattered about the kingdom. Yet Matilda often said that if she had to do it all over again, she'd make the same decisions.

"Matilda has known heartache, but she dwells on her joys," Judith said. "Her two children. The king's trust in her to rule in his stead when he is away. Her ability to fund projects and charitable acts dear to her heart. She enjoys being queen, and I think her a good one. Someday, I should like to do as she does."

Sister Mary Margaret huffed. "Then you may as well become an abbess. The queen spends more time here than in London, to escape her faithless husband."

Judith couldn't argue the point. Matilda retreated to Romsey as often as she could. Yet her marriage wasn't all bad. Henry was fond of his wife, and beyond his fickle ways, treated her with a measure of respect. Matilda, on the other hand, loved her husband with her whole heart.

Judith never tired of hearing the romantic story of their meeting, of how dashing Prince Henry had visited the abbey with a friend, of how he'd asked to pay his respects to the Saxon princess who resided there. Matilda's eyes would grow misty when she spoke of Henry's charm, of how he'd taken her heart with him when he left. Of how he returned, time and again, and finally asked her to be his queen.

Matilda held no illusions about her marriage. She knew it to be an astute move on Henry's part, uniting the noble houses of England and Scotland. Judith held no illusions, either. Someday her hand would be granted to a man with whom one of the royal houses wished to solidify an alliance. She could only hope for marriage to a man she could not only like but love, and who might love her in return.

"Not all husbands are faithless," Judith finally said.

"Mayhap not, but most men worthy of a wife of your rank think nothing of keeping a mistress or two. Then the wife becomes unhappy and turns shrewish. Best to avoid the unpleasantness altogether.''

Not all noble marriages turned sour. She had only to look to her friend Ardith, a Saxon lady who'd married Gerard, a powerful Norman baron, and was happy beyond belief. ''Could not a woman find happiness in her children?'' she asked, citing the Church's only acceptable excuse for marriage and consummation.

Sister Mary Margaret shook her head. ''Mayhap. But to have children, one must submit to a man's base urges and then give birth. I doubt children are worth suffering the pain of either the consummation or the birthing.'' The nun rose from her stool, her face flushed from discussing so worldly a subject. '''Tis overwarm in here. I believe I shall go out for a breath of air. Keep scrubbing.''

Judith scrubbed, not only to hurry the chore along, but to take her mind off submitting. It didn't work. It might have if talk of urges and submitting didn't bring to mind the face of one particular man. The male who had first, and last, aroused her curiosity and stirred her urges.

Corwin of Lenvil.

Sweet heaven, she hadn't seen Corwin in three years, yet could recall his startling blue eyes, a body wide at the shoulders and narrow at the waist, a smile that warmed her from head to toe.

Maybe, at the age of ten and five, she'd simply been ripe to feel those urges. Maybe she recalled Corwin's handsome face so vividly because Ardith frequently mentioned him in her letters. Unfortunately, she also remembered him because Corwin had shown her kindness and she'd repaid him with meanness.

Corwin had brought Ardith to Romsey, to see a nun whose skill as a midwife was unequaled. Poor Ardith had been so upset, and Corwin...well, Judith had never seen the like. Imagine a brother who so cared for his sister that he would risk the wrath of a baron to ease her mind.

She'd thought Corwin courageous as well as handsome, and her unfettered interest in the man had been so apparent that Matilda noticed and issued a warning.

"You must not encourage his attention," Matilda had said. "Corwin is a nice young man, but has neither the rank nor wealth to play suitor to a royal heiress."

Thoroughly disappointed, Judith had snubbed him the next time she'd seen him. Even now, after all this time, she felt a twinge of remorse for her crass behavior, and a greater twitch of embarrassment for her arrogance in assuming Corwin had given any thought to becoming her suitor.

He certainly hadn't pursued the matter. He'd never returned to the abbey to see her. Even if he'd tried, Abbess Christina or Queen Matilda would have turned him away.

Still, meeting Corwin had been a good thing. She'd learned for certain she wasn't suited to be a nun. Not that she'd harbored much doubt before then, but she certainly couldn't imagine any nun experiencing the tingles of awareness she'd felt when near Corwin.

The knowledge that she wasn't immune to a man's charm gave her a measure of confidence when arguing with Abbess Christina about taking vows.

Judith grabbed the biggest and heaviest of the iron kettles. She slid it gently into the tub, but managed to create a wave of water that splashed up and soaked the front of her robe.

Frustrated, Judith rolled down her sleeves and headed for the courtyard just beyond the kitchen door. High, gray stone walls loomed before her, blocking out nearly all of the sunshine that struggled to light the small courtyard. Sister Mary Margaret sat on one of the benches, her eyes closed.

Other nuns, also silent, were scattered about on others. A few walked about slowly, talking quietly to companions, making hardly a rustle in the never-ending peace.

No male ever intruded on this inner courtyard, not even the traveling priest who would say Mass in the abbey's chapel on the morn. Joy and laughter weren't allowed entry, either. Only when Matilda was in residence, and then only in the privacy of the queen's chamber could Judith laugh without censure.

Many of the nuns, like Sister Mary Margaret, had chosen this life and were content. But there was unhappiness here, too, among the daughters of noble houses who'd been given to the Church as children and had no hope of escape. The thought of being trapped here forever... Judith shook off the dire thought, knowing it would never happen. Someday she would leave this place, and doubted she would ever return. If she did, it wouldn't be by choice.

'Twas the quiet—the endless drone of days without change or color or laughter—that was driving her witless, she decided. That and the ceaseless pressure from the abbess. 'Twas beyond time to get out, to end these useless bouts of self-pity, to stop waiting for a prince to come to Romsey Abbey as Prince Henry had come for Matilda. Maybe 'twas time she went in search of her own prince.

With that intriguing thought in mind, Judith returned to the kitchen, rolled up her sleeves and went back to her pots.

If her fate in this world was to marry a high-ranking noble, then the best chance to meet her future husband was at court. If she wrote to Matilda and asked if she could come, would her aunt allow it? Perhaps. Judith had been to court before, though not in a long time. The prospect brightened her mood.

Getting such a letter out of the abbey would prove a challenge. The abbess would throw a fit if she learned of

Judith's plotting. Maybe the visiting priest would be willing
to deliver her letter, providing he was headed toward London.

Even if she didn't find her very own prince at court, once
there, if she begged the queen's grace, she might be able
to stay and not return to Romsey Abbey.

And she would never, ever, be forced to scrub another
pot.

Chapter Two

The crystal blue sky and early summer sun had called hard to Judith. Tagging along on an outing to gather medicinal plants, to escape the abbey's gloom for a morning, had seemed such a good idea. Until now.

Judith held back a strong curse directed both at the ruffian intent on kidnapping her and at herself for putting a group of innocent nuns in danger. If she'd remained in her cell, patiently waiting for an answer from Matilda, she wouldn't now be in this dire fix.

From atop his horse, an older man—obviously the leader—stretched out his hand toward her. "You have naught to fear, Lady Judith, if you will just come quiet like," he said.

Judith glared at the man, who shifted in his saddle, fully expecting her to relent. He appeared to be about her father's age, slightly grayed and life worn, sporting a full, shaggy beard. A warrior still, by the hard-muscled look of him. A Saxon, by the sound of him.

Several paces down the road, two young men, also mounted on fine steeds, held Sister Mary Margaret and four other nuns—who huddled together and prayed for deliverance—at bay.

If she fought, if she ran, would the ruffians harm her companions? Judith didn't think so. The men risked forfeiting their immortal souls if they harmed the nuns. Besides, 'twas she the brigands had come for. They'd singled her out, knowing her identity.

Sweet heaven, she'd been foolish to put herself at risk. She'd been warned of the dangers a royal heiress faced from those who would use her for their own gain. But she'd been outside of the abbey walls many times over the past years and nothing untoward had ever happened.

"What do you want of me?" she asked, her voice amazingly steady considering how her hands shook, hidden within the sleeves of her robe.

To her surprise the ruffian smiled at her. Almost tenderly.

"You have a destiny to fulfill, lass," he said. "We have not the time for explanations, but know that you will want for no comfort or proper deference."

Judith summoned every ounce of royal blood in her veins and tilted her chin higher. "'Tis a strange deference you show me, brigand. If you truly wish to give me my due, be gone!"

His smile disappeared. "I cannot, my lady. I have my orders. 'Tis for you to decide to come quietly or by force."

"By whose orders?"

"My lord's, soon to be yours, too." He stretched out a hand. "Come, my lady. We must be off."

So, some noble thought to force her into marriage to raise his standing at court, did he? 'Twas not an unheard-of practice. Judith had just never thought it could happen to her. Still wouldn't happen, if she could help it.

She slid her hands from her sleeves. "You may tell your *lord* to go straight to hell!"

She rushed the horse, slapping it hard on the rump. The brigand swore as his mount reared, but Judith didn't stop to admire her handiwork. Skirts hiked nearly to her knees, she bolted into the woods.

"Oswuld! Duncan! Catch her!" the man called out.

She didn't give a thought to being quiet about her flight, just to putting distance between herself and the ruffians. Twigs snapped beneath her booted feet. Tree limbs reached out to tear her black robe. Still she ran, leaping over logs and winding among the trees, in a headlong rush for a spot where she knew she could hide in thick underbrush.

If she lost her pursuers, she could later regain the road and make a dash for the safe haven of the abbey, the same abbey she'd been thinking of as a prison for so many weeks now. Amazing how one's view of the world could change so quickly.

Judith gave a brief thought to her companions and prayed that they would remain safe. She would have the ruffian leader's head on a pike, hoisted high over the abbey's door, if he harmed one hair on Sister Mary Margaret's head.

Over the noise of her panting she could now hear the two men who gave chase. They shouted back and forth at each other, directing the search. One even had the gall to call out to her, suggesting she be sensible and halt her foolish flight. She couldn't hope to escape them, he taunted.

Despite the ache in her chest and the pain in her legs, Judith quickened her pace. She ducked under a stout oak branch and headed down the steep hill beyond. She fell at the bottom and landed hard on the forest floor.

"I see her, Duncan! This way!"

Judith scrambled to her feet. She didn't look back. If she could make it over the next hill, she would be safe.

"To your left, Oswuld! Keep on her heels!"

Up she ran, slipping on the long grass, her entire being focused on the top of the rise. Sheer force of will got her over. Only a few yards off stood her refuge—a fallen oak, nearly hollow, smothered by vines and guarded by brambles. Quickly, ignoring scrapes and pricks, Judith crawled into the sanctuary of the oak and curled up as small as she could.

She buried her face in her robe to muffle her panting. Mercy, she hadn't run so hard since her early youth. She longed to draw a deep, refreshing breath, but didn't dare. From the rustling sounds, she could tell that the men had reached the top of the rise.

They came to a halt. Judith could almost feel their searching eyes pass over her hiding place, looking for some sign of her.

"Duncan?"

Silence stretched into eternity.

"This way, I think," he finally answered. "Aye, look here, a piece of her robe."

Judith closed her eyes and silently cursed.

The men resumed the chase, thundering past her hiding place in the direction they thought she'd run.

Acute relief trembled through her limbs. She'd done it. She was safe. Her heart still pounded, but it would calm. The fear she'd masked with anger began to abate.

The men would search for a while yet, but unable to find her, would return to their leader and report failure. By then, she'd be well on her way to the abbey. Until she was sure the men were gone, however, she would remain where she was, shooing away the bugs that made the rotted log their home, picking at the burrs that clung to her torn robe.

She wrinkled her nose against the stench of her nest. She could bear it, having no choice.

Abbess Christina was going to have a fit. Over the torn robe. Over her leaving the abbey without permission and then wandering so far away. Punishment, this time, would involve far harsher measures than scrubbing pots. But for all the abbess would bluster, she would also know how to proceed. These ruffians must be caught and dealt with before they could do further mischief.

Judith jumped when a thump reverberated through the log, as though something had hit it. A squirrel? Rabbit? An animal with sharper teeth?

"You might as well come out, my lady," said a voice she now recognized as Duncan's. "I would as soon not come in to drag you out."

Nay! This couldn't be! How had they found her? Why hadn't she heard them circle back? None of the answers mattered, for obviously they'd retraced their steps and found her hiding place. Or were they guessing? She didn't move.

Thump.

"Have a care with those stones, Duncan," Oswuld said. "If you hurt her…"

"I will not hurt the lady. Unless, of course, she makes me crawl through those brambles to drag her out of that log. What say you, Princess? Do you come out or must I come in?"

Whether they were sure of where she hid or not, they wouldn't leave without checking, and she'd be found. Judith sighed.

Thump. Thump.

Judith swatted at several agitated bugs. "Stop that!" she shouted, and crawled out of the log. She stopped short of wading through the brambles as she faced her tormentors.

The ruffian with the smug grin on his face had to be Duncan. He tossed several stones on the ground and dusted off his hands. The other, a lad barely grown into his beard, must be Oswuld. Oswuld looked malleable, Duncan no less than stubborn, but she wouldn't know until she tried.

"Could we come to a bargain?" she asked.

Both men caught her meaning and shook their heads. She tried again.

"You know who I am, so you must know that my uncle Alexander and aunt Matilda have the wealth of entire kingdoms at their disposal. Return me to the safety of the abbey and I will see you are both richly rewarded."

Oddly enough, 'twas Duncan who seemed to consider her offer. Oswuld didn't.

"We have our duty, my lady," the younger man said. "Besides, wealth would do neither Duncan nor me any good if my father hunted us down and carved out our hearts, now, would it?"

"Your father?"

"Thurkill, the man whose horse you pushed out of your way. He will not forgive you that for a long while, I wager."

Judith didn't care if Thurkill ever forgave her, and didn't plan to be in his company long enough to find out. Somehow, she must convince these two men to let her go, or escape them once more. Judith plowed through the brambles, this time feeling every prick and scrape. The men moved forward as she came out of the patch, one on each side of her.

"What you do is unlawful," she said.

"And for the greater good of England," Duncan stated with a gleam of righteousness in his eyes. He grabbed her elbow and steered her back toward the road.

She jerked away. "I fail to understand how abducting me can possibly benefit the kingdom!"

"Well, you see, my lady, we—"

Oswuld interrupted, warning, "Duncan, that is a tale for my father to tell."

Duncan took the rebuke with little grace, but said no more.

During the long walk back to the road, Judith looked for opportunities to escape. But with both men so close, she didn't find one.

Thurkill waited where she'd left him, as did everyone else. The nuns still huddled together, unharmed.

"Took you long enough," Thurkill complained.

Oswuld smiled. "She is a smart one, Father. Nearly gave us the slip, she did."

Mercy, Oswuld sounded proud of her!

Duncan nodded in agreement, then grumbled, "Aye, she did. Has a mouth on her, too."

Judith bristled, but kept her mouth closed.

"She can complain all she wishes and it will not change a thing. Let us be off," Thurkill said.

The dread returned, with full and shattering force. These men were truly about to take her away. She'd wanted to leave behind the bleakness of the abbey, but not as someone's prisoner.

"I beg you to reconsider, Thurkill," she said, her voice shaking, tears far too close to the surface. "Have you no mercy in your heart?"

"None. Hand her up."

Thurkill reached out a hand. Duncan and Oswuld grabbed her arms.

Judith screamed.

The woman's first scream rang with anger, the second revealed her fear.

Or so Corwin judged from the distant sounds—too far away to be sure and too close to ignore.

He reined in his horse and signaled the company behind him to halt. Sitting quietly, resting his gauntlet-covered hands on his thighs, he tilted his head to listen. No more screams—only the rustling of a summer breeze through the surrounding woodland and the shuffling of soldiers' feet on the dusty road.

William rode up beside him, with his sword already drawn. "Trouble ahead?"

"I hope not," Corwin answered, but he wouldn't be amazed if he found trouble, or at the least suffered another delay. The journey from Wilmont to Cotswold should have taken a sennight to complete, but had now dragged out to nearly a fortnight. A broken wagon axle. A horse gone lame. A nasty illness bringing most of the men low for days. The weather. All had conspired against him.

At least he'd been able to find a highly skilled carpenter in Romsey who, along with his assistants, now walked at the end of the entourage. The man could do with wood what a sculptor could do with clay or stone. Gerard was sure to be pleased with the man's work.

Now, so near to Romsey Abbey, another delay loomed.

He must investigate, of course, not so much to aid a woman in trouble as to ensure no harm threatened the company of men and wagons in his charge.

Corwin turned in the saddle and called to Geoffrey, "William and I will go ahead and see what is happening. Keep the company here until we return."

Geoffrey nodded.

Corwin nudged his horse up the road, setting a cautious pace, hoping that whatever situation lay ahead could be resolved quickly. He wanted to deliver his sister's letter to Romsey Abbey, then be off to Cotswold. If he pushed the company, he could reach the manor by nightfall.

He crested the hill to see a group of five nuns. One of them, the shortest, seemed to be sobbing into her hands. The others hovered over her as if comforting her.

William sighed. "Only nuns," he said, sheathing his sword.

"Aye, nuns," Corwin echoed.

To his chagrin, he wondered if one of the taller black-robed women might be Judith. Likely not, because all of them wore veils, and unless her circumstances had changed drastically, Judith wouldn't be veiled.

He'd thought of Judith too many times over the past few days, probably because of the letter he carried tucked securely between his chain mail and the padded gambeson beneath. Often, he'd envisioned her as the heart-faced, sweet-voiced maiden who'd been so kind to Ardith, whose dove-gray eyes had sparkled with interest in him. Then he would recall their last encounter—Judith's nose high in the air, firmly declaring him unworthy of her notice.

His embarrassment had stung hard, still rankled, even though he knew she'd been right. He might be Saxon, as was Judith. He might be an excellent warrior and a loyal servant of his lord, a man of good family and honorable reputation. Nothing, however, could change the fact that Judith was of royal birth and he wasn't.

Truly, he had no wish to see Judith Canmore again, not even to confirm if she'd blossomed from an adorable girl into a beautiful woman.

Corwin urged his horse to a faster pace, wondering what had made one of the nuns scream. Near them, several baskets lined the side of the road. A few were tipped over, the plants the nuns had been gathering strewn about. Obviously, something had caused one of them a fright, but he sensed no danger now.

As he and William approached, the nuns turned to look. Their expressions of stark fear caused him to slow again. He'd expect wariness—but fear?

True, he and William probably seemed fearsome, clad in chain mail and looking the worse for their troubled journey. To ease the nun's minds, he slowed his horse to a walk.

"Hail, good sisters," he called out. "Can we be of aid?"

The nuns looked from one to the other, still fearful of his intent. Then the one who'd been sobbing, her age-weathered face red and wet, held up a halting hand. Corwin honored her request for distance.

"We mean you no harm, Sister." Corwin dismounted and tossed his horse's reins to William. He held out his hands, palms up, in a gesture of peace. "We heard your screams. Are you in need of our help?"

"You are not one of *them?*"

Them?

"I am Corwin of Lenvil, knight of Wilmont, currently escorting a company of men and supplies to Cotswold." He smiled, hoping to ease her further. "Had I not come upon you on the road, we might have met within the next hour, for I intended to stop at Romsey Abbey. My men and I can escort you back there, if you wish."

The nuns bent toward each other, conferring, deciding on his trustworthiness, most likely. Soon their heads bobbed in agreement and the little wizened nun came bustling toward him. Her expression changed from fearful to merely guarded.

"I believe I have heard of you, Corwin of Lenvil," she said. "Your sister is Ardith of Wilmont, a friend of both Queen Matilda and Judith Canmore, is she not?"

"You have the right of it, Sister."

The nun glanced at the road behind him. "Have you many men with you?"

Thinking he understood her continued wariness, he shook his head. "Not so many, and good men all. You and your companions need not fear to be among them, Sister."

She dismissed his assurances with a wave of her hand. "I do not fear your men. I had only hoped…oh, dear." The nun looked both disappointed and confused for a moment, then continued. "We must return to the abbey to summon the sheriff. If you would be so kind as to let us ride in one of your wagons, we would be most grateful."

Wondering why the nun felt the need to summon the sheriff, Corwin took in the scene before him, paying closer attention. This time, he saw the fresh hoofprints from several horses.

"What happened here, Sister?"

"We were accosted by a group of ruffians." She went so pale Corwin thought she might faint. "They...they took Judith."

Corwin knew only one woman named Judith. As much as he hoped the nun referred to some other, he knew better. Still, he asked, "Judith Canmore? Those were her screams I heard?"

"Aye." Tears flowed freely down her wrinkled cheeks. "She tried to run away, but the men caught her."

Corwin could honestly say he knew what terror Judith must be feeling. When his twin had suffered being kidnapped, their link had flared. He'd felt Ardith's horror and fear, making his hands tremble and his brow sweat.

What he'd done then for Ardith he must do now for Judith. Effect a rescue. All manner of questions begged answers, but he asked only the important ones.

"How many men?"

"Three."

"All mounted? All armed?"

"Aye, and all Saxons."

The revelation didn't surprise him. Most of the brigands who roamed the roads were disgruntled or disavowed Saxons, keeping themselves alive by committing theft.

"They took the road?"

She nodded.

Corwin glanced up the road, then chided himself for

looking for a plume of dust. There wouldn't be one. The brigands had a good lead on him, but if he hurried while the trail was still fresh, he could catch up with them quickly.

Or was he moving too fast? If the queen's guards…nay, Matilda must not be in residence or the nun would be inclined to send the guards after Judith, not the sheriff.

"Was Judith hurt?" he asked.

Distressed, the nun crossed herself. "Her…her robe was torn. I fear the men who chased her did not treat her gently."

Resigned to the need for haste, Corwin turned to William. "Bring the wagons up and take the good sisters to the abbey. Have the abbess summon the sheriff."

William raised a surprised eyebrow. "You mean to go after them alone? Let me accompany you."

Corwin swung up into his saddle. "There are only three men. With luck I can have Judith back to the abbey within a few hours at most. If I do not return by morn, take the company on to Cotswold. I will join you there as soon as I am able."

He felt a gentle hand on his calf.

"We will pray. God go with you," the nun said.

Corwin reached down and covered her hand with his own. "Your prayers are most welcome. Is there aught else I should know?"

She was silent a moment, then said softly. "'Twas not happenstance the brigands took the unveiled one among us. They knew who Judith Canmore was and meant to have her."

He'd never doubted it. Not for one moment had he thought that a group of brigands had happened upon the nuns and decided to take the unveiled one among them for sport.

Corwin urged his horse forward, his ire rising with the horse's increasing speed. What the devil had Judith been doing out here, so far from the abbey, without a guard? Surely she knew of the dangers she faced if caught outside the abbey walls. The woman should know better than to be wandering about.

Judith certainly hadn't been given permission to leave the abbey, of that he was sure. Being of royal family herself, having had the duty of caring for Matilda as a young woman, Abbess Christina knew well the dangers and wouldn't allow Judith to leave the cloister without protection.

Judith had sneaked out disregarding not only her own safety but that of the nuns. Thoughtless of her. Irresponsible.

The tracks Corwin followed came to an abrupt end. The brigands had left the road and taken to the woodland. He entered the forest where the hoofprints ended, where the brush had been disturbed. A few feet off the road, he stopped to pick up a small piece of roughly woven wool. A piece of Judith's black robe.

Corwin rubbed it between his fingers, wondering if she'd purposely dropped it for someone to find or if it had simply torn loose.

He shouldn't have to chase after her. She needn't now be in the hands of rough men. This whole incident would have been avoided if Judith had simply used her sense and remained where she belonged.

Corwin was in the mood to tell her so.

First, however, he had to find her.

Chapter Three

Judith's hope for an immediate rescue dimmed along with the fading day. Thurkill obviously knew this area well. They'd long since left the road and ridden swiftly through the woodland, at times on trails and others not. Judith doubted that even a skilled tracker could find her now.

With no rescue imminent, she must devise her own escape. She prayed for an opportunity to arise soon, at a place where she might find aid, giving her a chance at success.

Heedless of her discomfort, Thurkill had pressed hard all day. They'd stopped only once for a brief rest and a meager meal. Her backside had gone numb from the constant abuse of the horse's rough gait. Her hands and arms grew weary from holding tight to Thurkill's leather hauberk to prevent herself from falling off.

A grunt escaped her lips when the horse stopped suddenly, tossing her forward against Thurkill's back.

"We will camp here for the night," he said. "Slide off, my lady."

Judith didn't hide her anger. "I do not think I can. I have no legs. For one who promised me every comfort, you do a miserable job of providing it."

"We will find you your own horse soon."

The prospect thrilled her, for with her own horse the odds for a successful escape rose.

Duncan helped her down. Her hands pressed to her lower back, Judith hobbled over to a nearby log and eased her sore, weary body onto it.

Thurkill had chosen a small clearing in which to spend the night. The men set about their chores. Thurkill took the horses to water in a nearby babbling stream, Oswuld gathered wood for a fire, Duncan set out rabbit snares.

"You should get up and walk about, my lady," Oswuld told her. "You will find your legs sooner."

Judith glared at him until he turned red and walked away. She wasn't about to move until she was sure she could walk about without falling on her face. She'd suffered quite enough indignities today and refused to suffer more.

Mercy, but she was tired. Beyond the physical pains, she'd also waged a heady battle with her emotions. She'd bounced from anger to frustration to fear far too many times today.

When the nagging pain in her thighs could no longer be ignored, she took Oswuld's advice. If she didn't walk, she would stiffen to stone.

Judith paced in front of the log, working out the stiffness and knots in her body. She cursed her idiocy, wondered how she could find her way back to the abbey, and said another prayer for the sheriff to come quickly.

Duncan returned with two rabbits dangling from his hand. Thurkill returned from caring for the horses. The evening meal wasn't long off now. For tonight, she was stuck here.

Back at the abbey, the nuns would be sitting down at the trestle tables in the refectory. They would give thanks for their food, then, in silence, eat what was put before them. Had Sister Mary Margaret returned safely to the abbey?

Had the abbess sent for the sheriff? Was anyone looking for her? Did anyone care enough to miss her?

Judith shook her head to clear the maudlin thoughts.

"A bite of bread, my lady?" Oswuld asked.

Oswuld's courtesy had her bristling once more. She took the crust of brown bread and ate it without thanking him. Just because he strove to be polite didn't mean she must also put on her manners. She would never forgive Oswuld his part in her capture, nor did one trade pleasantries with the likes of brigands.

"Mayhap a walk to the stream to wash away the road dust would suit you," he suggested, waving a hand toward the stream. "I will take you down, if you wish."

"I *wish* to return to the abbey where I might have a long, hot bath and clean, unripped garments!"

Oswuld sighed in exasperation. Judith didn't sympathize.

"I fear the stream is all I can offer, my lady. Do you wish to go or not?"

She did, and led the way.

"Guard her close, son," Thurkill called out from across the clearing, where he tended the cooking rabbits.

Oswuld nodded, not losing stride.

"Guard me close, he says," Judith complained. "Where does your father think I am going, I wonder? He batters me all the day long to the point of immovable joints, then worries that I might run away."

"He takes his duty and your care to heart, Lady Judith. Truly, none of us wish you to come to any harm."

She turned on him. "No harm? Every muscle in my body screams for mercy. The skirt of my robe is tattered beyond repair. I have been chased through brambles and frightened nearly witless, thanks to your nefarious band. You snatched me from the safety of the abbey and are taking me to…" Her voice caught. She took a deep breath and cleared her throat before she continued, "...I know not where. Think on all you have put me through today and tell me again that you mean me no harm."

He did think, for just a moment, his mouth curving into a frown. Then he shook off his thoughts and had the gall to say, "All will be well, Lady Judith. You will see."

She tossed up her hands in frustration and took the last steps to the stream. A splash of cold water drew the heat from her face but did nothing to ease her upset. Oswuld allowed her a moment of privacy to care for bodily necessities before they returned to the campsite.

The men sat near the fire, watching the roasting rabbits turn brown. Oswuld guided her to a nearby boulder, where she perched to wait for her share of the meal. Her stomach grumbled loudly, but no one paid it any heed. Mercy, the meat was taking a long time to cook. She dragged her attention away from the juice that dripped and hissed in the fire.

"You owe me an explanation, Thurkill," she said.

Scrunched down beside the fire, Thurkill gave the rabbit another turn before answering. "I do at that, Lady Judith, and I suppose now is as good a time as any to give it." He stood and scratched at his beard. "Where to start?"

"You might begin with why I have been abducted."

Thurkill smiled. "To make you our queen, of course."

"What?" she blurted out.

"You find that hard to believe?"

"'Tis possibly the most ridiculous thing I have ever heard!" she said, voicing her immediate reaction.

"But true, I promise you."

Judith opened her mouth to protest, but closed it again. Her reasoning simply wasn't keeping up with this absurd conversation. A queen, indeed! She thought back on all of the assumptions she'd made today about these men and their purpose. Obviously, she'd missed some vital link in her conclusions.

"Queen of what?" she couldn't help but ask.

"England."

She leaned forward. "England already has a queen—my aunt Matilda."

"Matilda will no longer be queen when Henry is no longer king. His reign will end soon if all goes well."

Judith trembled with horror. Thurkill calmly, with a smile on his face, spoke treason.

She could manage no more than a choked whisper. "You intend to displace King Henry."

"And put a Saxon on the throne." Thurkill's smile faded. "These Normans have ruled our land far too long. We intend to send them all back to Normandy and reclaim the lands they stole from us at the Conquest."

Unthinkable. Impossible! "You would need a vast army, well armed and trained and—"

"Aye, my lady, and a man capable of leading our army to victory. We have the leader and are amassing the army."

"Who would dare…?"

"I cannot tell you, not until we reach the safety of his holding," he said, and turned back to his rabbits.

Judith's thoughts churned, not wanting to settle on her part in these men's plans. But once it gelled, she felt compelled to confirm it.

"This leader of yours, 'tis he you wish me to wed."

Thurkill looked up at her. "He is of noble Saxon blood, but not royal. Marriage to you will strengthen his claim to the throne, make the shift of power more acceptable to the royal houses of other countries."

The royal house of Scotland would be the first to come to England's aid. "Acceptable to my uncle Alexander, you mean."

"And others."

"'Tis a foolhardy undertaking."

"'Tis England's only hope."

Judith closed her eyes and drew a long breath. Thurkill wouldn't be moved by her arguments, nor would the other men. If they'd followed Thurkill on this villainous adventure to capture her—to make her their queen, of all the ridiculous notions—they must believe in the rightness of what they did.

"My lady?"

Judith opened her eyes to see Thurkill standing before her, holding out a chunk of rabbit. Absently, she accepted it and took a small bite. Her hunger had vanished, but she needed to eat, if only to bolster her strength for the ordeal ahead. Mercy, she must not only find a way to escape, but to quickly warn the kings of both England and Scotland of the impending uprising.

She glanced from Thurkill—who'd taken a seat on the log she'd abandoned earlier—to Oswuld and Duncan. They all tucked into their portions of meat as if there would be no meal on the morrow, as most soldiers did. And these men were soldiers, though they fought for a hopeless cause.

Normans had ruled England for more than four decades, held every high position in the land, owned nearly every inch of England. Dislodging the Normans wouldn't take an army, 'twould take a miracle, and miracles came few and far between.

The meat went down hard and sat as a solid lump in her stomach, but she finished her portion. She turned to toss the bones in the fire, praying for her own small miracle.

Thurkill gasped. Duncan leaped upward.

"Sit you back down or your leader dies," commanded a male voice with steady and calm authority.

Recognition thrummed through her. She'd never forgot-

ten the sound of that voice, the deep, smooth tones of a
courageous, handsome knight. Even as she looked to confirm the man's identity, she wondered if her sight deceived
her.

Corwin! She would know his handsome visage and
azure-blue eyes anywhere. He wore no helmet, leaving his
shoulder-length brown hair free to frame his high cheek-
bones and strong, clean-shaven chin.

His highly polished chain mail reflected the orange rays
of the setting sun, giving him an aura of breathtaking
power. The hilt of his sword flashed from where it rested
in the scabbard at his waist. He was a sight to behold, to
be sure.

With one hand twisted into Thurkill's hair, the other
holding a dagger pressed hard to the helpless man's throat,
Corwin stared hard at Duncan.

Very slowly, Duncan obeyed Corwin's command, re-
suming his seat on the forest floor.

Judith stood up, her heart beating so fast she nearly
fainted. By the grace of God, Corwin had found her. Rescue
was at hand.

"If everyone remains calm, we may avoid bloodshed,"
Corwin said. "Especially yours, Thurkill. My dagger is
sharp, and I have yet to decide whether or not to let you
live."

To Corwin's relief, Thurkill remained tense but didn't
move. Killing the brigands' leader wasn't part of his plan,
a plan that had changed in extreme measure when he'd
overheard the rebels' treasonous intention to overthrow the
king of England.

Throughout the day he'd trailed this band with every
intention of snatching Judith from her abductors. They
hadn't been difficult to track, and had given him the op-

portunity. But now, with a kingdom at stake, he couldn't carry through.

Judith stood across the campsite, a smile gracing her lovely mouth. Wisps of hair had escaped her braid, which was about to come undone, giving a winsome quality to her classically beautiful features. Admiration and expectation shone in those sultry gray eyes he remembered so well.

Her unfettered glee had naught to do with seeing him again, he knew. She expected release from her ordeal. He was about to disappoint her, and the stronger her reaction to what she would perceive as betrayal, the better for both of them.

"You know my name?" Thurkill whispered, dragging Corwin's attention away from the woman across the campsite to the man held statue still by the dagger at his throat.

"Aye, I know your name," Corwin said, then glanced at the men who remained seated near the fire. "I know all of your names. You have been rather free with them all day."

"All day?" Oswuld asked with disbelief.

"A good portion of it. I heard Lady Judith's screams when you took her. By the time I finished questioning the nuns you left behind, I had to track you. 'Twas not difficult, despite your efforts to cover your trail." He looked down at Thurkill. "I wondered if you were actually that clever, or if you had simply become lost when you began going in circles this afternoon. You are lost, are you not, Thurkill?"

Thurkill neither moved a muscle nor answered.

Corwin continued. "Nor did you have any notion that I followed you. One should never leave one's rear exposed to attack, Thurkill. But then, given the circumstances, I may not have thought anyone could follow so quickly, either."

"Who are you?" Duncan asked.

"Corwin of Lenvil, knight of Wilmont. And if you will have me, the newest member of your band."

He heard Judith's stunned gasp. The men at the fire stared at him in surprise. Thurkill allowed himself a sharp intake of breath.

"You were also rather careless in voicing your purpose," Corwin said. "I heard it all and heartily approve."

"Then release me," Thurkill ordered, though softly.

"Not yet, I think. 'Twould be foolish to give up my advantage until I am assured I will not be murdered in my sleep."

Judith's hands clenched to fists at her sides. "How…how *could* you? Corwin, this is madness!"

Her distress was understandable, and he was sorry for it, but he couldn't back down. If there were any hope at all of stopping the rebellion before it started, he had to take this risk. Unfortunately, the risk extended to Judith, but he judged the danger to her slight. These men would crown her England's queen if they had their way. They'd do all within their power to keep her safe. And she was certainly in no danger from him. He, too, would protect her.

His duty, as he saw it, was to prevent a war by learning all he could of the rebellion, especially the name of the Saxon noble who would dare to be king. Mayhap, if Judith proved trustworthy, Corwin would ease her mind by taking her into his confidence. Surely she'd see the sense in remaining with the rebels long enough to glean the information.

Or maybe not. Certes, she hadn't shown much sense this morning. Too, he'd misjudged her before, three years ago—and paid a price. She'd told him with a harsh snubbing that she considered him beneath her notice. And now he gave her reason to believe him lower than the dirt beneath her booted feet.

"Madness? Nay, my lady. This rebellion may free England from Norman tyranny. If the leader is capable. If the army is large enough and well equipped." He looked down at Thurkill. "Is it? Or do I throw my lot in with you to find only men who travel in circles?"

Thurkill had the gumption to sneer. "You could do better, I suppose?"

Corwin smiled. "I can find the road you were looking for this noon."

"How do we know we can trust you?" Duncan asked.

They shouldn't, and making them believe would be the hardest part of his scheme.

"Do we all agree that, if I wished, I could take Lady Judith from you now, return to Romsey and set the sheriff on your tails?"

Judith's hands rose to rest on her hips, emphasizing her anger. The action also thrust her breasts forward, prompting Corwin to wonder all over again if a lushly curved female body lurked beneath the shapeless black robe. He suspected the rest of her would be as perfectly carved as her comely face and delicate hands.

"Taking me back to Romsey is exactly what you should do!" she stated.

Maybe he should take Judith and go. Even now the lady's face and form proved a mighty and unwanted distraction.

"But I will not," Corwin said. "I am Saxon, as are all of you, and am as ready to throw off the Norman yoke as you seem to be. As I see it, I need not prove myself to you, but you to me."

Duncan's eyes narrowed. "We do not even know if you are who you say you are."

Thankfully, that problem was easily solved.

"Ask the lady. Judith Canmore knows who I am, even

if she has ever disapproved of me. In fact, I carry a letter to her from my sister, which I may consider giving her if she does not cause us any further trouble.''

Judith's gray eyes smoldered, then flashed with fire that would have burned him to cinders had it been real.

"He is who he says," she said. "Corwin of Lenvil, vassal to Gerard of Wilmont, one of the most powerful barons in the kingdom, and one of the most fair and kind, and *most* undeserving of disloyalty! Why, Corwin? How can you betray the man who has given you so much?''

He almost winced at her condemnation, but then, he wasn't truly betraying Gerard. Never would.

"Given? Never. What land and privileges he granted me, I earned with the sweat of my brow and the edge of my sword. In truth, 'tis he who should be earning privileges at my hand. His castle sits on land once ruled by my forefathers. I would have it back.''

Not quite true, but the band needn't know that.

"Greed?" Judith shouted. "You would turn on a decent man for his land? What of your sister? Would you betray her, too?''

Now that truly hurt—which was probably why she'd tossed it in his face. Judith would use every argument she could muster to convince him of his folly, persuade him to change his mind.

"'Tis a naive notion that these men rebel for a mere ideal. In part, mayhap, but each looks for a reward at battle's end. With an entire kingdom to disperse to those who serve well, the rewards will be rich indeed. As for Ardith, she can do as she pleases, go to Normandy with Gerard or remain with me, so long as I am master of Wilmont.''

"I cannot promise you so grand a reward," Thurkill said.

Finally, Thurkill had begun to yield.

The rebel's hair was becoming wet with sweat, making

Corwin's grip less secure. He knew he must gain the band's acceptance soon, before the tide turned against him or he lost the advantage of holding Thurkill helpless.

"Nay, you cannot. Only the man you would make king can do so, and only if you win the battle. 'Tis to him I would pledge my sword for the price I ask. Believe me, Thurkill, you would much prefer to have me as friend than a foe. What say you?"

"If I say nay?"

"Then you die by my dagger, and your companions die by my sword. I am Wilmont trained. Never doubt that I could take them on and win."

"And Lady Judith?"

All day long Corwin had enjoyed ignoble but tantalizing visions of having Judith alone, beholden to him for her rescue, in need of him for protection and guidance back to safety. The concern in Thurkill's question prevented any glib answer, however.

"I would take her back to Romsey. I imagine, by now, a reward has been offered for her safe return."

"I will see you hung by your thumbs from the beams of the refectory," Judith threatened. "Flogged to within a beetle's breath of your life for your insults. Then drawn, quartered and hanged for treason!"

He wouldn't put it past her to try. He eased the dagger away from Thurkill's throat, far enough to let the man relax, but not far enough to remove the threat of a slit throat.

"Bloodthirsty imp," he remarked to Thurkill. "Are you sure we want her as our queen?"

"Aye." Thurkill's tension eased. He smiled slightly. "A right rare one, she is. She will make a grand mate for our lord, give him strong, healthy sons."

"The beast can get his unholy offspring on some other woman," Judith said firmly. "'Twill not be by me, I vow."

Corwin pushed aside a flash of anger that Judith had been chosen as a mate for an upstart rebel lord, much as one would choose a broodmare, albeit a royal broodmare. But then, she wouldn't suffer the obscenity. As soon as he had the information he wanted, he and Judith would leave the band.

"Have we reached an accord, Thurkill?"

"Our cause can use men with your training. If you truly wish to join us, I would be a fool to say you nay."

"Say me nay and you die."

"A consideration, but of little import. Sheath your dagger, Corwin of Lenvil."

The moment of win or lose had come. All depended upon Thurkill's decision. *Give some, gain some—with luck.* Corwin released his captive's hair, backed up a step and tucked his dagger beneath his belt—close to hand.

Thurkill rose from the log and shook away his tension. The other men started to get to their feet. Thurkill raised a staying hand, which his men obeyed.

With narrowed eyes, Thurkill proclaimed, "You may travel with us, but will be guarded closely. 'Tis for our lord to decide your worthiness."

Corwin didn't let his relief show. He wanted to ask the lord's name and whereabouts, but held back. He'd thoroughly embarrassed Thurkill, could understand the man's ire and wounded pride. Now was not the time to push for answers.

"Then I will fetch my mount and hobble him near the other horses."

"Duncan will go with you."

Judith sat on the boulder and put her face in her hands. If she cried, he couldn't see or hear her sorrow. 'Twas his fault she hid behind her hands.

Slowly, Corwin unfastened and lowered the flap of chain

mail that protected his neck and throat, then reached beneath to fetch Ardith's letter. A small consolation, maybe, but reading it might take Judith's mind from her troubles for a little while.

Corwin held up the piece of parchment and nodded toward Judith. "May I?" he asked Thurkill.

"Aye, but have a care she does not scratch your eyes out. I think she now hates you more than she hates us."

A wise and likely true observation. Corwin crossed the clearing and stopped before Judith. Her eyes were red rimmed and wet, but more with anger than misery. She snatched the letter from his fingers, then, with a mere look, consigned him to the darkest depths of the netherworld.

He couldn't think of anything to say that would ease her mind and not give himself away. As she unfolded the letter, he turned to leave her.

"Corwin!" she called after him.

He looked back.

Her hands were shaking. "Your sister writes of her kind and generous brother," she said in the Norman French that Ardith had probably used in the letter. "You will break her heart if you persist in your extreme folly."

Having had her say, she went back to reading. Knowing there was nothing he could do to ease her mind until after he won the confidence of the rebel band, he resumed walking toward Thurkill.

"What did she say?" the man asked gruffly.

Thurkill, or any of the others by the looks of them, hadn't understood the Norman French. That might prove useful.

"You are right, Thurkill. She hates me more than you. By the by, you will need to set a guard tonight. The nuns were intent on returning to the abbey to alert the sheriff."

Thurkill scoffed. "I doubt he could find us so soon."

So did Corwin, but he wasn't about to take the chance. Now that he'd set on this course, he wanted no interference.

"That depends upon how quickly the sheriff received the news," Corwin said, and glanced back at Judith. "And any man who brings her back will likely receive a hefty reward. I intended to brave the night, if necessary, to find her. The sheriff might, too."

Chapter Four

Judith longed for the comfort of a thin straw mattress on a small cot, within the confines of her meager nun's cell. No matter which way she twisted or turned, she couldn't convince her body that the ground didn't become harder or the night air less chilled.

Neither would her worry over what was to come ease, nor her disappointment in Corwin's betrayal lessen.

Giving up on sleep, Judith sat up and wrapped the rough woolen blanket—which Thurkill had presented to her as if it were a feather-filled coverlet—more tightly around her shoulders. Scattered about the campsite, the men slept. All but Duncan, who roamed the forest to watch for the sheriff who Judith doubted would come tonight. The best she could hope for was that Duncan might awaken a hungry bear so she might be rid of the most belligerent of her captors.

She rose and stretched, then took two slow steps in an effort to bring some feeling back into her legs.

"Going somewhere, my lady?" Corwin asked softly from where he'd bedded down several yards to her left. She saw no more of him than the bulk of his body lying on the ground at the edge of the clearing.

Earlier, she'd thought about stealing a horse and risking an escape. Wandering about in the dead of night in unfamiliar surroundings, however, didn't seem a good plan. She would only become hopelessly lost and might come upon the hungry bear she wished on Duncan.

Judith ignored Corwin's question to pose one of her own, not bothering to hide her disgust. "Does your guilt over betraying Gerard disturb your sleep?"

Corwin propped himself up on an elbow. "Nay, merely training. A soldier learns to sleep where and when he can, and then with one ear open and one hand upon his sword. I heard you get up."

"These other men are soldiers and they do not stir."

"Nay, they do not. They must trust Duncan to raise an alarm if the need arises. I do not have their confidence in him, so I listen for anything that might threaten our safety."

"Including me?"

With a low, rumbling laugh, he answered, "Especially you. Should you have a dagger hidden beneath your robe you might be tempted to slit our throats while we slept. Come toward me a few steps and you will find a patch of long grass that will make a more comfortable resting place than the one you chose."

Judith hesitated to move any closer to Corwin, a man who she should consider more her enemy than the rebels. Though she'd heard his reasons for wanting to join the rebellion, she didn't understand how he could so easily turn traitor. When this hopeless scheme failed—and it would come to grief as earlier Saxon rebellions had—Corwin would receive the same harsh punishment as the others.

If he lived through the battles. Or unless she convinced him to turn from this path he'd unwisely chosen.

Maybe some unresolved dispute between Corwin and Gerard had clouded Corwin's judgment, making him susceptible to a rash decision to seek a means of revenge. But by hurting Gerard, Corwin also hurt Ardith, and Judith knew he genuinely cared for his sister.

Judith thought back to the day they'd met. Corwin's concern for Ardith had been very apparent, and part of the reason Judith had been so drawn to him. True, she'd experienced a female's reaction to a handsome, well-put-together male. A woman couldn't possibly look on Corwin without noticing the brilliant blue of his eyes, the angled perfection of his strong chin or the seductive tilt of his smile.

His looks had captured her attention. His tender concern for Ardith had touched her heart. As much as her head said to be wary, her heart longed for another glimpse of the man he'd been then, the man Judith prayed Corwin could still be.

'Twas a practical thing she hoped for. If she could sway Corwin, he might aid her escape. Deep down, she admitted she wanted Corwin back as he had been for her own sake, too. She simply couldn't have so lacked in judgment as to have thought fondly of a man capable of villainy.

Slowly, she moved toward Corwin. His face became more visible and the shape of his prone body more pronounced as she drew nearer. No blanket covered his chain mail. His broadsword lay before him, just beyond his long-fingered hand, within easy reach.

He raised that hand and pointed to a spot a mere few feet from him. ''Your royal bower awaits you, my lady.''

Royal bower, indeed. His tone conveyed humor, as if he teased her over the rebels' plan to make her a queen. Judith withheld a rebuke. Any hope of swaying Corwin might depend upon how well the two of them got along. At one time she'd harbored no doubts they could deal with each other quite well. Now she wasn't so sure, but needed to try.

She settled onto the grass, noting the truth of his assertion of greater comfort. "My thanks, Corwin, for your thoughtfulness in pointing it out to me."

"'Tis not thoughtfulness but self-defense. Tomorrow will be a long day, if I guess correctly. I will get no sleep if your restlessness keeps me awake."

Again she bristled. "How can any day possibly be longer than today?"

"Thurkill will want to put as much distance between him and the sheriff of Hampshire as possible. We will need to take to the road, steal you a horse—"

"Steal? But that is unlawful," she said, hearing the lack of sense in her statement as soon as the words left her lips. Of course the brigands would steal a horse from its owner, just as they'd stolen her from the abbey.

"—and find you a different gown to wear," he continued. "You stand out rather sorely garbed in a nun's robe. Anyone who sees you will notice and question your presence in the band."

Corwin didn't look as if he belonged with the band, either. "And you do not stand out sorely in your chain mail? All the others wear leather hauberks."

He shrugged a shoulder. "People will see me merely as the leader of a group of soldiers, where you look more the bedraggled waif."

She'd given no thought all day to how she looked, only how miserable she felt. No doubt she appeared untidy, mayhap thoroughly mussed, and she didn't appreciate Corwin saying so. The man truly possessed no manners at all.

Judith took a deep breath to keep her calm. She, who took pride in remaining calm when faced with adversity, had lost her composure far too often today. Few people affected her so. Like Abbess Christina, when the nun pushed her beyond all patience. Now Corwin, who prodded her temper nearly beyond endurance.

But then, Corwin had no reason to treat her kindly, and the fault lay with her. Judith knew she'd been insufferably rude on their last parting. Though she'd regretted her actions afterward, she'd done nothing to correct the wrong. If their parting had been less harsh, would he now feel obligated to rescue her instead of joining the rebels?

No matter how Corwin felt or what he did, she'd been given the chance to apologize, if only to ease her own conscience.

Corwin had lain back down. Was he still awake?

"Corwin?"

"Hmm?"

Judith mustered her courage. Living among nuns allowed for few opportunities to do something she needed to apologize for, so she was sorely out of the habit. Certes, she also now owed a contrite apology to the abbess, so maybe practicing on Corwin wasn't such a bad idea.

"When last we met," she said, "I fear I was not as gracious as I might have been."

A weak beginning, and she knew it. To her own ears she sounded stiff and insincere. In the deepening silence she sought stronger words, but before she could continue, he rejoined.

"Truly? I did not notice."

His casual words didn't ring true. She'd hurt him, or at least dented his pride.

"You did not notice that when we last crossed paths in the abbey's passageway, I ignored your presence?"

"I must have been occupied with more important matters. 'Tis late, Judith. Go to sleep."

Not yet. She'd come this far, and the man would hear she was sorry whether he wanted to or not.

"When I informed Queen Matilda of your arrival, I offered to keep you company while Ardith spoke with Sister Bernadette. Matilda reminded me of my duty to my family, and bade me take care I not become too…friendly with a man not of my rank. I fear that in my inexperience with such matters I took her words to heart and treated you harshly. I merely wanted you to know I regret we parted on bad terms."

He was silent for a long time. "You make too much of the matter, Judith. We who serve have come to expect no less than harsh treatment from those who place themselves above us—unless, of course, that person seeks a favor."

"I ask no favor."

"Do you not? If I said we could leave this camp right now, would you not leap to your feet?"

"Aye, but Corwin—"

"Save your breath, my lady, for I will hear no more. Daylight comes soon. Sleep."

Judith plopped down onto the grass and wrapped the blanket around her. She'd wasted her breath. Let him join the rebels and hang with his fellows when caught in his treason. She no longer cared.

"Beast," she uttered, just loud enough for him to hear.

Corwin didn't refute her accusation as he watched Judith settle into the long grass.

Beast.

His words had been aimed at Duncan, who lurked in the forest not a few feet behind Judith, more guarding the lady—or watching him—than keeping a lookout for the sheriff. Corwin hoped Duncan would relay his statements to Thurkill. Not only would it aid his cause, it might prod the band's leader into finding Judith a horse and change of garments quickly. She would need both when the time came to make their escape.

To Judith's way of thinking, he'd probably sounded beastly, and that after she'd tried to make amends. Had she been sincere in her apology, or only attempting to sway him into aiding her escape from her kidnappers?

Her words had come out too stiff for sincerity. Yet he could well imagine the queen warning her niece about involvement with men of unsuitable rank. Nay, 'twas a ploy on her part, designed to soften his heart toward her so he'd change his mind about joining the rebels. Frankly, if he took her back to the abbey, she wouldn't then mind what he did at all.

Corwin started to roll to his other side, wipe his mind of all thoughts and drift back into a guarded sleep. Then Judith yawned, a long, indelicate sound, and he stayed where he was—to keep watch over her, of course.

Damn, but she intrigued him. With each encounter Judith showed him another facet of her personality.

She could be gentle and caring, as she'd been with Ardith. The day he and Ardith had ridden to Romsey Abbey had been a hard one for his sister. Judith had shown them to a private room and loaned Ardith one of her own robes. While Ardith changed, Judith led him down a long hallway to the kitchen, where she fetched food and drink.

Judith had talked to him the entire way down and back— of what, he couldn't remember. He'd been too wrapped up in his own worries over how Gerard was going to react if he returned early from his journey to find Ardith gone. But even now, Corwin could envision Judith's comforting smile, hear her soothing voice. Both had helped ease his turmoil before returning to Ardith and the sitting room.

Then Judith had left, obviously to tell Queen Matilda of Ardith's arrival and purpose—to see Sister Bernadette, who might be able to determine if Ardith could conceive, thereby satisfying the condition on which she and Gerard would be allowed to marry. Matilda herself had come to lead Ardith to the inner rooms of the abbey, consigning Corwin to wait in the priest's hut outside the abbey walls.

On his way out he'd encountered Judith again, in the passageway. She'd walked past him—eyes forward, chin tilted upward, lips pursed—as if he didn't exist. His saying her name brought no reaction, not even a hitch in her purposeful stride. All thoughts of thanking her for her tender care of Ardith had fled, and he'd carried that memory of her with him out the abbey door and through the years.

Then today he'd seen her temper—fiery indignation expressed with flashing eyes and vivid threats. No meek girl in evidence there! No haughty royal heiress, either. Simply a woman promising retribution for the wrong done to her.

Corwin smiled at the thought of Thurkill and his lord expecting Judith to meekly accept her fate. She found the thought of being used to further the rebel lord's aims abhorrent, and would fight.

But then, a woman's protests against ill use usually went unheard by men greedy for power and wealth. Corwin knew of several ways a woman could be forced to marry against her will, and no doubt the rebel leader planned to use such force against Judith if necessary.

Not that Corwin would allow it, or even let the situation advance so far. No matter what Judith truly thought of him, he wouldn't let the rebel leader abuse her. Once he learned the name of the leader and the location of the rebel camp, he and Judith would be off to London—Corwin to inform the king of the uprising, Judith to return to the protection of her royal family.

'Twas best, for now, if she believed him to be a beast. He could only hope that when he found the right time to tell her of his true purpose, she would believe him and cooperate.

Corwin led the company out of the forest and onto the narrow dirt road. After clearing the woods, he moved his horse aside to allow Thurkill to take the lead. As Corwin suspected he would, the man headed north toward Oxford. Likely they would travel far beyond the city, for no man could gather an army large enough to challenge the king within southern England without someone noticing. In the wilds of the far north, however, no one would be the wiser. Too, the men of that region had always been the most eager to challenge the Normans.

Corwin gave a brief thought to the company he'd led out of Wilmont, and hoped William would do as commanded and escort the wagons, lumber and carpenters to Cotswold. Then Corwin slid into line several paces behind Thurkill, knowing Gerard would approve of his abandoning that duty to take on this task of higher purpose.

Thurkill set a lively pace up the rough road, merely a wide path of dirt deeply rutted by wagon wheels. Corwin kept watch on Judith, who rode pillion behind Thurkill, just as he knew the two men behind him watched his every move.

As the morning wore on, watching Judith bounce on the horse's rump became harder. She would be sore this night, as she'd been sore the night before. There was no help for it. To evade the sheriff, they must keep up the pace.

Nearing midday, Judith's right hand released its hold on Thurkill's hauberk. She made a fist and hit him hard on the shoulder. Corwin bit back a smile. Had Thurkill refused a request to halt one too many times?

Corwin urged his destrier forward to come alongside

Thurkill. "I know of a cave not far ahead where we might take a rest."

"I have no wish to rest. The sheriff—"

"Will not find us there. 'Tis a truly secluded site." Corwin shrugged, as if uncaring one way or the other. "I think of your horse, Thurkill. He carries a greater burden than the others. But if you wish to go on, I will not object."

"Aye, think of your horse, Thurkill," Judith said in a sarcastic tone. "This *burden* he carries would be most pleased to cease bruising his boney backside."

Thurkill rolled his eyes heavenward. Had Judith been giving the man an earful of complaints and snide remarks all morning? Possibly.

The victim of a kidnapping, Judith had every right to protest. Her mind-numbing, hand-trembling terror had passed, but not her fear. She used anger to mask it, but Corwin didn't want her to goad Thurkill too hard. The man might be under orders to bring her safely to his lord, but every man had his limits. Coping for hours on end with Judith's sharp tongue might be more than Thurkill could tolerate.

"The cave is but a few minutes away if you care for a respite," Corwin said.

Thurkill studied him for a moment. "How do I know you do not lead us into the sheriff's snare?"

"You do not know if I lead you into a trap, just as I do not know if you lead me into one at journey's end. You will have to trust my word."

"Humph. How does one villain learn to trust another?" Judith interjected. "Neither of you deserves anyone's trust."

Through clenched teeth, Thurkill ordered, "Find the cave."

After a few moments of searching, Corwin found the

overgrown path he sought, and at its end, the cave. Brush hid the mouth of the cavern located halfway up a steep hill. A stream bubbled along at the base. The narrow sloping path from the stream to the cave proved a challenge for the horses, but all made it up without incident.

Corwin dismounted, planning to help Judith down from Thurkill's horse. Oswuld beat him to it. 'Twas probably for the best. The less he had to deal with Judith just now, the better. Her hands pressed into her back, she walked stiffly toward the mouth of the cave, with Oswuld a step behind her.

"How know you this place?" Duncan asked, his voice echoing in the large chamber. "'Tis rather far from where you say you live."

Corwin noted the suspicious undertone in Duncan's question. "'Tis far, but a friend and I once used this cave to shelter from a storm. Luckily, Stephen knew of its existence."

"This companion you speak of must travel much to know of so remote a spot."

Corwin slid his hands from his riding gloves, thinking of Stephen, his best friend and Gerard's youngest brother. Aye, Stephen liked to travel, rush headlong into one adventure after the other. Corwin had gleefully joined him on several of his journeys.

"He does love to travel, more than most men I know."

Duncan huffed. "He must be a Norman, then, to have the coin and time to waste roaming about the land."

Stephen did, but on that particular journey Stephen had performed a valuable service for Gerard, and Richard, their half brother. Having acquired several new holdings in a court judgment, Gerard had given most of the land to his brothers. Stephen had offered to visit all the holdings, determine the condition of each, then report on which needed repairs or where the people needed immediate assistance.

The Norman who'd previously owned the lands had been a cruel man, and Corwin saw firsthand how the peasants had suffered, then witnessed their joy when told they'd been placed under Wilmont protection. None had truly cared which brother became overlord. Each man had a reputation for fairness, even benevolence.

True, most Normans looked to their own wealth and comfort and never noticed any hardship suffered by the people who provided for them. Telling Duncan that some Normans could be generous and honorable, however, wouldn't aid Corwin's ruse.

"Aye, the Normans are a selfish, cruel race," Corwin proclaimed. "'Twas a sad day for England when King Harold lost the battle to Duke William of Normandy."

Duncan's mouth twisted into a sneer. "When the bastard invaded England he killed or maimed all who would not submit to his rule, burned crops and forests and huts at will until those country folk left could barely survive. A sad day for England, indeed."

Corwin now knew with certainty from where Duncan hailed. Only in the far north had the Conqueror taken such drastic measures to bring the old Saxon earls to heel. Corwin's ancestors hadn't joined in any rebellion, but had accepted the Conqueror as king and pledged fealty to the man the new king declared their overlord. The transfer of power had been peaceful, so unlike the experience of Duncan's family.

Corwin laid a hand on his destrier's neck, a fine example of Wilmont's herd. He'd benefited greatly from Norman rule. Would he be less complacent if his ancestors had lost everything, if his Norman overlord had been less honorable?

"This lord you follow, he has a plan to overtake the kingdom without any of the peasants suffering?" Corwin asked.

"Aye. We must first be rid of King Henry. Then the barons will give way in due course."

Duncan, clearly, knew nothing of the ways of war and less of Norman barons. Even with the king vanquished, the Normans wouldn't give way. Each would defend his strongest castle and challenge the Saxons for possession. A battle for the entire kingdom would be fought castle by castle, with the peasants suffering the most.

"Father!" Oswuld cried out as he ran into the cave. "She is gone! Lady Judith—I cannot find her!"

A cold fist gripped Corwin's innards.

"You were supposed to be guarding her!" Thurkill shouted.

"I allowed her privacy to take relief and she slipped away."

Cursing himself roundly for not anticipating this attempt at escape, knowing which way he would go if in Judith's situation, Corwin bolted out of the cave, hoping to get there ahead of her.

Chapter Five

She couldn't find the path.

With hands on her hips, Judith slowly turned in a full circle, looking carefully for any sign of her escape route. Four horses had ridden through this area not long ago, trampled down the grass and pushed aside brush. The *path* had to be here somewhere, and she must find it quickly before Oswuld noticed she'd fled.

Her plan was a simple one. Find the road and head north toward whatever town lay ahead. Send someone to take word of the rebellion to Scotland. Enlist a trustworthy person to act as her guide to London. Surely her kidnappers expected her to flee south, back toward the safety of the abbey. But she could trick her kidnappers, if only she could find the path.

Judith wiped away the moisture gathering in her eyes—from weariness. She wasn't crying. She wasn't afraid. She didn't have time for either.

She spun at the sound of rustling in the brush behind her. A small animal, gray-brown and furry, scurried into the heavier brush beyond. A squirrel, perhaps. Or a rabbit. Not a man.

She blew out a long breath and struggled to regain her

concentration. Nothing looked familiar, until she spotted a tree with two wind-snapped lower branches. Had she seen it before, during the ride to the cave? Aye, there, just beyond the tree the grass lay flat.

She hiked up her robe to run down the path to freedom. "Judith!"

Corwin.

She stared at the path. *Run!* A useless effort. Corwin was too close. He would catch her in a trice. She unclenched her hands, letting the fabric fall. At the edge of her vision, she saw the glint of a sunbeam flash off his chain mail.

Close. So very close to freedom.

Once again, 'twas Corwin who thwarted her. He would take her back to her captors, and they would watch her so closely now she might never get away.

Corwin closed the distance between them, until he was so near she could reach out and touch him if she chose.

"I beg of you, Corwin. Let me go," she said. To her own ears she sounded desperate. Perhaps she was. She looked up into the azure eyes she'd once so admired, still considered beautiful. The eyes of a traitor. "Join the rebels if you wish, but I want no part of their scheme. Let them find another woman for their queen, one who believes in their cause. I have no heart for it."

He smiled, almost tenderly. "'Tis not your heart they desire, Judith, but your name and womb. However, if someone asked me to choose a more perfect woman to make their queen, I could not come up with another's name."

His flattery fell far short of whatever mark he hoped to hit.

"Then you betray me again, force me to stay with the rebels."

"I cannot let you go, Judith." He sighed. "I will try to explain—"

Judith crossed her arms. "I heard your traitorous reasoning last eve, and have no wish to hear it again."

Corwin took a long, intense look around them. "I am no rebel, never will be."

Astonished and hopeful, Judith stammered. "But—but last eve you said...are you saying you have changed your mind?"

"My mind is set on joining the rebels, but not for the reasons I gave Thurkill. We have not much time before we are found, Judith. Come, this way. 'Twill give us a measure of privacy a moment or two longer."

He grabbed hold of her hand and tugged her toward the path. His hand was warm, large and encompassing. The strength of it didn't surprise her, but the tingling sensation that snaked up her arm at his touch set her mind to spinning and her knees to shaking. An unwelcome and unwise reaction to a man she needed to guard against.

"I go nowhere with you," she declared, and jerked her hand from his grasp. "I care not why you wish to join the rebels. I swear to you, Corwin, if you join them, I will ensure you are punished in suitable fashion."

The man had the gall to smile. "Chopped to bits and then hanged, or was it the other way around?"

She forced away a vision of Corwin hanging from a rope, not wanting to imagine the rest. How could she save him from that dreadful fate when he wouldn't listen?

"'Tis a gruesome punishment you risk, no matter the way of it."

Judith flinched when he put his hands on her shoulders.

He frowned and released her. "To my mind, the best way to thwart this rebellion is to join it. I need to learn everything I can—in particular the camp location, their numbers and the leader's name—before going to King

Henry. I could use your help, Judith. The more quickly done, the more quickly over.''

Corwin pretended to join the rebellion? Judith wanted so badly to believe him her heart ached. Except last night he'd made very convincing arguments to the contrary. She could have sworn he truly intended to join the rebels. Did he lie to her now?

"Help in what way?"

"I ask you to do no more than make this journey easier by not trying to escape. I cannot do what needs be done if I must chase after you each time you take it into your head to flee."

She'd been seized by strange men, bounced around on the back of a horse until her backside bore bruises, been forced to sleep on the ground—known fear and anger such as she'd never known before. Corwin now asked her to allow further indignities willingly. Of course, if the villains need not worry over her, the journey would go faster. But to what end?

"You want me to assist these knaves?"

"Only until I obtain the information I need."

"And how long might that take?"

"Depends upon how soon I can get them to trust me."

Judith voiced her greatest fear. "What if that never happens? What if you learn nothing of import until we ride into the rebel's stronghold?"

Corwin took a deeper than normal breath. "I am hoping that will not happen. I have no more wish to ride into their stronghold than you do."

"You only hope. There is no certainty," she said. "Last eve, Thurkill vowed to tell me no more of his lord or the rebels' plans until after we arrived at wherever we are going. I doubt he will reveal more to you, either. Then what,

Corwin? After we are in the rebels' camp, we may both be trapped.''

Corwin shook his head. ''I will not let that happen.''

Judith scoffed. ''So you say.''

''So I give you my oath.''

Last eve, he'd vowed to serve the rebels' leader in exchange for the reward of Wilmont. Which oath did Corwin truly mean to keep?

''Please, let us go now. We know enough to set the king's men on their trail. Let the soldiers find the camp and stop the rebellion.''

This time, when he put his hands on her shoulders, Judith didn't flinch, merely accepted the comfort offered in his massaging fingers.

''I know you are frightened,'' he said softly. ''I would take you away from here now, if I could. But Judith, if we flee, Thurkill will hunt us down to the ends of the kingdom if need be. And what would we tell the king if we managed to get to London? That we know of three men who *say* there will be a rebellion, who *may* have a large army gathered somewhere, with a leader who *might* be capable of leadership? I promise you, as soon as I know more of this rebellion, we will escape.''

He sounded so sure of himself, so reasonable. Yet...

''So we wait to make our escape until there is an entire army at hand and eager to hunt us down.''

''We wait until I have a solid plan and we both have horses. Try not to worry, and think on this. This Saxon noble they follow. Very likely he is, or was, connected with the court of the Scots. Have you any idea who the man might be?''

''Nay, I...'' *Oh, dear.* Shocked, Judith realized Corwin might have the right of it. She might very well know this person who'd ordered her abduction. She might have stood next to him in the palace hall, talked to him in the gardens, shared a jest during one festivity or another.

She'd been but a young girl when her parents sent her to the abbey, but she remembered most of the nobles, their names and faces. Which of them might have turned traitor?

"If it helps," Corwin said, "I believe we are headed for the far north, mayhap nearly to the border. The man may have a holding there. He may truly be Saxon or mayhap an exiled Scot. I know this is hard..." Corwin went very still, save for a brief, nearly imperceptible glance left. "Thurkill comes. I will turn you around and give you a push, toward the cave. We will talk more later."

Even though forewarned, Judith stumbled and cried out at the force of his shove.

She began walking, becoming angry all over again. "Was that necessary?" she said, tossing the words over her shoulder.

"It looked good to Thurkill. He needs to believe you and I are at odds."

"What makes you think we are not?"

Judith sat against the cold cave wall, trying to ignore Thurkill's loud, echoing voice, trying not to feel guilty for getting Oswuld into trouble with his father. She shouldn't care if Thurkill punished his son severely, as he threatened, for allowing her brief escape.

Corwin busied himself with the tack on his destrier, apparently also trying to disregard Thurkill's shouting. He didn't quite succeed. At times, he would glance at Oswuld with a puzzled look on his face, as if wondering how much more Oswuld could bear without fighting back.

Duncan hadn't yet returned. When he did, they would leave. She wished he would hurry. Then she wouldn't have to listen to Thurkill's ranting, and wouldn't wonder if his wrath would turn on her. He hadn't said a word to her since her capture, only thanked Corwin for his quick thinking and speedy action.

Thanks to Corwin's suggestion, names of Saxon nobles whirled around in her head, but she couldn't think of one she knew who had reason—and the means—to lead a rebellion against England's king.

Judith pulled Ardith's note from the folds of her tattered nun's robe. As always, the sight of her friend's lovely script proved soothing. Over the years, Ardith had written of her everyday life at Wilmont, of the trials and joys that came with the duties as chatelaine to so large an estate, as well as being a wife and mother. No matter how much she complained at the price of some commodity, or how difficult she found it to get everything done within the space of a day, Ardith sounded as happy as any woman could possibly be.

She'd married a wonderful man, both lover and friend, who treated her with respect and who she respected in return. The two of them worked and played, shared joys and sorrows, always together. To Judith's mind, they enjoyed the ideal marriage. What must it be like to know, deep within your heart, that one very special person would always be there when needed, would love and cherish you forever?

"Is aught amiss?" Corwin asked.

He stood before her, his arms crossed over the wide expanse of his chest. So much was amiss she didn't know how he could ask her such a question. But then, he wasn't looking at her, but at the parchment she held in her hands. 'Twas not for her that he voiced concern.

"Nay. What leads you to think so?"

"You looked...saddened. I thought mayhap Ardith wrote of ill tidings, and I wondered what they were."

On that, she could set his mind at ease. "Ardith writes of the boys' antics, of her husband's protectiveness and of not being able to see her feet. 'Twill please her greatly to have her child born."

Ardith also wrote of her brother, but Corwin already knew that. Judith had ungraciously told him so last eve after he'd handed her the letter.

The corner of his supple mouth curved into a brief smile. "She will push this child out with hopes of having another. Last I heard, she wants six at the least."

"And Gerard?"

"Will grant her every whim, so long as it does not harm her health."

Judith glanced down at the note. "Her happiness shines through in every word she writes. She and Gerard have the perfect marriage, do they not?"

Corwin shook his head. "She misleads you in her letters, then. Both are headstrong. When they argue, the rest of us stay well away."

The one time Judith had seen Gerard and Ardith together, Gerard had been in a fine temper, bellowing Ardith's name, plunging through the abbey's passageways as he looked for her. Upon finding her, he'd growled his displeasure. When Ardith had chided him, assured him of her well-being, that bear of a man had gentled almost instantly. Judith could well imagine the sparks that flew when Ardith's temper clashed with Gerard's. She doubted, however, if any argument could cause a permanent rift in the marriage. The two loved each other too well.

"Yet when their disagreement is over, their love remains undamaged, does it not?" Judith asked. At Corwin's nod, she continued, "'Tis as it should be, and worth bearing most any hardship. If there is a rebellion, Ardith will stand with Gerard, come what may. Be they in castle or hut, she will be happy so long as they are together. This assumes, of course, that Gerard does not die in the fighting.''

Corwin grinned. ''Do not worry over Gerard. The man is quite skilled at holding his own in any fight involving swords.''

In the ensuing silence—and there was silence, for Thurkill had ceased his tirade—Judith refolded the precious piece of parchment and tucked it safely away.

Duncan returned to the cave. ''Ah, the princess is found,'' he said, giving her a mock bow. Judith refused to acknowledge his insolence.

When she gave no retort, he turned to Thurkill. ''While searching for the lady, I spied a small village. One of the women was spreading garments over bushes, I assume to dry from washing. Now might be our chance to pilfer a gown for her ladyship.''

''Why did you not just take one?'' Thurkill grumbled.

''I was busy looking for the princess. Besides, what sense taking one if she had not been found?''

Judith took the hand Corwin offered to help her up. She didn't want to let go. The man did strange things to her mind. Though she wondered if she could trust him, she still felt safest when he was near.

''My lady,'' Thurkill said, ''I will warn you only this once. Should you attempt another escape, I will order you tied to one of us at all times. You will not know another moment's privacy.''

He said it without a dram of emotion in his voice. Not a plea for cooperation nor an angry threat, 'twas the statement of a commander of men.

Before she could express her outrage, Corwin spoke.

''Best heed the warning, Lady Judith. 'Twould be most uncomfortable for you, and bothersome for the rest of us to have you tied.''

Did she hear an underlying message—that Corwin would find it harder to arrange an escape if her hands were tied? Or did she imagine it, wanting to believe he had her best interests at heart and not those of the rebels?

"The next time I leave you, Thurkill, 'twill be for good." And with that, she headed for Thurkill's horse.

Oswuld stood there. He'd draped a blanket over the horse's rump. "'Tis not much, my lady, but may soften the ride."

His kindness touched her, especially since she'd caused him so much trouble. But she was the victim here and refused to treat any of her captors other than as villains. They might take any softening of her attitude as a sign of weakening her stance, and that she couldn't do.

"You have the right of it, Oswuld. 'Tis not much. A horse of my own would be much appreciated."

"Then you might wish to assure my father you are resigned to making the whole of this journey, or he may judge you too untrustworthy to let you have your own mount."

"I will not change my mind about assisting this nefarious scheme. I have no desire to meet much less marry your lord."

"Resist as you will, my lady." Oswuld glanced over at his father, who still conversed with Corwin. "Father will take you to our camp, willing or no. He has his orders and will see them through or…"

Die in the attempt. Judith finished the unspoken phrase so often uttered by men-at-arms faced with life-threatening duty—or in jest when they considered the duty no challenge. The tone of Oswuld's voice, however, made her wonder if the son didn't truly worry for his father.

The old man seemed healthy enough. Tired, aye, but they

were all tired. And flushed, but he'd been angry. Still, could Thurkill suffer some ailment that caused his son concern?

Corwin knew that stealing a horse wouldn't be as easy as stealing the gown had been—though Duncan had made fast and quiet work of it. The man had a talent for thievery, making Corwin wonder how Duncan had made his way in the world before joining the rebellion.

'Twould stand to reason that most of the men who'd joined the rebel forces were brigands, with nothing to lose if the rebellion failed and everything to win if it succeeded.

Corwin glanced around this evening's campsite at his traveling companions. Duncan had built a fire—over which he would roast the squirrels he'd caught, then toss Judith's old robe after she changed. Oswuld tended to the horses. Thurkill argued with Judith—an argument Corwin was trying to stay out of. If he came to Judith's aid every time she butted heads with one of the rebels, they might wonder at his attentiveness.

With renewed resolve, he applied whetstone to sword, gently grinding his weapon's edge to battle readiness.

"Thurkill," Judith said, irritated and struggling for patience, "if you tie a rope to my arm I will not be able to get the gown on. I give you my word I will not try to escape if you allow me the privacy to change."

"You have proven yourself untrustworthy, my lady. We will go back into the bushes a ways. I will not watch you change your garments, but neither will I allow you to wander far from my side."

Judith shoved the gown into his arms. "Then I will not put this on. Duncan stole it, let him wear it."

Thurkill leaned forward, his eyes narrowing. "Either change into the gown yourself, or I will do it for you."

"You would not dare!"

"Would I not?"

Corwin sighed inwardly and gave up on his chore. He stood up and sheathed the sword.

"This is the way you show me every consideration?" Judith shouted.

"I attempt to, my lady, but you try my patience at every turn," Thurkill rejoined, shoving the gown back at Judith. "Now change, either out here in the open where we can all see, or far back in the woods with only me for company and a rope tied to your arm so I know where you are!"

Corwin joined the combatants, who were getting nowhere on their own. "Just make Judith talk the whole time, Thurkill. If you can hear her, you will know where she is."

"Talk about what?" Judith asked, incredulous.

"Describe the plants and trees you see," he suggested. "Or simply continue to complain. You do so rather well and loudly."

"She does that!" Thurkill agreed.

Corwin ignored the glare Judith aimed at him. Sensing Thurkill's softening of temper, he continued, "Or she might sing. Since Judith has a lovely speaking voice I would think she can manage a song. Unless, of course, she cannot hit a note squarely. Then I would rather listen to her complain."

"A song," Thurkill said in a wistful tone. "Can you sing, my lady?"

"Certes, I can," she huffed. "But I will not serve as your evening's entertainment."

Thurkill shrugged as if he weren't disappointed. "Then think of something to say and go change. Do not go far, and be aware that the moment I cannot hear you I will come looking for you."

Judith's brow scrunched in thought. Then she smiled, too wickedly for comfort, and flounced into the woods. When just out of sight, she began a wholly unexpected recitation in Norman French. The minx! Corwin pursed his lips tightly to hold back laughter.

"What is she saying?" Thurkill asked.

"She recites *Beowulf*," Corwin said, his grin spreading despite his best efforts.

"*Beowulf?*" Thurkill exclaimed, frowning. "Why in French?"

Judith, too, must have noticed her captors didn't understand the language, and so could take no pleasure in the story's telling. "Well, she *did* say she wouldn't be your entertainment."

"Humph," Thurkill uttered. Slowly, a smile lit his face. "An imp, she is. Ah, if I were younger..."

Judith interrupted her tale to call out, "Can you hear me?"

"Aye," Thurkill answered.

"Can you see me?"

"Nay."

Judith resumed the story and, Corwin imagined, began to remove the nun's robe. She would gather fistfuls of the black robe and pull the garment up over her head, baring her body to the fading sunlight and warm breeze. Or did she wear a shift of fine white linen to protect her smooth, silken skin from the coarser wool?

He'd touched her but the once, this morning when halting her escape. When placing his hands on her shoulders, his fingers had momentarily brushed against her neck. Corwin didn't think she'd noticed his swift physical reaction, or how he'd struggled to focus on his purpose. If Thurkill hadn't come along... But he had, thank the fates.

After turning Judith around, he'd shoved her much harder than necessary, more to break contact with her than for Thurkill's benefit.

He must keep duty foremost in his mind. Not allow Judith's dove-gray eyes to distract him from his purpose. Ignore the apology that explained why she'd once turned him aside, an apology that may have been sincere and only delivered poorly. He shouldn't be standing here wondering if Judith, this moment, stood gloriously naked within hearing distance.

"Thurkill, I know where we can get a horse for Judith."

"I am not sure I want her to have one. I shudder to think of how far we will have to chase her if she decides to take off again."

Corwin could understand Thurkill's hesitancy, but when the right time came, a successful escape might depend upon Judith having a horse.

"Mayhap if she is not so sore at day's end her disposition would sweeten. Besides, if this journey will be as long as I think it will, 'tis asking much of your mount to carry the two of you the whole way."

Thurkill's eyes narrowed. "Think you know, do you?"

"Only time will prove me right or wrong. In the meantime, I know of a baron who lives north of Oxford who raises fine horses. I can purchase one of them for Judith."

"Buy? You carry so great a sum?"

"'Twill nearly empty my purse, but I should have enough."

"Humph. How do I know you will not give us away somehow?"

"Send Duncan or Oswuld with me. Either one could act as my squire and report my every move and word to you."

Thurkill grimaced as though pained, and rubbed at the area just below his ribs. "I will think on it."

"Something wrong?"

"Nay, I just need something to eat."

Oswuld came toward them, a metal cup in his hand. He

gave it to Thurkill, who drank it without comment. Only the scrunch of Thurkill's nose told Corwin that the cup contained something other than ale or water. Something bitter. A potion?

The melodic sound of Judith's voice drew Corwin's attention away from father and son. Her recital became louder, then stopped abruptly as she came out of the woods. Gray suited her coloring better than black. The lighter gown hugged her body more closely than the heavy robe.

Judith would be beautiful if draped in a flour sack.

She wore a shift. A narrow band of white hung below the hem of the gown. She hadn't bared her naked body to the sunlight and breeze. Knowing she'd remained covered didn't completely banish the erotic vision that had formed in his head.

"North of Oxford, you say?"

Corwin dragged his attention back to Thurkill. "We shall be near the castle by midmorn, I should think."

Thurkill swirled the potion in his cup. "Oswuld goes with you."

"Nay, I should go," Duncan protested. "Oswuld is too trusting. He would not know the baron's men were about to seize him until the deed was done."

"I would not send my son to a Norman holding if I thought he would be seized," Thurkill said quietly. "Besides, on the morrow you go into Oxford for supplies. I tire of rabbit and squirrel."

He quaffed the last dregs from his cup. To Corwin's surprise, Judith snatched the cup from the old man's hand. She sniffed at it, then stared at Thurkill for a long time. To his further amazement, she neither threw the nun's robe at Thurkill nor railed at the old man who she normally upbraided at every turn.

Instead, she returned the cup to Thurkill and very quietly

asked, "What will you and I do while the others are off on their errands?"

"Mayhap, if I plead sweetly, your ladyship will consent to recite *Beowulf* for me in a language I understand."

"I think not," she said, and walked off.

Thurkill followed at her heels, suggesting she consider *Song of Roland,* leaving Corwin to wonder what the hell had just happened.

What had Judith detected in the cup to affect her attitude so forcefully?

Chapter Six

The following morning, with Oswuld as his companion, Corwin headed for a manor belonging to an ally of Gerard of Wilmont.

"Who is this man we go to see?" Oswuld asked.

"Perrin de Saville, Lord of Aimsley."

"A Norman."

Corwin noted Oswuld's worry. "All you need do is sit tight and let me do the talking. All will be well."

Oswuld didn't look so sure, and Corwin couldn't blame him. There was much to worry over if something went wrong. For his part in the kidnapping, Oswuld could hang if caught. However, Corwin didn't want Oswuld riding into Aimsley looking as if he might bolt at any moment.

"We probably will not deal with de Saville. Most likely he is at court and leaves Sedrick, his steward, in charge." When that had no effect, Corwin tried another tack. "Oswuld, your father would not have allowed you to come with me if he believed you would not return."

"Father is beginning to trust you. I hope his faith is warranted."

"Well, he does have Duncan to remind him to have a care."

Oswuld's worried expression eased into a faint smile. "Aye, there is always Duncan, who trusts no one, not even Father, I wager."

"And you?"

"I will go along with whatever Father decides."

Corwin reined his horse to a stop, the better to question Oswuld.

"Over the past days I have noticed several things about this little band of ours. I gather your father joined the rebellion because he would prefer the rule of a Saxon king. Duncan simply hates Normans and anyone closely connected with them. But you...you do not seem to care. True?"

"True enough."

"Then why bother to join the rebellion?"

Oswuld shifted in his saddle. "When Father got it into his head to join, my brother and I discussed it. It seemed best if he stayed behind to look after...our interests and I go with Father."

Interests? A farm? Nay, more likely a place of business. Corwin could easily see Thurkill as a merchant of some sort. His other son, likely the elder, had stayed behind to mind the family's finances, sending the younger to look after their father.

Corwin thought back on last night. Thurkill rubbing his chest. The potion Oswuld had given him. "Your father is ill, is he not?"

"His heart ails him."

"Yet he risks his life."

Oswuld let his anger show. "Late one night a group of mercenaries downed a bit too much ale and talked of the rebellion they were on their way to join. After Father heard, nothing we said would stop him."

"So you take care of him."

"Someone must. He will not do so himself."

Corwin fought pangs of sympathy. During his own father's last years, he'd needed care. Ardith had borne most of the burden, both before and after marrying Gerard. She'd been both bereft and relieved at their father's death. As for himself, he'd grieved, but had the sole responsibility for Lenvil, and his other duties for Wilmont, to occupy his time and mind. Oswuld wouldn't have those things, not with an older brother to inherit.

Bah! Corwin mustn't let his feelings become entangled with these men. They were rebels, bent on taking over the kingdom. Men, women and children would suffer—and die—if war came. Peasants more than the nobility.

He kicked his horse into motion, realizing Judith already knew about Thurkill's ailment. Last eve, after taking a sniff of the potion in Thurkill's cup, she'd stopped shouting at him, as was her habit. A reminder to her, too, about becoming involved wouldn't be amiss.

Corwin had no sooner passed through Aimsley's gate when Sedrick, the short, paunchy steward, scurried across the bailey to greet him.

"Hail, Sedrick!" Corwin shouted in English, hoping the steward would follow his lead. He wanted Oswuld to understand every word said to report to Thurkill. To his relief, Sedrick answered in kind.

"Corwin, lad, there you are! Do you know that most of the shire is looking for you?"

Damn, so word had spread. It didn't surprise him. Judith's kidnapping would be juicy news, retold by travelers and peddlers as they went from town to manor to castle. The sheriff had probably also sent messengers to the larger towns and more important personages in the area, alerting officials to be on the lookout for a royal heiress. Corwin just hadn't expected the news to travel this far so quickly.

Corwin dismounted and tried to make light of the situation. "Surely, Sedrick, not most of the shire. How did you hear?"

"The sheriff himself was here yesterday, told us of the woman being kidnapped and that you were on the hunt. Did you find her yet?"

Yesterday? The sheriff moved fast—too fast.

"I am getting close, which is why I came to you. I need another horse, and next to Wilmont stock, Aimsley's is the best. What have you that is fit for a royal heiress to ride?"

Sedrick's mouth widened to a toothy grin. "There is a mare that will do. Sleek and swift. What you are after, right?"

"Dare I hope for gentle, too?"

"Come look."

Leading his horse through the busy bailey toward the stables, Corwin followed Sedrick—who looked at him strangely, then laughed.

"What is this? You grow a beard?"

Corwin rubbed at the growth on his face. When he didn't think about it, it didn't feel strange. He hadn't scraped his face in several mornings, thinking if he, too, sported a beard, he might fit in with his fellow Saxons better.

Had Judith noticed? Did she approve or not?

"Since embarking on this quest, I have had little time to eat or sleep, much less scrape my whiskers," he told Sedrick, who seemed to accept the explanation.

"Who is the lad?" Sedrick asked.

Corwin glanced back at Oswuld who, thankfully, didn't look ready to bolt. "Tracker."

Sedrick nodded his approval, then pointed to a mare at the far end of the paddock. "Will she suit your purpose?"

Oh, the mare would suit wonderfully. She was sleek and

firmly muscled, with a coat more red than brown, a mane of shiny ebony. Judith would be thrilled.

"She is truly a beauty," Corwin commented. "I imagine de Saville asks a fortune for her."

"He does," Sedrick acknowledged. "However, considering your purpose, I am sure my lord would be willing to give you the use of her." He chuckled. "If you do not return her in good order, he can always send a debt collector to seek payment from Gerard of Wilmont."

And Gerard would pay whatever price asked, with no hesitation, when given the reason for the purchase.

"Throw in a saddle and you have a bargain."

"Done." Sedrick shouted at a stable boy to saddle the mare, then said, "My lord might also be willing to lend you a few of his knights."

A generous offer, and one Corwin was tempted to take. He could leave Oswuld under guard here, and with a few knights, capture Thurkill and Duncan and force the two to lead them to the rebel encampment.

Could they be forced? Duncan would slit his own throat first, or fight until someone had to kill him. Thurkill would likely lead a company of knights on a merry chase all over England. Nay, without knowledge of where the rebel encampment might be, the easiest and fastest way to learn the encampment's whereabouts was to proceed with the plan he'd already set in motion.

Corwin shook his head. "I thank you for the offer, but believe I can travel more quickly without them. Tell me, has the sheriff a large company with him?"

"Twelve men, if I remember aright."

"Has he searched Oxford yet? I thought to, but if he already has, I will pass by the city and return to the countryside."

"I believe he planned to do so today."

While the sheriff searched the town, Corwin and the rebels could ride swiftly north. The irony—that he was thinking like a brigand running from the law—struck him as both uncomfortable and funny. But if he wanted the rebels to lead him to their camp, he must keep them from getting caught.

Then he remembered. Duncan had gone into Oxford.

Judith rose from where she sat as Corwin and Oswuld sped into the campsite. Both looked harried.

Corwin led a magnificent mare. Dainty and sleek, reddish-brown in color, she tossed her black mane in protest at the sudden halt.

"Has Duncan returned?" Corwin called out.

"Not as yet," Thurkill answered.

"Damn," Corwin said softly as both he and Oswuld dismounted.

"Is something amiss?"

"Aye. The sheriff is in Oxford."

Judith half listened to the details of Oswuld's report on how Corwin had obtained the horse and learned of the sheriff's whereabouts. She ignored the discussion that followed over whether or not to wait for Duncan. She'd become much too engrossed with the beautiful horse meant for her.

The last time she'd been on a horse of this quality she'd been a young girl. Her father kept a stable of fine horses, and she'd been allowed to ride any she thought she could handle. She ran a hand down the mare's sleek neck, remembering a gallop over the moors on another mare of fleet foot and high spirits. So long ago.

She hadn't thought of those days in so very long. Of her parents. Of a large, busting manor on a holding where she knew everyone and everyone knew her. Of feasts held in celebration of one thing or another, and afterward gossiping and giggling with her female cousins when they should have been sleeping.

Of home.

Judith dashed away the tear forming in the corner of her eye. 'Twas useless to shed tears over a moment of silly sentiment.

"Beautiful, is she not?" Corwin said.

Judith gave him a smile. "Most beautiful. Your friend keeps a fine stable."

"Not my friend, but Gerard's. And, aye, his stock is nearly as fine as that of Wilmont. Can you handle her?"

"Oh, I believe I can. I admit it has been a long time since I rode a horse of spirit, but 'tis a skill one never forgets."

"Hop up, then. Let us get the two of you acquainted."

She glanced over at Thurkill and Oswuld, who were watching from several paces off. Neither seemed ready to mount.

"We leave?"

"Not as yet. We will wait awhile more for Duncan."

"Mayhap the sheriff will capture him," she said softly.

Corwin chuckled. "Not likely, my lady. They look for three men and a woman, not a lone man who can blend in with the city folk."

Corwin boosted her into the saddle. Her gown had a generous skirt, but she had to pull it up some. Luckily, for modesty's sake, the hem covered the very tops of her leather boots. Still, she could feel Corwin's hands wrap around her ankles as he adjusted the stirrups.

"How is that?" he asked.

"Most comfortable," she said, and held out her hand for the reins.

Corwin didn't give them over. "Not yet, Judith. Thurkill still is not sure getting you a horse was a wise thing to do.

You may have to settle for being led all the way to the rebel camp.'' He tugged on the reins to urge the mare forward. "So, when was the last time you sat a horse?"

Judith buried her disappointment. Naturally, Thurkill feared she would use the mare in another attempt to escape.

"Five years ago,'' she answered, taking what pleasure she could in the ride. The mare possessed a smooth gait, and sitting in a saddle was a grand improvement over straddling the rump of Thurkill's horse.

"So long?"

"I was ten and three when my father sent me to Romsey Abbey. The only horses there belonging to the queen's guard, and then only when she was in residence. Not that it made any difference. The abbess forbade me to go near them."

"Why so? Most noblewomen can ride, and do it well. Did she worry for your safety?"

"She worried that riding would remind me of home, and that I was of royal blood, and…well…I think she may have feared as Thurkill fears, that I might escape."

Corwin led the horse around the campsite at an easy walk. For all she wasn't in control, Judith still enjoyed the ride.

"Would you have tried to escape?"

"Nay. I knew my duty. I was sent to Romsey as a companion to Queen Matilda when she visited. In turn, Matilda taught me the ways of the court and the workings of politics. My father wished me to become educated so I might one day be a helpmate to whoever is chosen as my husband. So I stayed."

"And were you content?"

She let out a light laugh, hearing the sadness in it. "I was given no choice."

No choice at all. Except the offer made by Abbess Christina, who'd wanted her to take the veil and eventually become an abbess, which hadn't truly been a choice. Judith knew she wasn't suited to life in a cloister. Corwin had played a part in that realization, though he didn't know it.

Handsome and agreeable, he'd made a grand first impression. Her young heart had fairly fluttered at his smile. His kindness was a quality she'd much admired. Corwin had seemed the answer to a maiden's dream. If someone had asked her that day to choose between Corwin and another, she might well have chosen Corwin.

Foolish thoughts. Her family wouldn't have allowed her to make such a marriage. 'Twas useless to dwell on what could never be, to wish for things one couldn't have. She reached down to pat the mare's neck.

"Her gait is so smooth I could ride for hours," she said, changing the subject from her past to the present. She didn't particularly want to think of the future, either—a future wrought with uncertainty.

"You might be careful of what you say, my lady. If Duncan returns soon, we might ride fast until the sun sets."

"With the sheriff on our tails."

"Mayhap."

Then she would have to make a choice. Follow Corwin, or make a dash for the sheriff.

Once more, Corwin made a circle of the campsite. When he finally stopped, he reached up to help her down. She braced her hands on his shoulders, so wide and solid. His hands warm on her waist, he eased her down as if she were featherlight.

"Judith?"

She looked up into eyes of startling blue, into a face touched by gentleness yet set in an intent expression.

"When this is done," he said, "I will take you to wherever and to whomever you choose to go. I swear it you."

Then he bent his head, and just as she realized what he was about, his lips were on hers in a kiss so gentle she nearly swooned, but so brief she wondered if it had happened.

Her tingling mouth knew, and her trembling body knew, though her mind needed a moment to realize he'd truly kissed her. When it did, she spun her head to look for her kidnappers. She needn't have worried. Corwin had placed the mare so Thurkill and Oswuld couldn't see them.

For the life of her, she couldn't decide if she should seek another kiss or berate him soundly for taking dangerous liberties. She reached up and touched his cheek.

"You grow a beard," she said, the roughness of it still a whisper of a memory against her chin.

"Like it?"

She didn't have the chance to answer. Duncan galloped into the camp as if Satan himself was snapping at his heels.

Corwin shifted in the saddle to ease his continuing discomfort and tried to concentrate on the task at hand: evading the sheriff.

They were traveling at a good pace, but not fast enough to suit him. Thurkill insisted on leading Judith's mare, which slowed them. Several hours remained before nightfall, time enough to get a good lead on the sheriff and his men—if Duncan was right about the sheriff making a thorough search of Oxford. With luck, the sheriff wouldn't leave the city until tomorrow morning.

Damn. Corwin shouldn't have kissed Judith, not even gotten near her. What if the mare had shied and exposed their brief touch of lips to Thurkill? What if Judith had cried out in either surprise or anger?

But neither had happened. The well-trained mare had stood her ground, and Judith...she'd retasted the kiss with the tip of her tongue and looked up at him as if she craved more of a sweet treat.

He'd kissed her more than an hour ago. The band had ridden several leagues to gain ground on the sheriff. Corwin purposely rode at the back, placing Duncan and Oswuld between him and Judith, hoping if he didn't see her clearly the kiss would no longer haunt him.

Useless gesture. Corwin didn't need to see the woman to know the feel of her palms braced on his shoulders, the warmth of her body against his hands, the sweetness of her lips pressed to his. He could tell himself from now until the second coming that he'd kissed her to give comfort and offer sympathy. To seal a promise given. Nonsense, all of it. He'd kissed her because she was there, in his arms, and it had felt so right.

On the day they'd met he'd wondered how Judith would taste, how she would respond. Since their reunion, thoughts of her had haunted his nights and brightened his days. He'd ached to hold her, press her close, feel her warmth, always wondering if her lips were as soft and moist as they looked. Now he knew, and doubted he would ever forget. His desire for her might lessen with time and distance. The sharp pangs of lust might fade into a sweet memory.

But he would never forget.

A low, distant rumbling set the hair on the back of Corwin's neck to tingling. Corwin never ignored his instincts; they'd saved his hide far too many times. The group of riders coming up hard and fast behind them might not be the sheriff's men, but he couldn't take the risk. Quickly, he overtook Thurkill and did what came naturally—gave orders.

"A large group comes up on our rear. Mayhap the sheriff, mayhap not. Judith, slide on with Thurkill. Oswuld, grab hold of her horse and remain behind with me. The rest of you head for the river and find a place to hide until the danger is past.''

''Why not just make a run for it?'' Duncan asked.

''Because if it is the sheriff, he will likely catch us. I may be able to misdirect him. If not, there is no harm done.''

''He is right, Duncan,'' Thurkill said before Duncan could voice another objection. ''If Corwin can cause a delay in his progress, we stand a better chance of evading capture.''

Corwin met Thurkill's evaluating stare head-on. It lasted only moments before Thurkill said, ''We will do as you say. Duncan will wipe out our tracks, so we will need to watch for you. If we are unable to rejoin, meet us at the White Swan Inn, south of Coventry.''

Duncan's horse pranced, reacting to his rider's anger. In disbelief, Duncan turned away from Thurkill and sidled toward Corwin. ''I obey because Thurkill orders me to,'' he said, spitting out the words. ''I swear to you, Corwin of Lenvil, if the sheriff catches us, *your* life is forfeit.''

''Protect Judith. I will see what I can do with the sheriff.''

The lady they all vowed to keep safe, though for different reasons, wore a strange expression. With her brow scrunched and her mouth forming a pout, Corwin couldn't tell if she expressed concern or was pondering on how to thwart his plan.

Thurkill spurred his horse. Duncan followed in his dust.

Corwin hated letting Judith out of his sight, entrusting Thurkill and Duncan with her well-being. If anything happened to her, the *rebels'* lives were forfeit. He watched until they disappeared around a curve in the road.

''Now what?'' Oswuld asked.

''We block the road. Keep your sword at the ready.''

"What do you want me to do?"

Sounds of the approaching horses grew louder. Oswuld was far more nervous now than he'd been when entering the Norman stronghold. "The same as you did at Aimsley. Stay on your horse and let me do the talking. If there is trouble, ride for all you are worth and take not to lead them to your father. And Oswuld, if this is the sheriff, he will be Norman and speak in his own language. You will not know what we say."

Oswuld sighed. "I guessed as much. One would think the rulers of a country would take the time to learn the tongue of those they rule, if only to give orders."

Corwin placed his warhorse in the middle of the narrow road and dismounted. He didn't have long to wait until the group appeared. At its head rode a man clad in chain mail, followed by only a handful of soldiers. Sedrick had said the sheriff led a company of twelve. Mayhap Corwin had worried for nothing.

His hope disappeared when the leader slowed and then stopped. The lank man of middling years leaned forward and asked in Norman French, "Might I assume you are Corwin of Lenvil?"

"Who asks?"

"Robert of Oxford, Sheriff of Hampshire."

"Then you assume correctly. How did you know?"

"Your man, William, gave me a rather detailed description of you—" his eyes darted about Corwin's person, "—and your horse and sword hilt. Would that I had received as good a description of our villains from the nuns. Three bearded Saxons. One old, two young. The younger men named Osgoode and Dunstan, or so they thought. Not much, hmm?"

"Ah, well," Corwin said, smiling. "At least to you they gave names."

The sheriff's gaze finally rested on Oswuld. "I expected you to be alone."

"I thought it wise to hire an extra set of eyes," Corwin said, staying with the same story he'd told Sedrick this morning. This man was smart, missed nothing. The sheriff truly had no reason to suspect Corwin of anything other than setting out to rescue Judith. Still, Corwin knew it best to draw no adverse attention.

"And the mare?" the sheriff asked.

"Purchased this morning at Aimsley, for Lady Judith if I find her. Sedrick told me you intended to search Oxford today. I gather you did not find her."

"Not as yet, but I will." The conviction in the sheriff's tone gave Corwin a moment's pause. "I left part of my force to search the city, but no one I talked with remembered seeing a woman in a nun's robe in the company of three men. 'Twould be an oddity people would remark upon. I suspect they are somewhere ahead of me yet, as you do, or you would not be here."

Corwin seized the chance to misdirect the sheriff.

"I begin to wonder if I am mistaken."

"Truly? Why so?"

"Obviously, our villains took Lady Judith in order to demand a ransom for her return. Agreed?"

"One would think so."

"Just because they headed north after the kidnapping does not mean they continued north for a long way. Did you lose their trail in the forest, not far from the abbey, as I did?"

The sheriff made a face, revealing his chagrin. "They seemed to travel in circles. But they did make the road, eventually. As you did."

"True. Since then, signs of their passing have been harder to find, and I wonder if we have not both been played for fools. Consider, Sheriff. One of them could have taken the lady to a place of safekeeping, and the others are leading the two of us away from her."

The sheriff thought about the suggestion, then shook his head. "'Tis possible, Corwin, but my gut tells me they all head north. If I do not find them by the time I reach Coventry, then I will have to give your suspicion more thought. For now, I will stay the course."

The man was both tenacious and cautious; Corwin would give him that. He swallowed his disappointment in not turning the sheriff around. "Will you follow the road?"

"Aye, for the most part. You are most welcome to ride with me."

A natural thing for Corwin to do if he were still in pursuit of the rebels, intent on rescuing Judith and bringing the brigands to justice. Instead, he had to find their hiding place to keep them from going to Coventry and possibly being caught.

"Consider this, Sheriff. I will do you the favor of searching the river from here to where it bends west. If I do not find them, I will head back to Cotswold and leave the search in your capable hands. If I do find them, I will send word to you in Coventry."

The sheriff smiled. "When William told me of you, he also bragged of your skill with a sword. If you find them, try not to kill them all. I want to see at least one hang."

Corwin gave a slight bow. "I shall do my best, my lord sheriff."

With a flourish, Robert, Sheriff of Hampshire, continued his journey north, along the road Thurkill had taken and Corwin prayed fervently that he'd left.

"How are your tracking skills, Oswuld? Think we can find your father?"

"Mayhap. I gather there is some urgency? I do not understand French, but understood the word *Coventry*. Is that where he intends to go?''

"I tried to alter his course, but to no avail. We need to warn Thurkill.''

Oswuld smiled. "I do believe you are truly a rebel now, Corwin. This makes the second time today you have misled a Norman. They will not be pleased when they find out.''

Inwardly, Corwin cringed. No matter what happened with the rebellion, there may very well be a penalty to pay for having lied to the sheriff. "Only one. Sedrick is Flemish, not Norman. Besides, the punishment for joining the rebellion will be severe if it fails. I do hope this leader of yours is a good commander or we will all hang right beside him.''

"Too true.'' Oswuld looked up the road. "I hope Duncan did not cover his tracks too well, but knowing him, he did a thorough job.''

Duncan certainly had. After two hours and as many backtrackings, Corwin finally found the spot where they'd left the road. After that, he counted on a broken twig here and a hoofprint in the leaf-carpeted forest floor there—and a good bit of luck—to guide his way.

Corwin was about to give up when he saw Duncan at the edge of the water—across the river.

"Duncan!'' Oswuld cried out. "Where did you cross?''

Duncan pointed downstream. "Back a ways, other side the man-height boulder. The horses will need to swim some.''

Corwin turned his warhorse around and retraced his path. By the time he and Oswuld crossed the river and found the campsite, Corwin was wet and tired, and wanted nothing more than a bite to eat and a patch of long grass on which to lay his head.

Judith came up, looking worried. She laid a hand on

Oswuld's leg as he sat on his mount. "I think you should have a word with your father. The ride this afternoon taxed him sorely. He does not look well."

Corwin swore inwardly. If the old man died, or even grew too ill to retain command, Duncan would certainly take over as leader. Given the man's distrust and animosity, Corwin didn't doubt that one of Duncan's first acts as leader would be to rid the band of its newest member.

Chapter Seven

Judith helped Corwin with the horses while Oswuld mixed a potion for his father. Duncan hadn't yet returned from his fishing, and Judith hoped he'd catch several trout. For their evening meal Thurkill wasn't the only one tired of rabbit and squirrel, and Duncan hadn't brought back supplies.

"How bad is Thurkill?" Corwin asked as he removed the saddle from Judith's mare.

"He tells me he needs something to eat and a night's rest, but I fear there is more to his illness than weariness. While we were crossing the river, he might have fallen off the horse had I not held him on."

"Oswuld told me his father has a heart ailment."

That explained why Thurkill had rubbed at his chest last night. Why he'd spent part of the mad dash to this spot slumped forward and had nearly slid off the saddle while crossing the river. She'd suspected he was in great pain after detecting hawthorn in his potion, though she hadn't known the pain was in his heart.

"Does Duncan know?" she asked.

"I think so. Why?"

"He pushed us hard," she said, her ire rising once more. "Neither Thurkill nor I saw any reason to cross the river—'' taxing the horses, getting her skirts wet, soaking her boots, which would take forever to dry out ''—but Duncan insisted. He believed the more obstacles we placed between us and the sheriff, the better. Was the sheriff behind us?''

"Aye." Corwin handed her his blanket. "Rub the mare down with this while I unsaddle the other two."

"You sent the sheriff on his way, I suppose."

"You knew that was my intent."

She'd known, but hadn't uttered a word of protest when Corwin ordered her off her mare and onto Thurkill's horse. She'd obeyed his command immediately, even knowing if she turned her mare around and bolted toward the oncoming riders, she might be headed toward a safe haven instead of still being held captive.

True, Thurkill had held the mare's reins, and he might have not allowed her to escape. But she hadn't tried.

The mare leaned into the rubdown, enjoying the scratch of wool against her hide. Judith found a measure of peace in the work.

Corwin chuckled. "If that mare were a cat, she would purr."

Judith smiled at the observation. "She enjoys the pampering. Has she a name?"

"Likely, but Sedrick did not mention one, and I was in so much of a hurry to get her back to you I did not think to ask."

"She is truly a beautiful mare. Mayhap that is what I will call her—Beauty."

When Corwin didn't comment, she looked toward him. He'd unsaddled the other two horses and stood near his destrier, staring at her.

"Aye," he said. "A true beauty."

His stare intensified, reflecting a raw animal hunger that

sent a warm flush through her body, head to toe. Corwin wasn't talking about the horse, she knew. Mercy, she was so disheveled she must look like the lowest of wantons. And she felt wanton, purely female, about to be pounced upon by the strongest, most virile of males.

Judith fought the desire that coiled low and deep. She shouldn't want Corwin's attention, or long for the press of another kiss, or wonder if he would caress her again if they were private.

Of course he would. He would do more than kiss her if she let him, and she very much feared she would let him do whatever he pleased. He'd been the first to arouse her female curiosity about coupling with a man. Her curiosity hadn't abated, and again she longed for Corwin to show her the ways of the world, what could happen between male and female.

At the moment, she wanted to be someone other than who she was, Judith Canmore, royal heiress. She longed to be a woman free to play the wanton, use whatever female wiles she might possess to lure the mate she desired to her bed. A mate strong, virile and intelligent—a man possessed of broad shoulders and a commanding voice.

She'd responded to Corwin's command, believing he knew what he was about, that she could trust him to do what was best. She'd listened with her heart, not her head. Was that wise? She didn't know, but she had to allow that at some time she'd begun to trust him, and had sealed her fate to his the moment she'd obeyed him.

Thurkill and Oswuld were beginning to trust Corwin, too. Not Duncan. Duncan trusted no one, not even Thurkill.

"You stare too hard, Corwin," she finally said, having become aware once more of the captors who watched. "Someone will notice."

"They can hardly be angry at me for what they do themselves."

"They do not stare at me as you do."

"Not for the same reason, but have you not noticed Thurkill's long looks? I think he begins to wonder if he has done the right thing by kidnapping you. Duncan stares, trying to guess when you might take it into your head to run again, I think. But Oswuld—the poor lad, I think he is half in love with you. Have you not noticed how he dotes on you?"

"He is just being kind."

"He is moonstruck, caught in the spell of a lovely, charming woman."

'Twas probably the height of foolishness to ask, but she had to know. "And you, Corwin, are you susceptible to spells?"

He tilted his head, his smile pensive. "Thinking of using one on me to help you escape? I cannot do that, Judith. You know why."

Corwin had every right to be suspicious of her motives for asking.

"Nay," she said softly. "I have decided to trust you, Corwin. I will not try to run away again. We will learn what we can, then take the news to whoever you think best. You lead, I will follow."

He raised a hand to reach out to her, then closed it into a fist and let it fall. "What changed your mind?"

Judith took the few steps separating them and gave Corwin the blanket. "I am not sure," she admitted. "All I know is that I did not try to escape this morning when I had a chance at success, and that I worried over you until you found us again. At some time I must have realized your plan is a good one, that only we can stop this rebellion. I stay with you, Corwin."

Nor could she bear the thought of being parted from him. On the verge of confessing her feelings, she walked off to check on Thurkill.

Oswuld hovered over his father, a worried look on his face. She, too, felt a pang of worry. Thurkill didn't look good at all, no better than he had since he'd slid off his horse and sat down on the ground. With his back against a log, he hadn't moved from the spot.

His smile for her was weak. "So, my lady, you have your horse back. I saw you rub her down," he said, his voice stronger than she'd imagined it would be.

"I will admit riding the mare is highly preferable to bouncing around behind you."

"I imagine it is," he commented, then told Oswuld, "Fetch Corwin. I wish to hear his tale of the meeting with the sheriff."

Oswuld looked from his father to her. Judith understood his concern.

"Go," she said, "I will sit with him."

Reassured, Oswuld turned and headed toward Corwin.

"I need no nursemaid," Thurkill grumbled. "Oswuld worries overmuch."

"Does he? I wonder," she said, making the log her perch.

"I need but rest and food."

"So you have said." She picked up the metal cup Thurkill had set aside. She sniffed at the dregs, noting the odors. "What herbs other than hawthorn are in this potion Oswuld gave you?"

"I know not. Oswuld mixes it, I drink it. Have you recovered from this afternoon's ride?"

Judith noted his attempt to change the subject and ignored it. "But for the discomfort of wet boots, I am fine.

You, however, possess the pallor of old flour and the strength of a newborn kitten."

"I will be fine by morn."

Judith had her doubts.

Corwin gave her only a passing glance before he settled in to tell Thurkill of the meeting with the sheriff. Duncan returned with two large fish and listened as he scraped the scales away with his dagger. After Corwin finished, Oswuld gave his own impressions of the meeting.

"The sheriff knew Corwin right off, but as he said, the nuns did a bad job of describing us. They even got our names wrong. The sheriff looked right at me and dismissed me."

"Humph, why would the sheriff pay any heed to you?" Duncan interjected. "If he catches us, he will be pleased. But we are not his quarry. The princess is. I imagine the royals will reward quite handsomely anyone who takes her back to Romsey."

Thurkill rubbed his eyes. "Aye, but if the sheriff finds Judith, he also finds us, and I prefer that does not come to pass."

"We should stay off the road," Corwin said. "The men the sheriff left to search Oxford may have orders to ride on to Coventry when finished. Can we get to...wherever we are going if we change our course?"

Thurkill looked from Duncan to Oswuld before he answered, "Aye. 'Twill take us longer, but it can be done."

"Not too much longer, I hope," Duncan said. "We must arrive within—soon."

Thurkill nodded, then leaned his head back and closed his eyes.

Judith watched Thurkill's chest rise and fall. "Oswuld, show me what herbs you give your father." With just a look, he questioned her request. "I know something of medicinal herbs. Mayhap I can suggest another that would further ease his pain.''

"Have a care, Oswuld. She may think to poison me for my sins against her,'' Thurkill said, only half teasing, Judith thought.

So Corwin was right. Thurkill was questioning her kidnapping, wondering if he'd made a mistake.

"Oh, I would not worry, Thurkill,'' she assured him. "I have no need to hasten your death. You do a good job of that all on your own.''

As Judith left, Corwin decided she had the right of it. The stress and exertion after kidnapping Judith were taking a heavy toll on Thurkill. Mayhap, with stronger herbs and more rest, the man's condition would improve. Or at least keep him alive long enough to complete the journey.

"She is right, you know,'' he told Thurkill. "You need to get more rest. I will take your stint at guard duty tonight.''

"I forbid it!'' Duncan shouted, getting to his feet.

"Forbid?'' Thurkill asked. "So long as I breathe, I am still in command, Duncan.''

Duncan backed down only slightly. "Strongly protest, then. He is not yet one of us.''

"Not yet, but he will be.''

"That, Thurkill, is not your decision to make, as you admitted when you let him ride with us. 'Tis…our leader who will decide. Yet you give Corwin liberties as if there were no question of his acceptance. Well, *I* question.''

Corwin got to his feet. "Duncan, I am at a loss where you are concerned. You are right about the reward for Judith's return. 'Tis likely hefty, yet I have not taken her back to collect it. I went into a Norman holding this morn and obtained a horse for her, without arousing a single suspicion. A few hours ago, I dealt with the sheriff. There have been several opportunities for me to turn you in, and I have not done so.''

"You say you aroused no suspicion. You say you dealt with the sheriff. Did you really, or will we wake up some morn to find the sheriff's men or Norman knights surrounding us?'' He shook his head. ''I trust you not, Corwin of Lenvil. You are not one of us. Your name may be Saxon, but you are far too Norman in manner for my taste. Not even the beard you grow will convince me otherwise.'' Duncan glanced at Thurkill before continuing. ''Take the guard duty if you must, but beware. I, too, know how to sleep with one eye open and my hand upon my sword.''

Guard duty proved boring when there was little to guard against. They were far from the road, well away from any town or village. Not even animals scurried about to break the dullness.

So Corwin watched Judith sleep.

'Twas a heady sensation, having her confidence. Something in her voice, and in the way she looked at him when she'd handed her care over to him, said she meant it.

You lead, I will follow.

Might she have also been sincere when she'd apologized for snubbing him all those years ago? Might the words have been truly meant but just delivered badly? Or was he fooling himself, wanting to believe?

She'd been subdued all evening. After finishing the evening meal, she and Oswuld had gone off hunting for some herb she claimed might help Thurkill. Corwin had given a brief thought to going along, not so much to help hunt, but just to be near her. To listen to the sound of her voice, to see her smile, to simply enjoy her company.

From somewhere, he'd found the willpower to remain in camp. 'Twould not be wise to become overattentive, which might raise suspicions among the rebels. They considered her the future wife of their lord and would become displeased if he paid undue attention to the woman they would make their queen.

Too, he couldn't trust himself not to find some excuse to send Oswuld off on his own so he could be alone with Judith. He wanted her, and if he judged her reactions to him aright, she wanted him, too. 'Twould be so easy, so pleasurable to wrap his arms around her, kiss her lush mouth until she moaned, strip her naked and caress every inch of her until both of them were senseless. When she cried out his name, he'd bury himself deep within her softness and stroke her solidly to the heights of ecstasy.

He could do it now. Remove his chain mail, lay down next to her, have her. Only the two of them would know.

Duncan's threat to remain awake had succumbed to the rigors of the day. Corwin gave him credit for trying, but the man's eyes had closed and stayed that way nearly an hour ago. The two of them were going to come to blows one day. Corwin knew it in his bones. Each time Thurkill allowed Corwin a new responsibility, Duncan's resistance increased. Someday, Duncan's anger would get the best of him and he would draw his sword.

As much as he was glad Duncan slept, Corwin almost wished Duncan didn't now snore. Resisting temptation was always easier if one feared one would get caught.

His current temptation moved her arm, a slight movement to gain comfort. Judith didn't wake, or reach out for him, or beckon him to her side. But he felt her pull.

You lead, I will follow.

And she would, right up to the gates of the rebels' stronghold, then down whatever road he chose to spread the news of the rebellion. He had no right to ask more from her, even if she was willing.

The risks were too great, both to their safety and his sanity. Duty demanded he complete his task, and he would. Fate had thrown them together; duty would pull them apart. So much the harder the parting if they became lovers.

And wouldn't King Henry just love that, if Corwin returned the royal heiress soiled. He didn't want to imagine the price they both might pay for his indiscretion.

So he would resist temptation. Best to concentrate on duty and get the thing done. Then he could get back to his own life. And Judith to hers.

She could feel him, just in front of her, only a few steps away. If she called out to Corwin, would he come? If she asked him to, would he stay?

He'd taken Thurkill's guard duty tonight, to let the old man rest. Even the smallest child knew better than to interfere with a man on watch. But out here, so far away from any danger she could imagine, what might he possibly be guarding against?

She understood why the others stood guard, more to keep watch over her than for trouble from without. Corwin knew she wasn't going anywhere but with him. Where better to watch over her than beside her? So she wouldn't truly be interfering with his duty if she distracted him.

Distract. Now, there was a genteel word for wanting his complete attention.

She heard him move, and opened her eyes. To her delight, he'd scrunched down in front of her.

"I did not mean to wake you, only to cover you," he whispered, and pulled the blanket up to her chin.

"My thanks," she said, preferring he toss the blanket aside, or crawl underneath it with her.

He nodded and put his hands on his knees as if to get up.

She grasped the first subject that came to mind. "Thurkill sleeps?"

"Aye. Let us hope the added rest does him some good."

"It should, though I fear no amount of rest will matter in the end."

"So long as he stays alive awhile longer. I would truly hate to make the rest of this trip under Duncan's command."

She hadn't reflected on what would happen if Thurkill died before they reached the rebels' stronghold. She'd been too mindful of easing his pain. "Thurkill is very ill but has some strength to him yet. He may surprise us all and recover."

"Ah, Judith, I do believe that is wishful thinking I hear. Have a care, my dear, that your sympathy does not run too deep."

She shouldn't care what happened to Thurkill, but she hated to see anyone suffer, and truth to tell, she'd come to like the old man.

"Is it so wrong to want him to live?"

Corwin chuckled. "This from the same woman who threatened gruesome deaths for all of us not long ago?"

Judith's face grew warm as she remembered. "I was angry and hurt and fearful…"

"I know," he said. His fingers brushed her forehead, soothing against her brow. "All I am saying is to hold on to some of your anger. You have a tender heart, Judith. Guard it well, or you will be hurt in the end. Sleep well."

Sleep was long in coming, and when it did, it wasn't easy. In her dreams Corwin kissed her again, not soft and briefly, but long and hard. He hugged her close, in no hurry to release her from his embrace. She reveled in his amorous attention and felt bereft when she woke to find herself alone.

The full night's rest had done Thurkill good. His color had improved, and his spirits were high. To her way of thinking, the man shouldn't be on a horse, wasn't well enough to take on a rough day's ride. Today would be rough, for Thurkill had decided to follow the river.

"If I remember aright," he told them all, "it will take a sharp turn west just south of Banbury. From there we will push through the forest toward Coventry. Mayhap by then the sheriff will have left and we can take to the road again."

"You had best let me have my own reins, then," she told him. "If we are riding through brush, there will not always be enough room for me to ride beside you."

"I do not trust you on your own."

"You have nothing to worry over until we come to a road. I have no wish to be lost in this forest." He didn't look convinced. "Besides, there are three men behind me who can give chase if need be, though I assure you there will be no need, at least as far as Coventry. *Then* you might worry that I may try to go find the sheriff."

She wouldn't, of course, having promised Corwin that she would follow his lead, not leave the rebels until he did. She couldn't very well give Thurkill any hint of her altered attitude, however. He would question her change of heart.

Thurkill glanced at the men behind her, ready and waiting to leave. "All right," he said, relenting, then waggled a finger at her and scolded, "but make one move to escape and I will tie your hands together and lay you over the saddle like a sack of grain. Understood?"

"Aye," she said, suspecting his threat all talk with no teeth.

Over the course of the morning, she followed the path Thurkill forged through the forest. More often than not, she heard the rippling, sometimes crashing sounds of the river.

Birds marked their passage with warning calls from the treetops above. At times the forest thinned, making the going easy. At others the trees grew closely together, giving Thurkill fits as he tried to pick a path.

Always she was aware of Corwin riding behind her. His destrier's hooves beat heavily upon the forest floor, unlike her dainty mare's. The tack of the horse's trappings jangled in rhythm. Whether he rode close or back a ways, she always knew where he was without looking over her shoulder to check.

She felt safer, more secure than she had since before the kidnapping. That had been, what…three days ago? It seemed longer, perhaps because she'd spent most of those days angry, battling her fears. True, she remained anxious about the future, but not as anxious as she probably should be.

Corwin wanted her to hold on to her anger, but that proved hard to do without the fear to fuel it. And her fear had fled when she'd decided to trust Corwin. What a muddle!

Thurkill raised a hand in the air, calling a halt. When he dismounted, Judith did, too.

"We will take a respite here," he called out, then pointed to the river. "Water the horses, and while you are at it, look for a good place to cross."

"Do you think you could find a bridge, Thurkill?" she asked, only half teasing. "My boots are still wet from yesterday's crossing."

He answered with a half smile. "I doubt we will find a bridge, my lady, but take heart. After today 'twill be a long time before we need to cross water again. Your boots will dry, eventually."

"So you say. You may never convince my shriveled toes, however."

Thurkill's smile widened.

Corwin's warnings were fresh in her memory, but despite her effort not to, Judith smiled back.

Chapter Eight

They weren't riding in circles, but weren't making rapid progress, either. They'd left the river behind two days ago.

Corwin leaned over in his saddle. "Tell me again your father knows where he is going."

Oswuld smiled. "He knows. Even I have a good idea of where we are. We should skirt Coventry soon now, just west of the town."

Corwin straightened, relieved. North of Coventry, they should be able to regain the road. A faster pace would be wonderful. At this rate, if they were going as far north as Corwin suspected, this ride would be very long indeed.

At least Judith seemed content. She'd not only ceased battling with Thurkill, but helped to nurse him, though in a manner Corwin didn't care for. Even though he'd warned her, she acted more like a daughter tending a father than a captive ministering to an abductor. The comparison, he supposed, came from watching his sister Ardith see to their father's needs during his prolonged illness.

But what could he say? As a man who intended to join the rebellion, he should be glad to see that she no longer prodded Thurkill into a temper. He should be happy she seemed to accept her fate. Or maybe he worried for naught.

Maybe her calm, her willingness to help nurse Thurkill, were simply her way of helping the rebels to reach their lord's holding as swiftly as possible.

The chill of an English mist wasn't helping his mood, either. It had settled in early yesterday, and as of today's midday respite, appeared too solidly entrenched to roll away. Somehow he had to prod Thurkill to a faster pace. When, some time later, the mist became thicker, Corwin urged his horse to the front of the line.

"Thurkill, do you think we have passed Coventry?"

"Aye. Mayhap," he answered with deep weariness.

"I believe I can find the road from here. 'Twould be easier going if we did not have to fight the forest for each league." Corwin glanced up at the sky. "'Twould also be nice if we found shelter for the night."

Judith moaned, a sensual sound. "Shelter," she said with reverence. "A roof above my head and mayhap a thick layer of straw for my bed. Do not speak of such things, Corwin, if they are not possible."

He'd certainly struck the right note. Even Oswuld and Duncan wore wistful expressions.

"There is an inn some leagues north of Coventry—"

"Too dangerous," Thurkill said. "We do not know of the sheriff's whereabouts, and one word from her ladyship to an innkeeper…"

"All right, then. If not the inn, then mayhap we can find a farmer willing to extend the hospitality of his loft. We shall simply have to keep him and Judith from speaking together."

Thurkill scratched his chin.

"Find me a soft bed for the night and I vow to turn mute till morn," Judith vowed.

"Ah, my lady! One should not make promises one cannot hope to keep."

Judith huffed. "I would swear 'twas you who promised me every comfort and consideration. I am wet, cold and so weary I may fall asleep in the saddle. Keep your word, Thurkill, and I will keep mine. If Corwin can find us shelter for the night, I will say not one word to the owner of either inn or loft."

Thurkill gave a sigh of resignation. "No inn, Corwin. Too many people to mark our passing."

Within the hour, Corwin found an abandoned hut, built of wattle and daub, covered by a thatch roof. The single room was empty save for a pile of straw in one corner and a stack of wood near the hearth. Perfect, Corwin thought.

They tied the horses far off the road and had begun to remove saddles and packs when the rain fell, cold as a witch's heart and sharp as a dagger. To the flash of lightning and the crash of thunder, they hurried to get everything into the hut, and were all soaked through by the time they shut the door a final time.

Judith stood in the middle of the hut shivering, dripping, forlorn. "Would that we had saved my nun's robe."

"I will get a fire going, Princess," Duncan said. "You will warm up and dry out soon enough."

"I have a tunic in my pack, my lady," Oswuld offered. "'Tis of rough wool, and will just cover your knees, though. Still, you may use it if you wish."

Temptation flickered across Judith's face, but Corwin didn't think he could bear seeing Judith's uncovered legs all evening and still be able to sleep.

"Mine is longer," he said, and unfastened the buckles on the pack that held a few of his belongings. From within a folded oilcloth he drew his full-length, midnight-blue dalmatic and shook it out. 'Twas heavily creased, but the garment was dry, the sleeves long and the linen heavy enough to keep her warm.

"Oh, Corwin, 'tis beautiful," Judith said with a sigh. She lightly fingered the embroidery on the sleeves—narrow bands of gold, red and green thread stitched in an intricate pattern. "Ardith's work?"

"Aye," he said. "She made it for me so I would have something other than chain mail to wear for her wedding to Gerard."

"Oh," she said, and took her hand away. "Then I should not wear so special a garment. If I should soil it—"

"'Tis a favorite of mine, I admit," he said, handing it to her. "'Tis also the oldest. Ardith has made me several since."

Her eyes darted around the single room. Having been raised in a household of females, Corwin understood. He pointed to a corner. "I will put up a blanket for you to use."

Judith resisted the urge to wrap her arms around Corwin's neck and cover his face with kisses. As soon as he had the blanket in place she slipped behind it. Her boots came off with a sucking sound, taking her short hose with them. She peeled off the gown and her shift. Her body was wet, her hair hung down her back in a sodden mass, but the dalmatic was dry, smooth and covered her down to her toes. She wrapped the leather girdle about her waist and draped some of the fabric over it, bringing the hem up far enough so it wouldn't drag on the dirt floor.

Judith came out from behind the blanket to find the men had done what they could to get dry, too. Hauberks and tunics lay spread out to dry beside Corwin's padded gambeson and black sherte. Boots stood lined up like soldiers before the hearth.

The men had stripped down to their breeches; only Oswuld wore a tunic. The sight of so much male flesh took her aback. Oh, she'd seen men's chests before. Mostly during high summer, in the fields surrounding her parents' home, when the men thought nothing of shucking their tunics as they worked. She'd never been confined to a small hut with partially clad males, however.

The hut was beginning to warm—and smell, of musty wool and old leather and men. Not entirely displeasing odors.

Judith glanced at Thurkill, who used his saddle as a backrest and drank his potion. She paused to notice the lank lines of Duncan's back as he poked at the fire.

Then she feasted on the sight of Corwin. He sat cross-legged on the floor, with a rag in hand, working oil around the metal rings of his chain mail. His long fingers worked quickly, the muscles in his arms rippling as he rubbed. She'd known him to be wide of shoulder and broad of chest, but hadn't dared think upon how beautifully sculpted those shoulders would be, or how smooth and hard the plane of his chest.

A rumble of thunder shook the hut as Corwin looked up at her, setting her knees atremble.

"I dare say you look better in that than I do," he said.

"Aye, well…" she managed to utter, flustered at the thought that Corwin looked magnificent in nothing at all, though she didn't dare say so.

To hide the flush that surely stained her cheeks, she lined her boots up with the others and spread out her gown and shift on the floor nearby. Maybe by morning they'd be dry. Then she could give Corwin back his lovely garment, put on the peasant gown, get back on her horse and endure another day's ride.

"Does anyone know where we are?" she asked.

"North of Coventry, would you say, Thurkill?" Corwin asked.

"A league or so," he agreed. "If the weather were not

so foul, I would post a guard to watch for the sheriff. I do
not think the man will be out and about tonight, however.
We can all get a good night's rest and be off at first light.''

Judith didn't voice her doubt. Thurkill slept more each
night, and by silent agreement, none in the group woke him
up on the morn, but let him awaken naturally.

"Father, are we now on the road we used to come
south?" Oswuld asked, drawing a puzzled frown from
Duncan.

"One of them," Thurkill answered. "From here either
of you should be able to find your way, if the need arises."

Duncan gave an exasperated huff. "Now I remember.
Damnation, if we had not been forced to take to the forest,
we could be in Sheffield by now!"

"Sheffield? Why that is—" she had no idea of how
many leagues "—so far!"

Oswuld smiled and shook his head. "Not so far, my lady,
when you consider how far—"

Thurkill touched Oswuld's arm. "Hush, son."

"Sorry, Father. I forgot they are not to know."

Corwin shifted his chain mail and continued polishing.
"'Tis no longer a secret, Thurkill. You may as well tell
her."

"Tell her what?"

"That in all of England, there is but one place where a
man might gather an army and not have someone take note.
Where every serious rebellion against Norman rule has also
begun. Am I right, Thurkill?"

Thurkill didn't answer, just sipped his potion.

With a sinking feeling in her stomach, Judith asked of
Corwin, "How far north are we going?"

"Have you ever been to Durham, Judith? I have, once.
Thought it a lovely place."

"Durham is almost on the Scots border!" She turned on

Thurkill. "You came all the way from Durham to Romsey just to kidnap me?"

"Aye," Thurkill admitted.

Judith tossed her hands in the air. "In the name of God, why? I have three female cousins who live in the south of Scotland, all unmarried, all as royally connected to two thrones as I am. Yet you cross the entire kingdom to get me. Why, Thurkill? Why me?"

Thurkill lifted a shaggy, gray eyebrow. "You would rather we had disrupted one of your cousins' lives than yours?"

"Aye! Nay!" Judith took a calming breath. "Nay, I would not have their lives tossed into upheaval to spare me. I am not so mean-spirited. I simply do not understand why one of them was not chosen. 'Twould seem the more practical thing to do."

"Not really," Thurkill said. "Your cousins are very well guarded, Judith. They live in keeps with thick walls and fathers who keep very close watch over those who enter their domain. You, however, lived in an abbey. 'Twas decided you were the easiest to abduct."

"I would not have been if the queen were in residence with her guards."

"We knew she had gone back to London some time ago. Also to our advantage, two days after we arrived near Romsey, you went out to pick herbs. Saved us from going into the abbey after you, as we were prepared to do."

"I see. I was chosen because I was most vulnerable."

"Well, not entirely. There were other considerations. 'Twas also thought you most suited for our purposes."

Something other than her name? This was news.

"How so?"

"Your knowledge of the English court, for one. Our lord felt he needed someone who knew most of the people, as well as the palace and hall. He also thought you most suited to his own nature.''

The chill that snaked down her spine had nothing to do with her wet hair clinging to her back. Corwin had asked her before if she knew who this Saxon noble might be. She'd thought of and discarded the names of several nobles who might have reason to turn traitor. Might Thurkill now give her a clue?

''In what way?''

''Because you are convent raised, 'twas thought you would be the more...quiet and reflective.''

Judith tossed back her head and laughed. ''Oh, your lord is in for a surprise, is he not? Is your lord quiet and reflective?''

''Nay, but I think he hoped his wife might be.''

She scoffed. ''He wants no wife, he wants a nun. That is truly why you came for me. This lord of yours thought I would sit quietly by the fire by day and do my wifely duty at night, all without complaint.''

''He will give you no reason for complaint at night, Princess,'' Duncan said with a lewd smile, handing her the chunk of bread that would be her evening meal. ''Those ladies who have shared his bed sing his praises. You might well be content to sit by the fire by day.''

A rogue, was he?

''Those *ladies* probably went to his bed to get a good night's sleep, and sang his praises so they might do so again.''

''You will know differently when you see him.''

''He is probably older than Thurkill, with no teeth. And no hair. And he likely smells.''

That brought laughter from all three rebels. Corwin wore a tight smile and continued polishing his chain mail.

Thurkill set his cup aside. ''If that is all that worries you, my lady, let me tell you our leader is both young and with good looks. We do not take you to some old reprobate who cannot produce his own heirs.'' He beckoned to Duncan. ''Give this old reprobate another chunk of bread, will you?''

Again the men laughed, and Judith knew Thurkill had signaled the end of her prying. He would answer no more questions, such as did the lord have light hair or dark? Brown eyes or blue? Was he tall or short?

She'd known too many young and handsome nobles for those clues to be of help in her pursuit of a name. There was no hope for it. Maybe come morn someone's name would pop into her head as the likely miscreant.

For tonight, she intended to sleep soundly. She tugged down the blanket Corwin had hung for her, and claimed the pile of straw in the corner.

One by one the men found places to lay their heads. All but Corwin. He sat within the light of the banked fire, his skin the color of burnished gold. The muscles in his back twitched with the motion of his hands as he continued to polish his suit of mail.

Judith tried turning over, burrowing deeper into the bed of straw, pulling the blanket over her head. Nothing she did worked. The man was too great a distraction. She wouldn't sleep until he bedded down and covered up.

Giving up, Judith joined him and lifted a mail sleeve onto her lap. ''Do you have another rag?''

Corwin ripped his in two and handed her one of the squares.

''Cannot sleep?''

She refused to tell him why. She plied the rag to the metal rings and whispered, ''My head whirls with names of young, handsome Saxon nobles who might have a holding in the Scottish lowlands or northern England, who might turn traitor and be their leader. I wish I knew if he were dark or fair, tall or short.''

"Not worth losing sleep over."

The odd note in his voice drew her head up. Corwin wore a deep frown. The muscles in his shoulders and arms had tensed, giving each a hard, well-defined form. They were very nicely formed. She could run a finger along the curve of each one and… She mentally shook herself to regain her focus.

Corwin didn't seem angry, just upset. Over what? She'd only been doing what he'd told her to do—pondering names of nobles, young and handsome men.

Silly goose, she chided herself, but the thought that Corwin might be jealous refused to go away, especially when she remembered Corwin's tight smile when Duncan related the tale of his lord's virility.

'Twas bad of her, she knew, but she asked anyway, "I wonder if Duncan overstates his lord's prowess?''

"At this rate you will never finish that sleeve. Have you ever polished chain mail before?''

Holding back a grin, she again plied the rag.

"Nay, but then, I have done many things on this adventure of ours I have never done before.''

"Like sleeping on the ground?''

Like sitting next to a half-clad man in the middle of the night, knowing he is disturbed if I think of other young, handsome men.

"'Twas not so bad once you pointed out to me that I should look for long grass as my bed. After that, I could almost pretend I was back on my cot in the abbey. 'Tis still fair strange, however, to sleep in the company of others, especially men.''

He turned to look at her, his eyes narrowed. "None of them have…approached you, have they?''

Only you.

"Oh, heavens no. 'Tis simply a change from having been in the company of women for so long." She shifted the sleeve to get a better grip. "Neither had I before washed my face from a stream, nor eaten fish so freshly caught. 'Tis also easy to lose track of the time of day when one does not pay heed. In the abbey, my days were ruled by the calls to prayer. Out here, only the need for food and rest rules."

"You make it sound like a grand adventure."

Judith admitted it was, in a way, and she'd grown stronger from the experience, both physically and mentally. She'd faced adversity and won—mostly. "Neither have I ever been so sore and stiff in my life. Or cold and wet. Or hot and parched."

Or so frightened that she'd screamed. Those screams had served her well, however. They'd brought Corwin to her.

"Your hardships will continue, I fear. We have a long way yet to go."

"Each day becomes easier," she assured him. "Truth to tell, I begin to feel a bit useless. You men take care of everything—the horses, catching and cooking our food. The only truly worthwhile thing I have done is help Oswuld with his father's potions. I wish I could think of another herb I might add to further relieve the pain, but have not."

"You polish chain mail rather well."

The sleeve she'd been working on did look good, though Corwin probably didn't need her help with this, either.

They worked in silence, side by side. Judith listened to the rain, feeling her eyelids grow heavy. Yet she stayed put, determined to finish the sleeve, unwilling to give up this time alone with Corwin. In the not too distant future, she would have him all to herself, which sent a thrill though her. First, however, they needed to learn the identity of the rebel leader. She wished she could come up with a name, because she didn't think Thurkill would reveal it.

"Corwin, if none of the men tells us the leader's name, then we must go into their encampment, true?"

He sighed. "I hope it does not come to that."

"But it might."

"Aye," he admitted. "Does that frighten you?"

Not as much as it had before.

"A bit, but I trust you to get us out. Besides, after all he has put me though, I want to know who this miscreant is, and let the man know just how very unsuitable he and I would be." She scoffed. "Quiet and reflective, indeed."

Corwin knew if he sat beside Judith much longer he'd do something stupid. Like kiss her again. Maybe more. He rubbed harder at his chain mail to keep his hands to himself.

Soon now, if he concentrated, he might be able to move the section he purposely kept spread across his lap.

Judith looked damn good in his dalmatic. She'd bloused it a bit at the waist, billowing the top, but not enough to hide the peaks of her breasts. He'd never be able to wear the garment again without remembering the woman whose body it had covered. And she smelled so good, of crystal rainwater.

She seemed content to sit beside him, to speak of her kidnapping in low, even tones. She seemed no longer afraid. She'd been through a lot, yet spoke of her ordeal in an almost lighthearted manner. It wasn't over yet. Corwin feared the worst was yet to come.

Judith had spoken of feeling useless, as if her mere presence hadn't been a boon to Oswuld, a pleasure to Thurkill—Corwin's own joy. She'd laughed tonight—with a bit of sarcasm and not out fully, but she'd laughed. He wanted to hear it again as an expression of glee. Maybe, once they were well out of harm's way, he could make her laugh again. Just for him.

She'd called him kind. If he were kind, she wouldn't be here, wouldn't have a reason to withhold her laughter.

Lightning lit up the hut, thunder shook it. She looked up at the roof.

"Praise be we are not out in this tonight," she said. "I do hope the horses are all right."

Corwin snatched at the excuse as a drowning man grasps for anything to help keep him afloat. "I should go check."

"But it is still raining."

"I will dry."

He shoved the chain mail from his lap and headed for the door. He would check on the horses and let the cold, driving rain cool his lust.

Chapter Nine

Five days later, within a few leagues of Durham, Corwin sensed a heightened urgency among the men. They'd stopped for a midday respite, and Corwin's instincts told him that by nightfall he would be within the rebel encampment.

He and Judith hadn't talked further about meeting the rebel leader. Both of them knew what would happen if Thurkill didn't reveal the man's name. He hadn't.

Judith currently sat near where Thurkill napped, reading Ardith's letter again. She found comfort in it, Corwin supposed, for on particularly hard days she would pull it out and linger over it. This morning's ride had been easy. She, too, must feel nervous, as if something were about to happen. Corwin didn't blame her. His own nerves were on edge.

"I wonder if Ardith has given birth yet," Judith said. "'Tis very near her time, is it not?"

"Very near, but not yet, I think." He hadn't felt the merest twinge that would tell him if aught were amiss with his sister. How odd that he'd left Wilmont in order to be half a kingdom away from Ardith when her babe was born.

He was now more than half a kingdom away, but in an entirely different direction.

"Mayhap she will have a girl this time," Judith mused, tucking the letter away. "'Twould be nice for her, since she already has a boy."

"I do not think Ardith cares, so long as the child is healthy," he said, not having heard his sister utter a preference.

Thurkill stirred, his hand rising slowly to brush against Judith's gown, drawing her attention. Even from across the campsite, Corwin knew something was very wrong. Judith bent down to hear what Thurkill whispered.

She shook her head. "I do not fear you, but—Thurkill?"

The man's hand dropped away, his eyes closing again.

For several moments, no one moved. The knot in Corwin's gut tightened as Judith tentatively put her hand to Thurkill's chest.

"He still breathes," she said with a rush of relief.

Oswuld hurried over to his father's side.

None of them had spoken to Thurkill, or to each other, about the leader's worsening health, of the amount of weight he'd lost—of the fear that he might one night go to sleep and not wake up the following morn. Thurkill dying now couldn't come at a worse time.

Corwin needed Thurkill to stand as witness for him during his meeting with the rebels' leader. Oswuld's good opinion would help balance Duncan's animosity, but Thurkill's words would carry the greater weight.

Getting Thurkill to a place where he could receive a physician's care became urgent. Corwin debated his options, then decided not to go into Durham, but to get Thurkill to the rebel stronghold. Unfortunately, Thurkill didn't have the strength to sit his horse.

As much as Corwin hated to do it, he saw no choice but to send Duncan to the stronghold for help.

"Duncan, I realize I am not supposed to know the whereabouts of the rebel encampment until the last moment, but I think, for Thurkill's sake, we need to act quickly," Corwin said. "He needs more expert care than we can give him, and soon. Can you reach the stronghold by nightfall?"

Indecision flickered in Duncan's eyes. Corwin understood the inner war he waged. Duncan hated letting Corwin out of his sight as much as Corwin wished he could keep Duncan within reach.

"Only you or Oswuld can go for help," Corwin said, pressing Duncan to cooperate. "And Oswuld should be here—just in case."

Duncan took a deep breath. "Aye, if someone is to go, it must be me."

"Then go," Corwin said, with the slightest inflection of a command. "Bring back a physician if there is one to be had. And a wagon. Thurkill will not be able to sit a horse."

"'Tis too far for me to travel both ways today, especially with a wagon in tow," Duncan commented, relenting.

Corwin had hoped the stronghold was closer. Duncan would now have the entire evening to speak with the rebel leader, and Corwin didn't want to think about the reception he would get after the man heard Duncan's tale. But that couldn't be helped. He'd have to deal with the leader when the time came.

"We shall look for you on the morrow, then."

"I should be back by midmorn." With the decision made, Duncan wasted little time saddling his horse and taking to the road.

Corwin joined Judith and Oswuld. The two had made Thurkill as comfortable as they could, and now watched the old man's chest, as if either of them looked away he would stop breathing.

Judith glanced up at Corwin. "I thought he told me not to be afraid. I now wonder if I misunderstood, if he was expressing a fear of his own."

"I doubt you misunderstood," Corwin said. "Thurkill strikes me as a man who fears very little, not even death."

"Corwin has the right of it, my lady," Oswuld said, his gaze never leaving his father. "His words were for you, not for himself. Had he feared dying, he would not have joined the rebellion or made the long trek to fetch you."

"'Twas your father's idea to kidnap me?" Judith asked.

"Nay, my lady. He argued against it, but when the decision was made he *insisted* on going. He would trust no other with the task for fear you might be hurt or misused." Oswuld got to his feet. "I will mix another potion, for when he wakes. My lady, if you would remain near him...?"

In answer, Judith reached down and picked up Thurkill's hand. The action wasn't startling, but brought home just how attached she'd become to the old man.

As soon as Oswuld was out of hearing range, Corwin crouched down next to her. "Judith, for all he is a likeable man, Thurkill is your enemy, the man who kidnapped you."

She answered softly. "I know. If this heart ailment does not kill him, then he might die on a battlefield or at the end of a rope. I should not care, but I do." Tears formed in her eyes, but didn't fall. She waved a hand, as if dismissing her heartbreak. "You need not worry over me, Corwin. My silly emotions are my burdens to bear, and I will."

He wanted to wrap her in his arms, hold her close and assure her that her emotions weren't silliness to be waved aside, that the tenderness of her heart was one of her most endearing traits. Even when she cared for a man who didn't deserve her affection.

Unable to hold Judith in the way he wanted to, Corwin settled for brushing back a strand of her hair that had come loose from her plait. The better he got to know her, the more deeply he fell under her spell. The longer they were together, the harder it would be to let her go. On the morrow, he would find out what he needed to know. Then he and Judith would ride hard and fast, probably to London, to their own destinies.

Duncan arrived with a wagon and an escort of six men.

"I do not need the wagon. I can ride my horse," Thurkill declared.

Corwin hid a smile. The old man had awakened this morn with enough vigor to complain about the plans they'd made for him. While Corwin understood the man's desire to conceal the extent of his infirmity, he wanted Thurkill strong enough to act as counsel, if necessary, when he faced the rebel leader.

"Father, you cannot ride so far," Oswuld argued, a mark of his worry. Oswuld had never raised his voice to his father during the entire journey, not even when Thurkill had loudly berated him for allowing Judith to escape from near the cave. "Your heart cannot bear the strain. I doubt you can even walk from here to your horse. 'Tis your stubborn pride that makes you speak foolishly. Do you wish to return to camp alive or not?"

Thurkill leaned forward slightly. "I wish for my son to heed his father's wishes and bring my horse to me."

"You ask me to hasten your death, and that I will not do. You want to ride? Then get you on your own horse."

Thurkill rose on an elbow. Sweat broke out on his brow. When he dropped back down, exhausted from so slight an effort, Oswuld waved for the wagon driver to come forward. Thurkill didn't say a word as several men gently lifted him. Corwin jumped into the wagon to help settle Thurkill onto a thick layer of straw covered with a wool blanket.

Once he'd done so, Corwin found Duncan blocking his way down.

"You, too, are to ride in the wagon," Duncan said. "I have orders to bring you into camp unarmed, with your eyes covered."

Corwin tamped down his momentary alarm. So Duncan had done a good job of prejudicing the rebel leader's opinion. Though Corwin considered it a compliment that the man thought him so dangerous, he couldn't obey such a senseless order.

He glanced at Judith, who'd overheard. Her eyes had gone wide with both surprise and fear. He couldn't protect her if he didn't see danger coming. Besides, he'd known all along he and Duncan would come to blows. Better here and now than in the encampment.

"Duncan, if your leader thinks I would ride into his camp in so vulnerable a position, he is mistaken."

"He is not pleased we brought you with us, distrusts your motives, as I have all along. Those are his conditions for your entering the camp. If you do not do so willingly, we are ordered to force you, or kill you if we must."

Corwin glanced around the campsite, at the men who stood ready to follow Duncan's orders if necessary. Brigands? Thieves? Farmers? He didn't know, but never doubted that his skill with a sword was far superior to any of theirs. Nor did he need to fight them all, only make an example of one or two.

"You can try."

Duncan stepped back and drew his sword. Corwin recognized the stance he settled into as one of a soldier with a bit of formal training.

"Duncan! Do not be a fool," Thurkill called out. "Corwin will separate your head from your shoulders."

"I follow your orders no longer, old man," Duncan retorted. "From the moment he held a dagger at your throat you have believed his tale, but not I. Come down, Corwin. I have been itching to test these skills you say you have."

Corwin held out a hand toward Judith. "Come into the wagon with Thurkill, out of harm's way."

She made slow work of crossing to the wagon. Corwin reached down, clasped hold of her wrists, braced his feet and soon had her safely inside the wagon.

She said softly, "Mayhap you should do as he asks."

"The leader tests me, is all. No man worth having in his company would submit to such a demand." He turned to Thurkill. "I will try not to take Duncan's head off, just nick his hide a bit. You are both to stay put and remain calm. Understood?"

Judith didn't doubt she would stay put. But remain calm? Her insides churned at the very thought of Corwin taking on six men—seven including Duncan. She'd never been so frightened for anyone in her entire life. If anything happened to Corwin...

"Take care," she managed to say, and squeezed his hand hard, a poor substitute for the fierce embrace she longed for. She took what comfort she could in the warmth and pressure of his grip, and in the fact that he wore chain mail. 'Twould protect him better than the leather hauberk that covered Duncan's chest.

"Not to worry. 'Twill be over in a trice," he said, then turned and jumped from the wagon bed. "Oswuld, your assistance if you will."

Duncan was pacing, sword in hand. He snickered. "For what do you need Oswuld's help?"

"If you are ordered to kill me, I should give you the opportunity," Corwin answered.

With growing horror, Judith watched Oswuld help Corwin shrug out of the chain mail. Down to breeches and padded gambeson, Corwin hefted his sword and took a stance opposite Duncan.

Corwin's eyes narrowed, giving his accompanying grin a feral quality, like a hunter toying with his prey. "Whenever you are ready, Duncan," he said in a low, lethal voice, sending a shiver down her spine.

Duncan leaped to the attack, his sword raised high for a brutal downstroke. She covered her mouth to hold in a scream, nearly swooned as the sword slashed downward. Corwin never raised his sword in defense. In a swift and graceful move, he ducked the blow and threw an elbow into Duncan's ribs.

Duncan doubled over. With both hands on the hilt of his sword, Corwin swung the flat of his blade against Duncan's backside and sent the man sprawling in the dirt.

"Too fast, Duncan," Corwin said. "Try again, but keep your sword a bit lower."

She groaned. Duncan was out for blood and Corwin was telling him how to go about it!

Thurkill tugged on her skirt. "Sit, my lady. I cannot see when you move around."

She obeyed, only because she knew her wobbly legs wouldn't hold her upright much longer. Duncan was on his feet and making another run at Corwin. She covered her face with her hands, heard a single clash of steel against steel and peeked through her fingers.

Thurkill chuckled. "If Duncan has a brain in his head, he will learn from this."

Duncan looked too angry to learn. He circled Corwin, who stood his ground, moving only as much as needed to keep his opponent in sight, bringing his sword up when necessary to deflect the occasional jab of sharp, pointed steel.

"Keep this up and we will be here all day," Corwin observed, sounding bored.

If he'd done so deliberately to prod Duncan to action, it worked. A flurry of blows followed, fast and furious on Duncan's part, with hardly an effort on Corwin's.

"Ah," Thurkill sighed. "To be young again."

Incredulous, she looked down at the old man, who was thoroughly enjoying the sword fight, watching Corwin and Duncan slash away as if they did so for his entertainment.

"I suppose you could have bested Corwin," she said, chiding Thurkill.

"Nay, not even on my best day. Look, my lady. He ends it."

Corwin had, indeed, taken the attack. One step at a time, he advanced on a backward-stepping Duncan, his sword dipping into whatever hole Duncan left open to take thin cuts of flesh and leave deep gashes in leather. Duncan was clearly out of his element and knew it. The anger on his face had been replaced with sheer determination to survive the encounter.

Corwin allowed it, as he'd told Thurkill he would. With a lightning swift series of blows, Corwin soon had Duncan backed up against a tree, the tip of his sword pressed against the vulnerable hollow of an exposed throat.

"Toss your sword toward the wagon," Corwin told Duncan. "I would hate to have you die because you moved too fast."

Duncan tossed the sword. Corwin kicked it under the

wagon and backed up a step, dropping the tip of his own sword to the ground, allowing Duncan room to breathe.

"Bastard." Duncan spat the word, fingering a bloody scratch on his neck.

Corwin tilted his head. "If I remember aright, 'twas you who sought to kill me. Be thankful you still live!"

Duncan showed his appreciation with a fist flung at Corwin's jaw. It didn't connect. In one fluid movement, Corwin dropped his sword and used Duncan's forward momentum against him. A punch, a kick, a hearty shove—and Duncan lay sprawled on the ground once more, his nose spilling blood into the dirt. He didn't get up.

Corwin grabbed his sword and spun around. "Anyone else?" he shouted fiercely.

Judith held her breath as three foolhardy souls rushed him.

Corwin was everywhere, his sword flashing in short, sharp bursts or long, curving arcs. They chased around the campsite. Oswuld jumped into the wagon to get out of the way, and was quickly told to get out of his father's line of sight.

Corwin changed tactics. He kept the men right where he wanted them, giving no ground. Like tightly penned cattle they bumped into each other, getting in each other's way. One by one they lost their swords to the force or finesse of Corwin's blows.

Finally, all was peaceful. Corwin tossed his sword onto the wagon bed and hefted himself up to sit on the edge. Breathing hard, he looked over his shoulder. He spared a glance for Judith, then smiled at Thurkill.

"I have not had that long a practice session since leaving Wilmont."

"But you could still take on the others."

Corwin's laugh rang through the campsite. "Aye, but I

would rather not. Oswuld, shake Duncan. He should be ready to wake by now. We need to get your father to the stronghold, and I could surely use an ale.''

She wanted to touch him all over, make sure he didn't bleed—and he wanted an ale. Men.

''Frightened?''

Did it show so much? ''Aye,'' she admitted, swallowing hard.

''Try to remain with Thurkill. I shall stay as close as I can.''

The odd comment took her aback, until she realized they were talking about two different things. She'd been frightened nearly out of her skull while watching him fight, not thinking about going into the rebel encampment. No matter, her answers might have been the same.

Duncan gained his feet and shuffled over to the wagon.

''Duncan, I will make you a bargain,'' Corwin said. ''I will ride in on my own horse, with nothing over my eyes. I will, however, go in without my sword. Thurkill, will you do me the honor of guarding this for me?''

Judith wanted to snatch up the sword, tell Corwin to keep it in his hand and be very careful of his back. But she didn't. She had to trust that he knew what he was doing.

And that he hadn't missed the look of pure hatred in Duncan's eyes.

From the middle of the company, Judith could see over the wagon to the road and rebel stronghold beyond. She tightened her hold on her mare's reins and sidled so close to Corwin that he would be able to hear her if she whispered.

On a hill stood a keep, built of wood in the square, three-floored style commonly found all over England. The structure screamed power and wealth, and if she didn't know it belonged to a Saxon, she would have assumed it was built and lived in by a Norman. Or maybe the keep had been a Norman's seat of power, and the rebels had captured it and made it their own.

No timber palisade circled the keep. Earth works built up to the height of three men stood between the keep and the surrounding fields—fields swarming with men, horses, tents and weapons.

Hundreds of men. Stack upon stack of weapons.

Judith knew nothing of armies. 'Twas impossible for her to judge whether or not the army was large enough to overthrow the English throne. But far too many men camped within the long shadow of the keep to mistake them for anything other than an invading army. Too many discontented Saxons ready to take up arms and fight for a hopeless cause. Too many who paused to stare at her as the company passed through the encampment.

Her stomach turned at the stench of unwashed bodies and decaying waste. Fields that should be green with crops had been churned into muddy ruin. The men wore somber looks—but their weapons gleamed. Axes and maces stood stacked and at the ready. Lances had been arranged in circular towers, tips pointing toward the sun.

Corwin didn't seem the least concerned. Nothing in his posture or expression revealed his thoughts, as if entering a rebel encampment was an everyday occurrence for him. His seeming indifference, and the reassuring smile he shot her way, helped ease her disquiet. But she couldn't help wonder if he feigned calm, if deep inside he wasn't also terrified that once they reached the heart of the camp and entered the keep they might never get out.

He'd given her his word they would escape. But as Judith once more looked out over the sea of men now surrounding them, she couldn't foresee escape, only entrapment.

"Take heart, Judith," Corwin said. "Remember these men think of you as their future queen. They will not harm you."

"Mayhap not, but neither will they let me go."

"They will not be given the choice. We will get out."

"How?"

He chuckled. "Give me a day or two, my lady. In the meantime, enjoy the pleasure of decently prepared food and the comfort of a soft pallet. Just take care you do not come to like the lodgings and deference so much you do not want to leave."

He teased her, she knew. Maybe he had the right of it, that all she must do was bide her time and wait for Corwin to gather the information he wanted and then arrange for their escape. Sweet heaven, she looked forward to that day, and not only because she would be free of her captors.

She would be alone, completely alone, with Corwin. In the midst of her turmoil over whatever she must endure during the next few days, the utter certainty of having Corwin all to herself afterward thrilled her to her very core.

To be able to talk to him, say whatever she would, without a care to being overheard. To touch him, maybe share another kiss, without fear of being observed and judged.

Aye, she craved those things—and more.

She trusted Corwin's promise. Knew him to be both an intelligent and an excellent warrior. But more, she placed her fate in those very capable hands because she loved him.

Unwise, certainly, for there was no future possible for them even if she wanted one. Yet she trusted and respected Corwin beyond any other man. And while a niggling voice in her head advised caution, her heart urged her to both romantic and sensual visions of her and Corwin—entwined bodies, whispered endearments, ecstasy. Her desire to know him fully, as a woman knows a man, had become a merciless ache that only he could ease.

Was that not love? And if so, how did one guard against it if one wished to?

Corwin need not worry about her willingness to escape. For many reasons, she was more than eager.

"What of you, Corwin? You, too, will have a soft pallet."

He shrugged one of his broad shoulders slightly. "That will depend upon the leader, which is one of the reasons I want you to remain as close to Thurkill as possible. The old man is fond of you and will see to your well-being when I cannot."

Judith didn't like the sound of that. "But you will be in the keep," she said, hearing the near desperate hope in her voice.

"Likely," he said.

Only likely? But where else...? Out here, among the throng of men-at-arms. Where she wouldn't see him. Where she couldn't look to him for a comforting word or reassuring smile. Where no one would watch his back.

She closed her eyes as dread took hold and shook her until her hands trembled. Her concerns had all been selfish. Only now, on the edge of the keep's bailey, did she think of what could happen to Corwin.

What if the rebel leader didn't believe that Corwin truly wished to join the rebels? And Corwin had already defied the man by entering the camp with his eyes uncovered.

If the rebel leader ordered Corwin chained, or killed...

Judith fought the darkness threatening to overwhelm her.

"Judith?"

She clung to the sound of his voice, calling out to her from beyond the swirl of terror in her head. She opened her eyes and searched him out. Right there, immediately beside her—so terribly far away.

"Courage, my sweet," he said. "If I had thought you endangered, I would not have—"

She shook her head. "Not me. You. Corwin, what if the leader does not believe you truly wish to join the rebellion, or decides that the price you ask is too high? He cannot let you go because you already know too much. What if he throws you in chains or...worse?"

The wagon stopped. They'd reached the keep. Corwin swung down from his horse and came around to help her dismount.

Judith longed to fall into the arms of the knight whose hands wrapped about her waist, on whose shoulders she placed her hands, whose very life stood imperiled by the whims of a single man. Mindful of the men whose curious looks added to her fright, she quelled the urge to cling to Corwin as he lowered her to the ground. He smiled an almost victorious smile. How could he? Here she was, on the verge of tears, praying that he wouldn't be killed, and Corwin was grinning. She didn't understand at all.

"You must not worry over me, Judith," he said, removing his hands and backing up a step, out of her reach. "I truly am quite capable of taking care of myself. Now, take the worry from your eyes and the frown from your lips. 'Tis not wise to show fear to an enemy."

She tried.

"Raise your chin a bit higher," he ordered. "There. Perfect. Now, let us see how Thurkill fares."

As she turned toward the wagon, she caught sight of the keep's stairs. Coming down those stairs was a man—a young and handsome Saxon noble.

Corwin had warned her that she might know the rebels' leader. She did. With dread twisting in the pit of her stomach, Judith told Corwin the man's name.

"Ruford Clark."

Chapter Ten

Corwin peered at the blond, bearded man striding toward him with Duncan at his side. Ruford Clark? Corwin couldn't place the name, so knew he must not be a member of one of the more important noble families.

"Last I saw him," Judith said quietly, "he was leaving Scotland for France on the King's orders, or so was the rumor. Banished for attempting to murder his elder brother."

Not an unusual happenstance. A second son often found himself without a living when his father died and an older sibling inherited. Many attempted to do away with elder brothers. The crime proved Ruford a ruthless man, but Judith's actions confirmed his prowess. In the seconds before Ruford reached her, she tucked stray wisps of hair back into her braid and slid the tip of her tongue over her lips. Her spine went lance straight, her shoulders back—a true picture of a royal heiress about to greet a noble, a peer.

Corwin's gut tightened, knowing she cared what this man thought of her—the man who'd ordered her kidnapped. The man who planned to marry her and make her his queen.

He cannot have her! Corwin's vow came fast and furi-

ously. Never would he allow Judith's marriage to this upstart. He'd kill Ruford first.

"Lady Judith Canmore," Ruford said, bowing over Judith's hand. "Do you remember me, my lady?"

"I believe so," she said, as if she wasn't sure, making
no move to reclaim her hand. "Are you not supposed to
be in France?"

Ruford gave her a strained smile. "I visited, for a time."

She looked up at the keep and around the bailey. "What
is this place?"

"A keep once known as Norgate. I have not yet decided
if I should change the name."

Corwin knew of Norgate, and the Norman who owned
it. Apparently, Ruford's forces had conquered it and made
it their own. He would have to find out when and how, and
whether the Norman and his family still lived. He didn't
hold much hope.

Judith smiled at Ruford with a dainty shrug, *finally* pulling her hand away. "I fear I know it not," she said, then
tilted her head in inquiry. "Is this keep, then, your reward
for joining the rebellion?"

Corwin almost winced at the low blow to Ruford's pride,
delivered with a velvet fist. He knew Judith wasn't that
naive. She knew Ruford was the rebels' leader, not a fol-
lower. Thankfully, Ruford believed Judith's question innocent, for he hastened to correct her mistake.

"My reward, my lady, will be the crown of England and
all the lands that go with it."

With her expression one of disbelief, she asked, "You?
But that is impossible! Oh, dear. You are quite serious, are
you not?" She barely paused when Ruford nodded. "This
is very unexpected. I had thought the leader would be a
baron, at the least. Or mayhap an earl. Someone whose rank

more fitted mine, not the second son of a lowland laird. How…disappointing.''

Corwin could think of several stronger words she might have used. So could the man she'd just proclaimed unworthy of her.

Ruford tilted his head and studied Judith. ''You are no longer the pleasant child I remember,'' he finally said.

''One changes as one comes of age.''

''You have certainly become a beauty.'' With the comment, Ruford reached out to touch Judith's face.

She avoided the offensive hand by backing up a step—and collided with Corwin. He gripped her upper arms to steady her.

Ruford's eyes narrowed. ''You must be Corwin of Lenvil. Unhand the lady.''

Corwin obeyed, if slowly. He couldn't afford to anger the man unduly. For the moment, Ruford held the upper hand.

''I also wished for you to be brought into the keep with your eyes covered,'' Ruford said, his ire apparent. ''For one who seeks to serve me, you do not heed my orders well.''

''Only a fool would enter an armed camp blind,'' Corwin said. ''I assure you I am no fool. And as I am certain Duncan has told you, I have not yet decided whether or not I wish to serve you.''

Ruford's hands clenched into fists. ''I should have Duncan run you through for your insolence.''

Corwin scoffed. ''Duncan has already tried and failed. Nor would a man who wishes to conquer a kingdom take so rash an action against a man who can be of great aid to him, insolent or no.''

''So great an aid as to warrant the reward of so grand a prize as Wilmont? I wonder.''

Corwin knew exactly how valuable he could be to Ruford. "I have fought with and against Normans. Under both Wilmont's banner and King Henry's. I know how Normans fight, how they plan strategy. Tell me, Ruford, have you another in your camp who has fought by the king's side? Is not Wilmont a small price to pay for such knowledge?"

"Wilmont is a very large fief."

"So is England, which you seek to rule. Prove to me you are worthy of it and I will help you get it."

Ruford stared at Corwin for an interminable moment before he said, "Come into my hall. We will talk." Then he turned his attention once more to Judith. "I have women waiting to attend you. They will see you to the solar, where you may bathe and don suitable clothing."

Several men bore Thurkill—and Corwin's sword—up the stairs behind Ruford and Judith. Once inside the hall, Ruford waved two women forward.

Corwin watched Judith climb the stairs, wary of letting her out of his sight, though he knew she'd be safe. No matter what happened to him, unless Judith did something extremely ill-advised, she would be treated in a manner befitting her station.

The hall looked like most Norman halls. Tapestries and banners hung from the rafters, where the hawks resided. Dogs snuffled about the trestle tables, searching among the rushes for scraps of food.

One would never guess that this hall was occupied by people who didn't belong here. But then, maybe some of them did. Ruford may have done away with the Normans, but might have allowed the peasants and soldiers to live— if they joined his rebellion. Many would.

Still, something wasn't quite right here, though Corwin was at a loss to give it a name.

Ruford pointed to a table near the end of the hall. "Put

Thurkill on a pallet near that table," he told the bearers, then turned to Duncan. "Call out my captains. We will meet as soon as they all gather."

Duncan rushed off; Ruford headed for the hearth. Left to his own devices, Corwin followed Thurkill. After laying the old man on a pallet, the bearers left. Oswuld went in search of large mugs of ale, leaving Corwin to watch over Thurkill.

Corwin lifted his sword from the old man's chest. He gave a moment's thought to putting it in his scabbard, but Ruford might take offense, so he laid it at the foot of the pallet. He would reclaim it when Ruford accepted him into his rebellion.

"What think you of our stronghold?" Thurkill asked.

"I think you misled me, Thurkill. From what I observed riding through the encampment, your army is far from ready to take the field."

"One of the reasons I thought it a good idea to bring you with us. Given your training, you could get them ready."

Aye, he probably could. But that wasn't why he'd come.

"Now that we are here and I know who the leader is, I need some answers, Thurkill."

"Such as?"

"For one, what happened to Norgate's Norman lord?"

From behind him, Oswuld said, "I can answer that one. The story goes that the Saxon soldiers rose up against their lord—though I have not heard why." Oswuld handed over a mug of ale. "Duncan, Ruford and two of the men you will soon meet were a part of the uprising. 'Tis said Duncan was the one who killed the Norman lord."

Maybe that's what had bothered Corwin. He saw no signs of a long, hard-fought battle from without. Treachery had come from within, though he could hardly imagine Ruford as a soldier in a Norman's service.

"How did Ruford become involved?"

"'Tis said he was a guest here at the time," Oswuld said.

A guest? Ruford had betrayed the lord of Norgate, a man who'd offered him the hospitality of bed and table, by using the lord's own soldiers against him. Corwin could well imagine Ruford's tactics.

He voiced his conjecture aloud. "Ruford sensed displeasure among the soldiers and approached the most vexed—Duncan—and convinced him and his fellows to rebel. Once done, being of noble blood, Ruford set himself up as lord. Then he convinced the soldiers that if they could bring down one Norman, they could bring low all Normans, including the highest of them all—the king."

"Quite possibly. By the time Father and I arrived, this keep had been well secured and most of the army you saw outside was in place." Oswuld nodded toward the doorway. "The rest of the captains begin to arrive."

"You are a captain, are you not?" Corwin asked of Thurkill.

"Aye," he said quietly, probably knowing he wouldn't be one for long. Even if he didn't die, he wouldn't be of much use to Ruford if his heart ailment kept him abed. Ruford would have to assign someone to take his place.

Like me, Corwin thought.

As each captain arrived, Oswuld made an introduction. Some greeted him, others didn't. Each went over to Thurkill and asked after his health, some with genuine concern, others as a mere formality. Corwin noted it all while his head reeled with the notion of becoming one of them.

As a captain, he would be privy to the rebels' planning sessions. By the time he left, he would know every detail of how they intended to overthrow the crown. And possibly, he could cripple those plans, maybe cause dissension among the captains. Use Ruford's own tactics against him. First, however, he had to convince them that they couldn't possibly win this rebellion without his help.

Eight captains had assembled by the time Ruford joined them, again with Duncan trailing behind. Corwin likened him to a hound, sniffing around his master in hopes of a bone or a pat on the head.

Ruford sat on a bench and waved a hand at Duncan. "Repeat the tale you gave me last eve," he ordered.

Duncan paced as he told of Judith's kidnapping, saying how he, Thurkill and Oswuld had watched the abbey for several days. Satisfied they wouldn't meet with armed resistance, they'd decided to enter the abbey to take Judith. She'd made it easy for them, however, by venturing outside the walls.

With a self-satisfied smile, Duncan said, "She tried to escape. Oswuld and I caught her, though, and we made off with her without incident." His smile faded. "Unfortunately, Corwin heard her screams and tracked us."

Corwin remembered Judith's screams, filled with anger and fear. If he'd been closer, or had answered her distress more quickly, neither of them would now be in the far reaches of northern England in the midst of a rebel stronghold. Judith would be safely ensconced in Romsey Abbey, and he overseeing the structures being built at Cotswold.

He wouldn't have gotten to know Judith for the intelligent, charming, desirable woman she'd become. She wouldn't now be in a chamber at the top of the stairway, probably fretting about what was transpiring down here in the hall. He suppressed a satisfied smile at the depths of the concern she'd expressed on the ride through the encampment, and chose not to examine too closely whether

Judith fretted because she cared deeply for him or because he'd vowed to help her escape.

"Your intent was rescue," Ruford said, dragging Corwin's attention back to the business at hand.

"Aye," Corwin said. "Then I overheard Thurkill tell Judith of the reason she'd been kidnapped, of the purpose of your rebellion. I decided not to kill him, but to join him."

"A rather swift decision, one might think."

"Mayhap, but one not made lightly, nor one I will regret if this rebellion succeeds and the price of my service is met."

"Wilmont."

Corwin nodded.

Duncan snickered. "So he says, my lord. I still mistrust him."

After a moment's silence, Ruford said, "I will keep that in mind, Duncan. Pray continue."

Duncan obeyed, relating the journey's progress—Judith's second attempt to escape, obtaining her gown and mare, and the group's close brush with the sheriff of Hampshire. Ruford seemed to pay little heed. Judging by the direction his gaze continually wandered, Corwin guessed where the man's thoughts strayed—up the stairway to the chambers above, where the maids had taken Judith.

His own thoughts had strayed up that same stairway far too often, pulling his concentration away from determining the rebellion's troop strength and the quality of the rebellion's leadership. Especially Ruford's.

From their conversation upon arrival, 'twas obvious Judith knew Ruford Clark, might know him well. At some point, Corwin wanted to hear Judith's opinion of the man.

Duncan neared the end of his tale. Corwin prepared to

answer whatever questions would come his way. He also had a few questions of his own.

"As you saw, my lord, Corwin refused to cover his eyes, in direct *disobedience* to your order," Duncan said. "For that insolence alone he should not be allowed to remain among us."

"How answer you that charge?" one of the captains asked.

"Duncan has the right of it. I refused to enter your camp with blinded eyes." Corwin waved a hand toward his sword. "As a sign of my goodwill, I put aside my sword. However, I felt no obligation to obey the orders of a man I had not yet met, to whom I have not sworn my loyalty."

"You swore loyalty to Gerard of Wilmont," Ruford said. "Yet now you seek to betray him. How do I know you will not betray me?"

Corwin smiled. "You do not," he admitted. At Ruford's frown, he chided, "Come now, Ruford. Your rebellion is rooted in betrayal. Does not everyone here betray an overlord by his presence in your stronghold?"

"Not I," another present said, taking umbrage.

By the frowns on a few faces, Corwin knew he offended more than one of the captains. If they didn't betray their overlords, then they obeyed an overlord's orders—and Ruford couldn't be their overlord. Could he? Corwin pushed that quandary to the back of his mind to mull over later.

"Do we not, each one of us, betray the overlord of us all—the king—by plotting to hand Ruford his crown?"

Corwin wanted to rail at them for falling under Ruford's spell, to jolt their consciences once more. And maybe he would—later. A carefully placed word here and there could go far to cause dissension within the ranks. For now, however, he desisted.

Corwin leaned forward. "And I, Ruford, can help you

obtain that crown with less bloodshed. I know many of the Norman nobles, have visited their holdings. I can tell you whose forces are the weakest or strongest. In many cases, I can enter a keep without being questioned.''

"'Tis true, my lord,'' Oswuld interjected. "When we bought Lady Judith's mare, no one stopped us at the gate. Truth to tell, the steward greeted Corwin with pleasure by name, as one would a friend.''

"And think on this,'' Corwin added. "I could lead a company of men right up to the doors of Westminster Palace or the royal residence in White Tower. I can damn near hand you the crown of England.''

An exaggeration, to be sure. The king's guards were not so complacent. The lie, however, brought a spark of greed to Ruford's eyes.

"My lord, I must protest—''

Ruford cut off Duncan's words with the wave of a hand. "I will hear more,'' he said.

Corwin knew he had his man.

Judith lounged in the tub of steaming hot water, a jewel-encrusted, gold goblet—nearly empty of wine—dangling from her fingers. She tried hard not to think about what could be happening in the great hall between Corwin and Ruford, tried to simply enjoy the luxury of a bath in a comfortable bedchamber. She was almost succeeding.

A tapestry depicting the hunt covered nearly a full wall of the chamber, overshadowing the large bed with its invitingly thick mattress, on which lay a huge bear pelt. Her gaze skimmed over the heavy oak table, two chairs and a low-burning brazier. In the corner of the room stood an intricately carved chest, from which the maids had pulled an amber silk gown. She didn't ask about the gown's former owner, fearing the woman had died, along with her husband.

Somehow, Ruford and his forces had managed to capture a Norman keep. Ruford wouldn't have let the Normans go free, not if he wanted his shameful acts to remain secret.

When Corwin had asked her to think about who might be the leader of the rebellion, Ruford Clark's name had been one of the first she'd come up with, then promptly discarded. Not only had she believed Ruford still in France, she simply hadn't envisioned him as a man with the means to take on so grandiose an undertaking as the overthrow of England. Though Ruford could be charming, he didn't have the forceful personality necessary to draw followers. She doubted he had the funds to pay them all. Unless, of course, Ruford had simply promised huge tracts of land to each of his soldiers. In land was power, and those who craved land would do most anything to get it.

If so, then these soldiers were fools. Once Ruford obtained England, he'd be loathe to give up a hide of land to anyone.

But then, Ruford would never sit on the throne, so all this conjecture was for naught.

All she need do was get through the next day or two until Corwin arranged their escape. Then they'd warn the kings of both England and Scotland, dooming Ruford's rebellion.

Judith glanced over at Emma, a woman of about her own age, who sat on the bed and busily plied a needle and thread to the silk gown, taking tucks where necessary so the garment would better fit Judith's form.

Nan, the older of the two maids, poured rose-scented oil into the bath. The aroma drifted up with the steam, filling Judith's head with visions of a flower garden at summer's height.

"Here now, my lady, you must not fall asleep," Nan said kindly. "After your bath, his lordship wishes you to go down to the hall. The cooks are preparing a special meal to celebrate your arrival."

Judith opened eyes that she hadn't realized she'd closed—shouldn't have closed. Though the maids seemed harmless enough, she shouldn't let down her guard while in Ruford's sphere.

Mercy, she shouldn't be enjoying this pampering so much, either, but as Nan slid a brush through her freshly washed hair, Judith submitted without protest.

As Corwin had suggested would happen, these people treated her with all of the deference due her rank. A bath in scented water. A gown of silk. A feast prepared in her honor. Would there also be entertainment in the hall this night? Likely. Ruford wanted her to feel as if she were a guest, not a captive.

Her first inclination had been to rip Ruford apart for his presumption, to be uncooperative and let everyone know of her displeasure at being kidnapped and brought here against her will. As much as she wanted to rage, now that she knew the identity of the rebel leader, she thought better of it. She must be more subdued in her rebuke.

Acting the shrew would only grate against Ruford's thin layer of patience. If he became angered, he might punish her by locking her away, which would only make it harder for Corwin to get to her when the time came for their escape. Having to be somewhat nice to Ruford galled her. She'd make no secret of her vexation at his high-handed tactics, but she wouldn't invoke his temper, either.

Corwin and Ruford were down in the hall, supposedly talking about Corwin's desire to join the rebellion. She heard no loud voices or clashes of steel coming up the stairway. A good sign.

Emma rose, shook out the gown and inspected her stitches, then held it out.

"'Tis finished, my lady. What think you?"

"'Twill do," she said flatly, bringing a frown to Emma's face.

"You are not pleased?"

The woman looked fairly crushed. Judith stopped herself from apologizing for hurting Emma's feelings. She held out a hand toward the maid. "The chemise, if you will."

Emma helped Judith into a chemise of fine white linen, then the gown of amber silk. Both felt smooth and soft against Judith's skin, so different from rough peasant weave, but not comforting. She sat on a stool, allowing Nan to plait her hair and weave into it ribbons of the same color as the dress.

Emma fairly beamed. "Ah, my lady! You look just as a queen should. Lord Ruford will be so pleased!"

Judith doubted that Emma had ever seen the likes of a queen. As for Ruford's pleasure, the man could go hang. Judith couldn't help wonder, however, if Corwin might take notice of her much changed appearance.

Ever since the day of the kidnapping she hadn't taken many pains with how she looked. Not that she could have, lacking so much as a brush for her hair. Neither her black nun's robe nor the gray peasant gown had done a thing for her—but the amber silk did. The silk molded to her body in places the robe was designed to hide. The fabric moved in soft, subtle folds when she moved, unlike the shifting bulk of the peasant weave.

Her hair shone with renewed vibrance, reflecting the gleam of the amber ribbons, and felt as soft as the down on a duckling.

Such vanity, she chided herself, but not too harshly. For the first time in her life she wanted to look good to impress a man. To draw his attention and hold it captive. See appreciation, perhaps desire in his eyes. For just one moment, she wanted to be the center of Corwin's world, make him forget about his quest and see only her.

Emma and Nan looked at her with such pride in the changes they'd helped wrought, thinking she would be the woman to help their lord rule England. They wanted her to be their queen. 'Twould never happen.

Yet the pretense might work to her advantage over the coming days. Just as had happened with her kidnappers, if Ruford thought her complacent, she might not be guarded tightly.

As for his followers, if they wanted a queen, Judith could give them one. Heaven knew she knew how, having had the best teacher—her Aunt Matilda, Queen of England, the woman these people wanted Judith to replace.

Chapter Eleven

"Gor, and will you look at *her*," one of the captains said.

Corwin noticed the sweet suffering in the man's voice. Indeed, Ruford and all of his captains took note and looked toward the stairway.

Obviously, Judith had come into the hall.

A silence ensued, bordering on reverence. Corwin carefully steeled his resolve to show no untoward reaction to Judith. He shouldn't even look, but couldn't help himself.

Lovely. Delicate. Regal. Each word accurately described the woman who stood at the bottom of the stairway.

Gowned in flowing amber silk, the vision that was Judith began a slow glide across the rushes toward the table where Corwin sat motionless, held captive by her beauty.

Like a butterfly emerging from a cocoon, Judith in her transformation was stunning. She'd been beautiful when draped in a nun's robe, and no less lovely when garbed in rough peasant weave. The silk, however, hugged her body as none of her former garments had, revealing a shape molded to please the eye and invite a man's hands.

Judith held her head high and her shoulders back. Her steps landed firmly. To those who shuffled aside to let her pass, she gifted nearly imperceptible nods of acknowledgment, accompanied by a faint smile.

A smile to die for.

She approached the table. For a short, painful moment Corwin's gaze locked with hers. Then he turned away, fearing she would see unerringly into the depths of his heart. She already possessed his loyalty and devotion. 'Twould be foolhardy to let her know she could have far more.

'Twould be foolhardy to allow the rebels to see how much he desired the woman Ruford planned to marry.

Ruford looked pleasurably stunned at the change in Judith's appearance. He rose and held out his hand. "My lady, words fail me."

"You may save your flattery for some other, Ruford," she said. "I do not forget I am a prisoner here, not a guest."

Ruford's hand dropped back to his side. "Truly, my lady, you are my most welcome guest. Did your maids not perform their duties to your satisfaction? Is not the chamber given you one fit for a lady?"

"From the moment your men captured me I have been a prisoner. I spent several long, hard days on horseback on a journey I did not wish to make. You bring me here against my will. Did you expect me to be pleasant about it? Surely you did not believe a bath and a decent chamber would allay my distaste at being kidnapped!"

"Did not Thurkill tell you why?"

"Oh, he spouted some silliness about my becoming queen of England. Truly, I do wish you had chosen another and let me be."

Judith flounced around Ruford, coming into Corwin's line of sight. She knelt down in the rushes next to Thurkill, in flagrant disregard for her silk gown, and put a gentle hand on the man's shoulder.

"How fare you?" she asked.

"I will live," he said.

Corwin wasn't sure Thurkill would last the night. No physician had been summoned, leading him to believe there wasn't one within the rebels' encampment. A mark against Ruford. Every army should include several healers.

Judith beamed down at Thurkill. "I am gladdened to hear so. You and I have a score to settle, and I want you healthy enough to bear the brunt of my anger."

Thurkill patted Judith's hand. "Do not fight so hard, my lady. All will be well. You will see."

"Thurkill speaks true," Ruford said. "When our task is done, and you sit on England's throne, I believe you will forgive us the inconvenience we caused you."

Judith rose and sighed. "How many Saxon rebellions have there been over the decades? Three, mayhap four? I see no reason why yours should succeed where others failed."

Lord, Corwin hoped Judith knew what she was doing. Hoped she knew Ruford well enough to know how far she could push him without drawing an angry response. To his relief, Ruford looked at her quizzically.

"Is that what bothers you? You think this rebellion will not succeed, that you will not obtain the crown? Believe me, my lady, I have studied those rebellions and know why they failed. I will not make the same mistakes."

Judith crossed her arms. "I find that very hard to believe."

Ruford smiled. "Then I shall endeavor to convince you. Come, our meal is nearly ready. Mayhap, over wine and venison, I can give you hope."

Judith glanced around the table at the captains, at Corwin, but didn't linger on any one man. "I did not mean to interrupt. You are finished here?"

"We can resume our talk after we eat."

The captains rose from the benches at the dismissal. "My lord," the more vocal of the captains said, "we have not decided Corwin's fate."

Corwin wondered why the man thought he had any say in the matter. True, Ruford had called the captains together, but from what he'd observed, concluded that the summons had been a token gesture. Only Ruford's opinion mattered.

"For now, Corwin's sword remains where it lies. He does not leave the confines of the hall," Ruford said.

Corwin nodded slightly, an agreement to the terms.

The captains also nodded, then walked off toward tables already set with trenchers holding dark brown bread in preparation for the meal.

"Judith, you will join me at the high table," Ruford said, his order given in a polite but firm tone.

For a moment, Corwin thought she might refuse. Instead, she looked down at Thurkill, her true worry apparent. "I will be back later," she told him. "You had best be breathing."

Thurkill managed a chuckle. "I shall do my best."

Judith then set her features in regal indifference and walked off ahead of Ruford with the same poise she'd displayed earlier.

Alone now with only Thurkill and Oswuld, Corwin rolled his shoulders, easing the tension that had set hard in his muscles when entering the encampment.

He was still alive, and hopefully well on his way to acceptance, despite Duncan. Judith seemed to have found a way to cope with the situation, knew how to handle Ruford to her advantage. All in all, today had gone very well.

Oswuld got up and brushed pieces of broken rushes from his breeches. "I will fetch us something to eat," he told Thurkill. "Are you up to more than broth?"

"Broth will do," Thurkill said. "Bring food for Corwin, too. I am sure he would prefer to take his meal with us."

As Oswuld turned to leave, Thurkill patted the rushes where his son had been sitting. "Come, Corwin. I imagine you now have more questions than when the meeting began. Where did we leave off?"

Corwin thought a moment. "When you and Oswuld came, this army was already in place."

"Most of it, aye. Some came after us, but not many."

Thurkill closed his eyes. Corwin wondered if he should continue or let the man rest. Except this might be his last chance to get answers from Thurkill.

"Among these men are brigands and mercenaries, those who look only for reward—like me. There are also men like you, who would truly like to oust the Normans and put a Saxon on the throne." Corwin shrugged a shoulder. "Each man has his place in an army. So long as he wields a weapon with some skill and stands his ground in battle, it does not matter why he fights."

"Aye, but fighting is easier when one has the skill to do it, good leaders to follow and hope of success. 'Tis why I agreed to fetch Judith."

"You just confused me, Thurkill. I cannot imagine Judith training or leading troops."

"Nay, but besides reward or an ideal, men will also fight for someone they admire and respect. Men might fight to make Judith Canmore their queen. Especially if a strong, worthy Saxon stands by her side."

Corwin wasn't sure he succeeded in hiding his revulsion at the pairing of Judith with Ruford. But he saw Thurkill's point. Out of respect and admiration alone, Corwin would fight for Gerard of Wilmont.

Dare he ask the question now uppermost in his mind? Would Thurkill give him an honest answer?

"Thurkill, do you truly consider Ruford a worthy Saxon?"

Thurkill sighed. "I believed so. But during our journey, away from the stronghold and Ruford's influence, I had time and reason to rethink my beliefs. He does have noble blood, which works in his favor, but now I believe another man might be the better choice."

"Who?"

Thurkill opened his eyes and turned his head slightly. His eyes were clear, his voice firm as he declared, "You."

Shocked speechless, Corwin stared at the old man in utter disbelief, noting only on the edge of his awareness that Oswuld returned.

"From the look on Corwin's face, I gather you told him," Oswuld said, setting a large platter on the nearby table.

"I did," Thurkill answered. "Here, help me sit up. My back is sore."

"'Twill take another hour off your life."

"Son, I am dying. We both know it. At which hour no longer concerns me. Corwin, give me your hands."

Still dazed, Corwin took Thurkill's hands while Oswuld moved to support his father's shoulders.

Once he was upright, the old man's grimace turned to a smile. "Much better. Now I can drink my broth without it running down my chin."

Corwin finally found his voice. "Surely you jest!"

Oswuld handed his father a tin cup. "You drink. I will talk," he said, then sat on the other side of Thùrkill's pallet. "Father does not jest. He feels the force here may be large enough to take a holding or two, but not London. Others may yet come, rally to a Canmore. But this rebellion is doomed unless a strong leader takes it in hand." Oswuld smiled wryly. "Too, we noted that you and Judith make a

handsome couple, and from the way you look at each other
when you think no one sees, neither of you would oppose
a marriage. She may have grown fond of Father, but she
seeks you out when fearful or otherwise needs someone to
talk to. She has forgiven you for not rescuing her, just as
she no longer hates us for kidnapping her.''

Chagrined, Corwin said, ''I thought I had hidden my
attraction to her rather well.''

Oswuld shrugged, as if it mattered not. ''I doubt that
Duncan saw, and you must take care around Ruford. Be
that as it may, Father feels that since you are willing to
fight a war for the reward of Wilmont, he sees no reason
why you should not take the entire prize—both the woman
and the kingdom.''

Corwin shook his head. ''You want me to begin a rebellion within a rebellion.''

Thurkill drank the last of his broth and handed the cup
to Oswuld. ''King Corwin and Queen Judith. Has a nice
sound to it, do you not think?''

''I think you have gone mad, Thurkill.''

''Then think on it some more. Oswuld, wake me when
the captains and Ruford return,'' he ordered, then lay back
down on the pallet.

Oswuld got to his feet. ''Come to the table. Our food
grows cold.''

On the platter lay two trenchers filled with chunks of
meat covered with thick, brown gravy. While Oswuld
tucked heartily into the meal, Corwin picked at his. His
stomach hadn't yet settled from the jolt of Thurkill's suggestion.

At the dais, Judith sat next to Ruford, sharing his
trencher. She looked neither happy nor unhappy—just sat,
and ate, listening to whatever Ruford was saying. She
should be here, next to him, sharing his trencher.

"Corwin, I should like to ask a favor of you."

Corwin gave a burst of laughter. "I hesitate to ask what it is."

"Nothing so profound as my father's request, I assure you."

"All right, what then?"

Oswuld took a deep breath. "After Father…dies, I want to bury him next to my mother. Some here will object to my leaving, even if I swear to tell no one of what I have seen or heard here, so I do not intend to tell them."

Corwin wondered why Oswuld trusted him with his secret, but didn't ask. The young man needed help now, not questions.

"You want me to help you find a way to get your father out of camp without being discovered."

"I know the way of it," he said. "What concerns me is what will happen when they realize I have left. I should like you to show me how to wield a sword as skillfully as you do."

Corwin pushed aside his trencher, no longer interested in eating. He almost couldn't believe that the answer to one of his main concerns might have just come his way.

"You know a way out of the encampment?"

"Aye."

Dare he trust Oswuld with his own secret? If he had only himself to consider, he might, but with Judith's safety involved, it might be best to wait before taking the risk.

But he could help Oswuld.

"I cannot teach you all I know within a practice session or two, but I can show you a few moves to give you some advantage over an opponent."

"That is all I ask. My thanks."

* * *

"You look delightful in that gown, my dear," Ruford said. "The color suits you."

Ruford's effusive compliments were beginning to grate on Judith's nerves. But then, Ruford had at least noticed the change. For all the reaction she'd received from Corwin, she may as well be draped in black robes. Still, she resisted the urge to ask Ruford if the gown's color had also suited its former owner.

"I believe blue is a better color for me."

"Then by all means, you shall have blue, in whatever fabric you fancy. The women in our court will follow your lead, and we shall look out from our thrones over a sea of blue."

So far, she'd also managed to resist his attempts to elicit a smile or ignite a spark of interest in his plan to make her his queen. Throughout the meal he'd talked more than ate, feeding her while reflecting on how glorious her life would be when his rebellion ended.

No argument of hers could shake his confidence. Ruford hadn't a doubt that the rebellion would succeed and he would be crowned king. He had even chosen the man he would name archbishop of Canterbury, who would thus preside over the coronation ceremony.

Ruford speared a tidbit of venison with his eating knife and brought it to her lips. Judith took the meat with her teeth, being careful not to touch the knife, avoiding the anticipated brush of his fingers against her cheek. He'd done so twice, bringing an embarrassed flush to her cheeks and a shot of revulsion to her stomach.

She truly hated sitting at the dais, next to Ruford. She would prefer to sit at the table at the far end of the hall, where Corwin and Oswuld now partook of their meal.

Corwin had looked out of place among the captains, his gleaming chain mail a sharp contrast to their leather hauberks. Though he'd let his beard grow to better fit in, the very set of his shoulders placed him above the others. Strong. Confident. Intelligent. All showed in his demeanor, from the way he held his head to the manner in which he spoke.

Corwin didn't appear ill at ease, either then or now, even though Ruford had yet to pass judgment, even though Corwin's sword still lay near Thurkill's pallet. She would feel much better when that sword once more rested within its scabbard, the hilt within easy reach of Corwin's hand.

"More wine, Judith?" Ruford asked, already pouring the ruby liquid from a silver flagon into her goblet. When he speared another piece of venison, Judith put the goblet to her lips. No more would she play his game. Better not to eat.

"Not hungry?" he asked.

"I have grown accustomed to eating quite late in the day. Mayhap later I will have more."

"The food is quite good, do you not think?"

"I am not fond of venison."

He put his knife down and leaned back in his chair. "How long do you intend to suffer this ill humor? It will not make a difference, you know. You are here. You will be my wife. Why not accept your fate?"

"Accept the fate you have decided should be mine?" Judith clasped her goblet more tightly. "You bring me here against my will. You intend to wage a war, with the outcome of usurping the throne. In doing so, you will harm people I love. I know you put no value in family, but I do. I do not understand why you believe I can look favorably upon your scheme."

"Your approval is not necessary. Nor, truly, is your cooperation. I had hoped that on your journey here you would become content. Indeed, Duncan led me to believe you were warming to the idea of becoming queen.''

''You were misinformed.''

''I believe not. Once given a horse, you no longer tried to escape. Why, if you truly find my plans for you so abhorrent?''

Because Corwin had convinced her not to, but she couldn't tell that to Ruford. There were, of course, other reasons.

''The farther north we came, the less sure I was of my surroundings. Wandering about lost in a forest with wolves and bears did not appeal.''

'''Tis my belief the wolves frightened you less than returning to the abbey,'' he countered. ''You came because you began thinking like the royal personage you are.'' His tone became more urgent. ''Envision yourself not as the niece of a queen, entrapped in Romsey Abbey by a family who has let you waste away there. You are free now. Free to do as you are meant to do. To rule. See yourself in the palace at Westminster, with a vast treasury from which to draw funds. Servants to attend your every whim. No one to tell you what you may or may not do, where you may or may not go.''

Except you.

''Judith, had I not sent Thurkill to fetch you, how long would you have remained imprisoned in the abbey until your *family* decided to let you out? And to whom would they have given you? Some lord who cannot offer you anywhere near what I can, no doubt.''

He would never understand, she realized—no matter how many times she protested she hadn't been fetched, but kidnapped. No matter if she declared she loved the members of her family, despite their lack of action on her behalf.

But most of all, he simply could not understand she had no desire to be his queen.

No matter a woman's rank, be she a queen or a peasant, the man who she married gained full power over his wife. What he gave, he could take away.

Ruford had always been ambitious, had always sought things he couldn't have. He'd been banished after attempting to gain his father's lands through murder. Now he sought the crown of England. His greed knew no bounds or restrictions. He wouldn't hesitate to kill anyone who stood in his way, or have another do the deed for him.

Heaven forbid if Ruford found out what Corwin was truly up to... She pushed thoughts of the certain consequences aside. Ruford wouldn't find out until after she and Corwin were well away.

She gave him the response he craved. "As you say, Ruford, you offer much. I will consider what you have said."

With a smug smile, he said, "You will not be sorry, my lady, I vow."

Judith saw no reason to comment, so took another sip of wine, and was glad she'd taken a small sip when Ruford unexpectedly said, "I understand from Duncan that you have known Corwin of Lenvil for some time. Is he to be trusted?"

How to answer without damaging Corwin's efforts or raising Ruford's suspicions?

"As I am sure Duncan must have told you, Corwin is the brother of a friend," she said softly. "He happened to be on the road where I was kidnapped, heard my screams and came after us to rescue me. Only he didn't, instead deciding to join Thurkill—and you."

"He says he does it for Wilmont. A steep price."

She shrugged a shoulder. "That is for you to decide. I

only know I was quite disappointed in him for not rescuing me.''

"Yet not so disappointed that you spurned him. Duncan said you spoke often with Corwin."

She had, but that was easily explained.

"As I did to Thurkill, and a bit to Oswuld. With Duncan, there was truly no point. Corwin and I spoke mostly of his sister. He also tried to convince me that all would be well— mostly, I would wager, so he would no longer have to listen to me complain. Besides, Corwin is a knight, and is brother-by-marriage to a Norman baron. Given my choice of companions, naturally I spoke most to the person closest to my own rank.''

"Duncan does not trust him."

She gave a short, sharp laugh. "Duncan trusts no one!"

As if he'd heard his name, Duncan rose from his bench. The captains did, too. Apparently they had finished their meal, for they all headed toward the table where Corwin sat with Oswuld.

She nodded toward them. "Your captains await you," she said, hoping to divert Ruford. She feared getting caught in a lie, or a truth.

"They can wait. We are not yet finished."

Deliberately mistaking his meaning, Judith glanced down at the trencher, where two pieces of meat remained on the bread. He might not be finished with his questions, but she was determined to give him no more answers.

"I want no more," she said. "You may toss the rest to the dogs if you wish. I should like to speak with Thurkill again before you resume your meeting with your captains."

If he realized she was purposely being dull witted, he gave no sign.

"Very well," he agreed. "However, I would prefer that

you do not speak with Corwin anymore, at least until I can decide if he is trustworthy.''

So, as his queen she could do what she wished, could she? Unless, of course, Ruford objected.

Two days, she thought. Only two days.

"As you wish," she said, rising from her chair.

"How long has Thurkill to live, do you think?"

Judith wished she knew, wished there was something more she could do to prolong his life, or at least make his passing less painful.

"I shall be surprised to find he yet breathes."

"I think he does. Only moments ago he sat up to drink."

Surprised that he had noticed, Judith took it as a warning to take nothing for granted where Ruford was concerned.

"Come," he said. "You may have your talk with Thurkill and I will make you known to my captains. After I finish with them, we shall talk more, get to know each other better."

His last phrase made her skin crawl. Maybe he merely wanted to talk, but Judith had the distinct feeling he wanted more. The upper floor had been divided into two chambers and a garderobe. She'd been given one bedchamber; the other must be Ruford's. Judith squelched the urge to run up the stairs to her chamber and throw the bolt on the door.

Corwin had told her to remain near Thurkill, but truly, the old man was too weak to be of much help if Ruford decided to share her bed. Nor could she remain down in the hall for the rest of the night—Ruford would be angry if she refused the comfort of the bedchamber.

As she pondered the dilemma, she watched Thurkill turn to his side, trying to get comfortable. He shouldn't be on a pallet on the floor, but in a bed.

What better bed than hers?

The thought struck and settled, almost making her smile.

She could ease Thurkill's discomfort and keep Ruford from her bedchamber simply by having Thurkill hauled up the stairs.

Of course, Ruford's bedchamber was up the stairs, too.

Judith took a resolving breath and decided to deal with that unpleasant reality later.

Chapter Twelve

Removing Thurkill to her bedchamber might not be easy. He would need to be carried, and Ruford must give his permission.

As she neared the table where Corwin and Oswuld and the captains awaited Ruford, Oswuld once more seated himself on the floor beside his father's pallet. His grim look tore at her heartstrings.

No matter that Thurkill was a rebel, no ill man should be lying on a pallet at the far reaches of a hall, with no physician or priest to attend him, his breath ladened with the odor of rushes in want of changing.

If she were in charge here… Judith glanced about the hall. Why shouldn't she be in charge?

Ruford could hardly complain if the woman he considered his future wife took charge of the keep's hall. Or oversaw the meals. Or tended the sick. All duties naturally within a woman's purview. In doing so, she might give Ruford pause over his choice of a wife, and yet give Thurkill a bit of comfort at the end.

"Oswuld, is there a physician or priest here?" she asked, voicing her thoughts as her plan took form.

"No physician," he said, then snickered. "As for a priest, well, we have what passes for one."

"If he is ordained and therefore able to hear your father's confession, he should be fetched. No man should die unshrived."

After giving her his hand to help her stand, Oswuld went in search of the priest.

"Ruford, I ask a boon of you," she said, managing to convey that she fully expected him to grant it.

"Of course, my dear, but hold a moment. I would like you to meet my captains."

She bit her bottom lip at the delay, but held her peace as the captains stood. Ruford rattled off names that she wouldn't remember for lack of concentration. But it didn't matter. If what she had in mind for the remainder of her stay at Norgate took place, she would never see any of them again.

"You honor us with your presence, my lady," one of them uttered.

Judith graced them with a brief, dismissing nod, then turned back to Ruford. "I realize soldiers consider it most glorious to die on the field of battle. Since Thurkill is denied the honor, I believe we should make his passing more comfortable. Might I borrow a few of your men to carry him up the stairs?"

Ruford's brow furrowed. "Up the stairs? To what purpose?"

"To put him in the bed in my chamber."

The furrows deepened. "My lady, I know you mean well, but...the maids worked hard to prepare the bed and chamber for your use."

He could not care less about the tender feelings of the maids. Truly, he objected to the honor she did Thurkill.

She looked pointedly down at the dying man, then back up at Ruford.

"Would *you* care to breathe your last down on that pallet? This man has served you well. He does not deserve to die among overripe rushes."

He took a moment to answer. "Nay, mayhap not, but neither should you give up the comfort of your bed."

She scoffed. "For the past seven years I have made do with a hard, narrow cot. During the journey here I slept on the ground. A thick pallet will do me fine. Besides, I do not intend to sleep, but keep vigil. I have sent for the priest. In the absence of a physician, Emma can help me tend Thurkill, and no doubt Oswuld will wish to remain by his father's side. Naturally, anyone who wishes to join us in prayer may do so."

Ruford's dark look conveyed his wish to deny her request, but Judith doubted he'd do so. Not in front of the very people he wanted to have accept her as his wife and their queen. To do that, he must give her the rights given by any noble lord to his lady—the care of hearth and home, the tending of his vassals.

He lowered his voice to just above a whisper. "Then have your vigil, Judith. But beware, I have no liking for how you went about it. We will talk about this later, you and I."

She matched his volume and tone. "Make up your mind, Ruford. Either I am to be given the rights due me as your wife, or denied them as your prisoner. I *did* do you the favor of seeking your permission when I could have commanded—and been obeyed."

"You gave me little choice."

"As you have given me *no* choice. Does it sit hard in your mind, Ruford, ignite your anger? Then mayhap you can understand how I have felt since your men tore my world apart.''

To his credit, his features smoothed as his anger faded. Somehow, she'd hit her mark, but didn't rejoice. Matching wits with Ruford drained her of energy.

Ruford turned and pointed to two of his captains. "Her ladyship needs your help to take Thurkill up the stairs. Be quick."

Thurkill woke slowly when she shook him gently. "We are taking you up the stairs. We will have you in a clean bed soon."

He groaned when the captains picked him up by his hands and feet. Before Judith could reprimand them to be more gentle, Corwin rose from his seat and came around the table.

"Let us not hurt him more than he already hurts," he said gruffly, getting down on one knee. "Give him to me."

Oh, Ruford wouldn't like this one bit, Judith thought. He said nothing, however, as Corwin took Thurkill into his arms. Thurkill wasn't a big man, but neither was he small. Yet Corwin fitted the dying man into the cradle of his arms, then smoothly and gently rose to his feet as if lifting a child.

"Lead the way, my lady," he said.

"Go. I shall be along directly," she said.

If Corwin was coming up the stairs, she had one more thing to do. With both hands and most of her strength, Judith managed to lift his sword.

"Have a care, Judith. 'Tis finely honed," Corwin said.

She'd never had a doubt, not after she'd watched him use the whetstone on it on several evenings. Not after she'd seen the deep sword bites in Duncan's leather hauberk.

She'd known Corwin was strong. He'd just proved so once again when he lifted Thurkill. But she hadn't realized how much weight his muscles could bear until she held his sword—the hilt in her right hand, the flat of the blade across her left arm. Only hours ago she'd watched Corwin wield this weapon with one hand, watched it flash with swift strokes as if it were a mere extension of his arm.

Only hours ago, yet it seemed like days.

"I gather there is some purpose to this?" Ruford said, staring at the sword.

So you do not steal it. Though maybe she shouldn't have worried. She very much doubted Ruford could heft it without difficulty.

"Corwin yielded his sword to Thurkill," she said, as if that explained all, then turned to call the maids. "Emma, go up and turn down the coverlet on my bed. Nan, to me."

Emma scurried up the stairs, Corwin following at a sedate pace. Nan obeyed, too, if more slowly.

"The rushes need changing. Gather whatever brooms can be found and put them into people's hands. I will not eat another meal in this hall until I smell only the food."

Nan glanced over at Ruford, seeking permission. Judith held in her temper, vowing that if Ruford did not support her order, whatever words passed between them later would be quite heated.

To her relief, he gave Nan a hesitant, brief nod.

With a bob of a curtsy, Nan said, "As you wish, my lady."

Judith slowly made her way up the stairway. With Corwin's sword balanced in her arms, she couldn't lift her skirt, making the ascent clumsy.

'Twas silly to feel so good—more in control of both herself and her fate than she had in a long time. In a moment or two, if she could once again manage to arrange things to her satisfaction, she would have time alone with Corwin.

* * *

Corwin entered the chamber, amazed that Judith had arranged things to suit all of their needs so perfectly, unable to remember when he'd last been so proud of anyone. Judith's handling of Ruford had been nothing short of magnificent. The man was arrogant and overbearing, dangerous and ruthless to be sure, but could be made to back down when caught unaware.

'Twould make sense if Ruford conceded more to Judith than any other person in the encampment. Her rank surpassed his—one of the reasons he'd brought her here—and he would always be aware of her value to him as a result. Too, Corwin had the feeling Ruford wanted Judith to think highly of him, both as a potential king and as a husband.

Handsome, with courtly manners and charm, Ruford was likely far more accustomed to dealing with adoring females than obstinate ones. He would court Judith, try to control her.

But if Ruford thought she'd gone too far, that he'd been made to appear foolish, he would extract revenge in an underhanded manner. Up here in her chamber, with Thurkill to nurse and with Oswuld and a priest to keep her company, Judith might be safest.

"Rather nice, is it not?" Thurkill said, surveying the room.

Corwin looked down at the man he still held in his arms. "I thought you had passed out again."

"Hardly, though I feared I might when those two oafs picked me up. I thank you for a timely rescue."

"Aye, well, Ruford may have my head for it."

The young maid, Emma, stood near the bed. She'd turned the coverlet down as ordered.

Corwin smiled at her. "Emma, you may wish to leave the room while I put this old man to bed. Unless, of course, you are accustomed to the sight of naked men."

Her mouth forming a shocked, silent "oh," she fairly sped from the chamber, closing the door behind her.

Corwin eased Thurkill down on the edge of the bed and began working on the fastenings of his hauberk. Thurkill breathed heavily. Just the small exertion of being carried up to the chamber had taken a toll, and removing his garments would take more.

"I truly hate this," Thurkill said, grimacing as Corwin removed the hauberk.

Thurkill meant being weak. Dying.

"I must admit I would prefer to have a young female take my clothing off, too, but you will have to settle for me." Corwin bent down to pull off Thurkill's boots. "You realize you are now the envy of every man in the hall. They know you are in Judith's bed, that she will make a fuss over you. I swear, before long every male in the place will be lined up outside the door professing one ailment or another."

The tunic, then breeches and hose. There was little left of Thurkill. All that had gotten the man through the past week had been the strength of his will, for there was none left in his body.

"They shall have to wait their turn," Thurkill said, and lay back in the bed, making hardly a dent in the feather-filled mattress.

Corwin tossed a coverlet over him. "Make them wait awhile, will you?" he said, then shook his head at his foolishness. This man was a rebel, and dying, and the sooner done the better. Judith would be loathe to leave here otherwise.

"I may linger for days," the old man said, then closed his eyes.

Corwin sighed inwardly, torn between liking for this man and the duty he must perform. He opened the chamber door to let Emma back in, and found Judith standing there with her.

Magnificent Judith, with his sword in her arms and a smile on her face. Would that he were his sword, secure in her embrace, warming to her hands. Would that he were in the bed, the object of her gentle care, the focus of her attention.

Damn, but he wanted to sweep her up, hold her close, tell her how very proud he was of her. He couldn't. Emma watched. Thurkill would hear.

Nor did he have the right. For all Corwin hated to admit it, Ruford's noble blood made him a more suitable match for Judith than a mere knight.

"Finished?" she asked.

He stepped aside, allowing the women to enter. Both walked over to the bed—Emma to the head, Judith to the foot. She laid his sword at the end of the mattress, at Thurkill's feet.

Judith glanced at Thurkill, then turned to Emma. "Fetch some clean towels."

Emma's large eyes expressed her surprise. "You intend to bathe him?"

"I intend to let Oswuld do so. Go quickly, Emma."

With a nod, the maid obeyed.

Judith turned to Corwin, her smile fading. "You should go quickly, too."

"Aye," he said, but didn't move. "Why did you bring my sword up?"

"I had this foolish notion that Ruford or maybe Duncan would steal it. Then I picked it up and realized neither of them could wield it as you do," she said, and glanced down at the sword. "Still, I am not sorry it is here. This way I will know all is well when you return to fetch your sword."

She walked toward him, a vision in amber silk. Through

no conscious thought of his own, he held his arms open. To his utter delight and sorrow, her steps didn't halt until she stood firmly against him, fingers hooked into the rings of his chain mail, her forehead resting lightly against his chin.

"Hurry back," she whispered urgently.

"I will," he promised. For more than his sword. For Judith.

"Ruford is yet angry at me, Corwin. Have a care."

"*You* have a care. Do not allow yourself to be alone with him. Bolt the chamber door if you must."

"I will."

He had to let her go, face Ruford and the captains. He slid his hands to her shoulders, intending to push away. His resolve deserted him when she moved, tilting her face upward. Tears welled in her eyes, but didn't fall.

"If you are going to kiss me, Corwin, do so now. Ruford is waiting. Emma will return. Oswuld and the priest—"

She sought reassurance; he tried to comfort. They ignited passion. The kiss quickly flared from a gentle touch of lips to an urgent melding of mouths. Hot. Sweet. Heaven and hell.

He'd kissed Judith once before, but not like this. Not with her wanting it as much as he did, with her kissing him back.

He gave himself up to his burning desire. The moist heat of her mouth and the sweet taste of her lips. The sheer wonder of a fantasy come to life in his arms. He wanted Judith more than he'd wanted any woman. He would hurt for hours, but couldn't bring himself to care. He couldn't have her, but didn't let the fleeting thought stop him.

Right now, for this moment, Judith was his. All his. And he all hers.

Judith felt her knees wobble, her whole body begin to

melt. She clung to Corwin and struggled to stay alert, unwilling to wither away into nothingness and miss a single moment of pure bliss.

'Twas all she'd dreamed of and more. She felt his power—over her body, over her senses. She gave herself to him willingly, completely, knowing he wouldn't abuse her. Not Corwin. Never Corwin.

She'd been misled. By her elders. By the church. Submitting to a man couldn't be wrong if he were the right man. A man like Corwin. Her right man. She'd found him, longed to keep him, and promptly brushed aside the contrary thought that she wouldn't be allowed to.

Then all thought fled as Corwin's hands moved, skimming over her shoulders and her back, down to cup her backside. Just when she'd recovered from the shock of it, his hands moved again, retreating along their former path but coming higher, to frame her face.

His mouth gentled, then deserted her.

Of course, the kiss must end. Corwin must leave. But it took a long, deep breath and a great amount of willpower for her not to pull him back.

"Have a care," he whispered.

She couldn't find the voice to answer, so simply looked deep into his azure eyes and hoped he'd find her agreement there.

"Corwin?" Thurkill's voice from the bed startled her, making her leap out of Corwin's arms.

Mon dieu, she'd forgotten about Thurkill. His eyes were closed. Had they been all along or had he seen?

"What?" Corwin answered.

"Are you thinking?"

Thinking? About what? Corwin wondered, still dazed. Then he remembered. Rebellion within rebellion. Be a king. Marry Judith. He shook his head at the man's audacity, and at his own for having probably proved to Thurkill that his feelings for Judith went far beyond attraction to a beautiful woman.

"Aye, I am thinking, Thurkill. Very hard."

"Thinking about what?" Judith asked, her confusion apparent.

Corwin thought of explaining, but could hear footsteps on the stairway. There wasn't enough time. And maybe it was best that she didn't know. Well, 'twas Thurkill's ridiculous idea, and he'd brought it up. Let him deal with it.

"Ask Thurkill—later."

Oswuld entered the chamber, followed by a priest.

"Ruford grows impatient," Oswuld told him.

"Poor man," Corwin said, and as he'd hoped, the sarcasm brought a smile to Judith's face. "I will be back."

He'd tossed the phrase out to the room in general, but Judith knew Corwin meant to reassure her. She listened to his boots hit the steps and fade away, hoping he'd be back soon. Already she missed him. With a short prayer that Ruford wasn't so angry at her that Corwin would suffer for it, she turned her attention to her next task.

Oswuld and the priest had crossed to the bed to attend Thurkill. The priest plopped down on the edge crossed himself and bowed his head. Oswuld backed away so he wouldn't overhear his father's recitation of sins.

The young man looked at her, his face etched with pain. She motioned to him to follow her out into the hall, knowing nothing she could say right now would ease him. Maybe, however, she could lead his thoughts elsewhere, give him a bit of relief. She left the chamber door cracked open.

"I see you found the priest quickly."

Oswuld stared at his feet.

"Oswuld, what troubles you?"

He hesitated yet another moment. "The worst sin my father will confess is kidnapping you. Mayhap I should talk to the priest, too." Finally, he met her eye. "Both Father and I should ask your forgiveness, my lady."

Judith had come to like both father and son. Aye, they'd committed a crime and hauled her across England. But the experience hadn't been all bad. She'd learned much about herself, her strengths and weaknesses, and had even decided that roast rabbit could be a feast. More, she'd found Corwin again.

Of course, if Corwin were not already planning their escape, if she was truly forced to marry Ruford, she might not feel quite so forgiving.

"Both you and your father have become dear to me, Oswuld. 'Tis not terribly hard to forgive you."

"My thanks, my lady," he said, a sad smile touching his mouth. "I must also thank you for bringing Father upstairs."

"No thanks needed there. I could not bear to have him breathe his last in that foul air."

"A kindness I am sure Father appreciates. But I also have a task to perform…after. Having him up here will make it easier."

"What task?"

Oswuld glanced at the stairway. Judith saw Emma making her way up, towels in hand.

"I would rather not say just now, my lady, but when the time comes I believe you will approve."

She might, simply because she had the feeling that whatever task Oswuld was set on doing, Ruford wouldn't approve at all.

Chapter Thirteen

While the servants swept out the hall, Ruford and the captains had gone out into the bailey and gathered near the stables, a place Corwin wanted to visit soon to check on his and Judith's horses. He wanted them properly treated and fed. A successful escape might depend upon their speed and stamina.

Ruford glanced at the scabbard at Corwin's waist, looking for the sword that now lay at the foot of Thurkill's bed. Satisfied, he said, "Took you long enough."

Obviously, the man was angry, but angry at Judith or because he'd been kept waiting, Corwin didn't know.

"I did the ladies the favor of undressing Thurkill and putting him into bed. Surely you cannot object."

Ruford looked like he wanted to, but instead got to the business at hand. "It seems we are divided, Corwin. Some for you, some against."

Expecting it, Corwin crossed his arms and ignored all but Ruford. "And you?" he asked.

"I am of two minds. I could certainly use you, but you ask a large reward. Would you settle for less than Wilmont?"

Corwin raised an eyebrow. "Would you settle for less

than England? Come now, Ruford, what is Wilmont compared to it? A small piece, indeed. With me at your side, you stand a better chance of winning the throne.''

''I have an entire army to win me the throne. One man more will make no difference.''

Corwin scoffed. ''When I rode through the encampment, I saw no army, only a gathering of men and stacks of weapons. No one practiced with those weapons. All sat idle. 'Tis no way to prepare for a war. I sense a lack of discipline that would not be tolerated in a Norman holding. When was the last time you called your soldiers into ranks and marched them across a field?''

Ruford's eyes narrowed. ''We are not Normans here, but Saxons. These men will fight hard and long for our cause.''

''They may fight hard, but I warn you, Ruford, they will not fight long if unprepared. The king's troops will slaughter them. But first they must get to the palace. Let us test them, shall we? Call your men to ranks, with weapon in hand. Let us see if they can march across a field, much less the length of England.''

''I do not need to prove anything to you!''

''Then prove it to yourself. See if this army can truly put you on the throne of England. My guess is they cannot.''

Ruford took the bait. He rounded on his captains. ''Have the footmen form ranks in the field south of the keep. We will march them to the woodland.''

The captains looked from one to another. One stepped forward. ''My lord, I believe this action unnecessary. The men—''

''Your lord just gave you an order,'' Corwin said, halting any argument that might sway Ruford. Too, the soldier in him took offense at a captain arguing at a commander's order. ''Why do you not obey?''

''The men, they will not like—''

"Soldiers do not have to like what they are told to do, they must simply do it," Corwin stated firmly. "On the field of battle, if Lord Ruford gives you an order to attack, will you say him nay because the men do not like it?"

He'd angered the captains but didn't care. The soldier in him found the lack of discipline appalling. Never had he seen the like. If he were actually considering joining this rebellion, he would advise Ruford to replace his captains.

"I do not appreciate your interference," Ruford said as the captains walked away.

Corwin decided to tutor Ruford on the finer points of leading an army. "As commander, you need not justify your order or be forced to give it twice. Once should be sufficient, especially for a king. Shall we watch how it goes?"

Ruford turned on his heel and headed for one of the earthworks. Corwin followed. From atop the work he could see the field and the woodland—and the odd manner in which the men gathered, in separate groups, not as a whole. Corwin could tell which men were true soldiers and which had little training, both from the way they carried their weapons and how they reacted to the captains' shouted commands to form lines.

One large group of men had apparently decided they need not participate. They stood on the side of the field, chiding their fellows for the walk they were about to take.

"Who are they?" Corwin asked Ruford.

"Knights," Ruford answered absently, watching the progress on the field.

Corwin hid his shock at learning so many of Ruford's soldiers would be mounted. "Have they all horses and chain mail?"

"All have mounts, and I expect all will have chain mail before we march."

It took far too long for the men to form ranks and amble across the field. Long enough for Ruford's anger to turn to dismay, and for Corwin to accurately count the troops.

Not every man carried a weapon. The lines formed weren't neat. In a true battle formation the bowmen had to be separated from those with lances or maces. Few men here carried shields.

Still, where Ruford saw disorder, Corwin saw potential. Given direction, if the men possessed a measure of skill with weapons, this group could be a formidable army—not large enough to severely threaten the king's highly trained forces, but able to create havoc wherever it marched.

Corwin realized he would dearly love to see the horsemen in action. Nearly thirty in number, the mounted soldiers were likely mercenaries. Men skilled with both weapons and the use of horses, mercenaries fought for whoever paid their price. Corwin guessed that Ruford must be paying well to have gathered so many.

Thurkill was right. With proper leadership, with good training, with a cause to fight for... Corwin shook his head at the treasonable thought that he could do what Thurkill suggested. Maybe all that raw ability spread out before him made his instincts itch to take a hand in the army's formation.

He wouldn't, of course. Nothing could induce him to betray Gerard or the king. Still, if a man had a mind to, here in the north, with this group of soldiers, a would-be king could make an excellent start.

Corwin didn't want to be king. True, there were laws he would like to see changed. Plunging the kingdom into chaos seemed an extreme way to go about it, however.

Thurkill's suggestion to marry Judith and take over this army might well be why Corwin saw potential in Ruford's army.

Judith didn't want to be queen. She'd said so often enough. Not that she wouldn't be a good one. She'd certainly shown a talent for it today—taking charge of Thurkill, bringing Ruford to heel.

Then she'd shown Corwin her true power, that of a woman, in the depth and passion of a too-brief kiss. For the duration of their embrace, the barriers between them had vanished, leaving only a man holding a woman—not a lowly knight kissing a royal heiress.

If not for the impossibly high obstacle of Judith's royalty, Corwin would pay suit. But even if she cared for him, there was nothing either of them could do to change her heritage, or his.

"How long until they can be ready?" Ruford asked.

"'Twould depend on how hard you are willing to work them and who commands them," Corwin said.

Ruford hesitated for only a moment. "If you command them?"

To fight one battle against a Norman baron's forces, Corwin figured he'd need a month, maybe more, depending on whether or not the soldiers possessed the necessary skill with their weapons. They might never be ready to take on the king's guard.

"When must they be ready?" Corwin answered.

"A fortnight."

Corwin shook his head. Impossible. 'Twould take the first week alone to get them accustomed to answering a call to ranks and to line up in proper order, and the second to begin testing each man with various weapons and working out times for training.

Why a fortnight? Had Ruford set the date for some solid reason or just on a whim?

"You look for a miracle, Ruford. No one could have them ready in so short of time. In a month—perhaps."

Ruford looked out over the field, where the men began straggling back to their tents. "I have no choice. We march in a fortnight."

No choice? A chill accompanied the sudden realization that Ruford didn't act alone. Damn. Corwin should have guessed that earlier.

Ruford had taken over this keep and its stores. He'd used the coin, food and material goods at hand to provide for the men who rallied to his cause. No keep's stores, depleted from the past winter and awaiting replenishing from the next harvest, could support a large number of men for weeks on end. Food must be coming in from elsewhere.

The stacks of weapons should have made Corwin suspicious right off. The arms didn't belong to the men, who would keep personal weapons with their other belongings, not piled in a common stack.

And the number of men. Aye, word had spread of the rebellion, but to carefully selected ears only, to keep the possibility of discovery low. Someone of means—or more likely several such persons—supplied Ruford with food, arms and men—some going so far as to send trained soldiers.

Who would dare? Corwin could name several Norman barons who would seize the chance to cause King Henry trouble if their identity remained a secret. Henry wasn't on the best terms with the Church hierarchy at the moment either, having been threatened with excommunication from Rome over several differences of opinion with the pope. Too, a wealthy merchant, or several, might finance this rebellion to drive prices up to wartime levels. Even a foreign king wouldn't be adverse to upsetting England's finances.

The possibilities were endless, and all disturbing. So was the question of whether or not Ruford's conspirators expected the rebellion to succeed, or just cause a disturbance to irritate Henry—or distract the king while some other piece of vital government business was going on.

Did Ruford expect to succeed? Was the rebellion his idea or had he been talked into it? Was he a willing participant in a farce, or being duped by those who supported him?

And if the whole rebellion turned out to be no more than a ploy to irritate the king, then why kidnap Judith and risk angering two royal houses, both of England and Scotland?

Corwin bit back the multitude of questions, mostly because he wasn't sure which to ask first. Maybe after he'd had a chance to sort things through, observe the camp and men more closely, he'd be better prepared.

"I will do what I can," he finally told Ruford. "You will have to have a talk with your captains. I want no one questioning my orders or hesitating to carry them out."

Judith stared out the window at the two men coming toward the keep—one fair-haired, one dark. They were deep in conversation. Apparently, Ruford had decided in Corwin's favor. The two had stood side by side on the earthwork, observing a practice march—which had revealed a lack of order on the soldiers' part. They certainly lacked the snap and polish of any royal guards.

"A handsome devil, is he not?" Emma said with a sigh. "And to think you two will soon be wed."

Judith ignored Emma's reference to a wedding that wouldn't happen. To either man.

Both Corwin and Ruford were handsome, but only one appealed to her. Corwin, with his dark hair and blue eyes, the power in his kiss and the gentleness in his touch... Aye, Corwin appealed, with the lure of a calm harbor to a storm-tossed ship.

Judith chided her faulty comparison. She felt anything but calm whenever Corwin came near. If her observation was correct, Corwin would come up the stairs shortly, to fetch his sword.

"'Twas a truly pitiful display," she heard Oswuld tell Thurkill. "'Tis a wonder they made it across the field."

"Does Ruford accept Corwin?" Thurkill asked his son.

"Corwin stood by Ruford's side the whole time. I would think that a good sign."

"A good sign indeed. Corwin will know how to prepare the troops, if only Ruford will allow him to."

Judith didn't disabuse Thurkill of his fantasy of Corwin training Ruford's army. Corwin wouldn't be preparing troops, but preparing to escape.

She turned away from the window. "Corwin and Ruford are on their way back to the keep. If all is well, Corwin will be here soon to collect his sword."

Thurkill gave Oswuld a wry smile. "Then we shall see how things truly stand, shall we not?"

Oswuld winked at Thurkill. "Aye, Father, that we shall."

Servants and well-wishers had drifted in and out of the room all afternoon, giving Judith no privacy to question either father or son about all of the secrets being hinted at and not explained. After Corwin fetched his sword, she would set Emma to some task in the hall and have answers from these two.

Through the open chamber door, she heard footsteps on the stairway. Men's voices. Corwin and Ruford.

Ruford entered the room ahead of Corwin. Both men walked straight to the bed, Ruford to the head, Corwin to the foot.

"How fare you, Thurkill?" Ruford asked.

Judith paid little heed to the answer. With a satisfied gleam in his eye, Corwin slowly picked up his sword, his hand wrapped firmly, lovingly around the hilt. He turned the blade over as if inspecting it for damage, then slid it into the scabbard at his waist. She could almost feel his relief, so great was her own.

"Ah, that is good to hear," Ruford commented. "I must also give you thanks for having the foresight to bring Corwin to us. His experience in the king's service will prove invaluable."

"As will his skill with a sword," Thurkill said. "I thought he might be of best use in the practice yard."

"Aye, there, too," Ruford said, sparing a glance for Corwin. "He has already pointed out problems of which I was unaware. They will be corrected with due haste."

Judith wondered at Ruford's manner. One would think he'd be embarrassed by his army's lack of grace in the field. He didn't seem uncomfortable. Nor did he appear upset that Corwin had obviously told him that his army was less than perfect, suggesting improvements, just as she'd implied that he ran a less than tidy hall by ordering the rushes changed. Maybe the man now saw all of this as helpful, but she doubted it. She mistrusted Ruford's gracious mood.

Thurkill turned his head to smile upon Corwin. "I knew from the first he could lead this army to victory. I can die easy now, knowing that the crown of England will soon sit upon a Saxon head."

In response, Corwin rolled his eyes heavenward but said nothing.

Not seeing Corwin's odd action, Ruford puffed out his chest. "For tonight, rest easy while we celebrate our good fortune. You have brought us a knight to lead us and a lady to grace us with her presence. We shall have a grand feast, with good food and wonderful music. Would that you could join us."

"Ah, entertainment, say you?" Thurkill said wistfully.

Judith could almost hear the thoughts running through his head—and put a quick halt to what he was surely planning.

"We will have food brought up, Thurkill. I will leave the door open so we can hear the music. 'Twill be as much celebrating as you can bear."

Ruford frowned. "Surely, my lady, you plan to join us."

No, she didn't. The very last thing she wanted to do was again join Ruford at the dais. Listen to his effusive compliments. Avoid his wandering hands. She'd had her fill of it for one day.

"I will remain with Thurkill," she said.

"There is no reason for that, my lady," Oswuld said. "I will stay with Father so you can enjoy the evening. Should you be needed, I will send for you."

"A most suitable solution," Ruford said. "After all, Judith, the feast is in your honor, and the servants have changed the rushes as you requested. If you do not come down, they will think you find fault with them."

She felt outmaneuvered. Maybe she could put up with Ruford for a short while. And Corwin would be in the hall. Maybe Ruford would be too busy discussing his army with Corwin to pay her any heed. Or so she hoped.

"All right, then, but only for a short while."

"Wonderful. I look forward to your company, my lady," Ruford said, then turned to Corwin. "Come. We have work to do. Where do we begin?"

Corwin shook his head. "All can wait until the morrow. Let the men rest tonight, for tomorrow I intend to work them hard and they will need their vigor. For now, I want to check on my horse, then have a good wash and get out of this chain mail. 'Tis not suitable attire for your celebration."

Judith knew what he would wear. Corwin would don his midnight-blue dalmatic, trimmed with Ardith's artful embroidery. A garment soft, warm and imbued with precious memories. She was suddenly glad she'd relented about joining in the feast. She could hardly wait to see Corwin in his finery.

"When you go to the stable, would you also check on mine and Father's horses?" Oswuld asked. "I have not had the chance."

"Of course," Corwin answered. "Is there aught else you require?"

"Nay, just to ensure our horses are in their proper stalls and well cared for."

"Then I shall see you next on the morn, in the practice yard."

Oswuld grinned. "Aye, with sword in hand."

"'Tis good to see you take an interest, Oswuld," Ruford said. "I had nearly given up hope you might one day show enthusiasm for our efforts."

Oswuld's grin faded. Corwin's hand came up to near his waist in a brief, halting motion. A caution to Oswuld?

After a pause, Oswuld said, "'Tis a day of discovery for us all, is it not, Lord Ruford?"

"A good day all around, I should say." Ruford turned to Corwin. "I will have one of my guards show you to the armory."

Corwin nodded, and Judith realized where he would sleep tonight—on the first level of the keep with the household guards. He would be close by if she needed him.

Ruford left the bedchamber with Corwin on his heels.

"'Tis truly a day to rejoice," Thurkill said. "Ah, what lovely delicacies will be laid on the tables tonight, I wonder?"

"Oh, the cook prepares a true bounty!" Emma said. "There be roasted boar and pheasant. And sweets—all manner of sweets." She lowered her voice to a whisper, as if conveying a secret. "She makes pastries filled with apples and nuts and cinnamon. 'Tis a sinful confection."

Thurkill groaned.

Oswuld chuckled. "You have hit upon Father's true weakness, Emma. I suppose I could go down and pilfer one from the cook."

"Do that," Thurkill said. "And bring me a large mug of ale to wash it down with."

Judith saw her chance to be alone with Thurkill. The man had some explaining to do.

"Emma, go down with Oswuld. Have pallets brought up for our use this night."

Judith closed the door after them.

"All right, Thurkill. What is going on?"

"My lady?"

"Do not play the innocent with me. Earlier today you asked Corwin if he were thinking hard. He said he was, and that you would explain. I sense you two share some secret."

"Ah, that. Come sit so I need not shout."

Judith settled onto the foot of the bed.

"Oswuld tells me you have forgiven us your kidnapping," he said.

"'Twas a grievous sin I hope you confessed and received a hefty penance for."

"Aye, but 'is to you I hope to make amends, of a sort." He shifted slightly. "If Corwin proves agreeable, and I dare say I think he might, then you may not be so averse to having been brought here. Answer me this, my lady. If the Saxon destined to become king, the man you are to marry, were Corwin, not Ruford, would you accept the crown of England's queen?"

A jolt of shock stiffened her spine. "Surely you jest!"

He chuckled. "Corwin gave the same reaction to my

suggestion.'' Then he sobered. ''I am quite serious, my lady. After meeting Corwin I realized how unsuited Ruford is for the task. He has noble blood, but little else to recommend him. He has not been able to pull the various factions of the army together. Corwin, while not noble, can control the captains and make this army a true force. He also knows the politics of the kingdom, and would work hard to make England a better place for all.''

Thurkill wanted Corwin to usurp Ruford, to use the army gathered at Norgate to take the crown for himself. The vision of Corwin doing so simply refused to take solid form.

''Oh, Thurkill,'' was all she could manage to say.

He smiled. ''You would not be averse to marriage to Corwin, would you?''

''Well, no, but…'' She shut her mouth, realizing what she'd confessed.

''I thought not. The more Corwin sees here, the more I think he will realize he can have more than the prize of Wilmont. He could have all of England.''

Seductive, indeed. But Corwin didn't want Wilmont. He only pretended to in order to thwart the rebellion. Corwin wouldn't betray Gerard of Wilmont, or his king. Wouldn't betray her.

''Thurkill, when did you propose this scheme to Corwin?''

''After the first meeting with the captains.''

''And his answer?''

''He scoffed at first, as you did. But I asked him to reconsider. As you heard yourself, he is thinking hard on the matter.''

Judith closed her eyes, remembering a kiss filled with passion, with possession—mind-bending with seduction. She'd practically begged him for it. All the while she'd thought he yielded to his emotions. Could he merely have been thinking of binding her to him, with another purpose in mind?

Aye, he'd told Thurkill he was "thinking hard" on some matter, and now she knew on what. Had he been placating a dying man or giving Thurkill's suggestion serious consideration?

How ridiculous! Corwin wouldn't agree to this foolishness of Thurkill's. He wouldn't give in to temptation. He couldn't.

Judith got up and walked over to the window. The field was now empty of the soldiers who'd marched across the grass, with Corwin watching. He must now know everything he needed to know to report to the king. Escape would come soon.

Where would they go? Scotland wasn't far off. London would be a long trek. How long would they have alone together? A day, maybe two? More?

Oswuld entered the bedchamber, a pastry in one hand, a mug in the other. "Still warm," he said, laying the pastry on Thurkill's chest.

"Ah, you are indeed the best of sons," Thurkill said as he broke off a piece of the flaky delicacy. "Tell me, what is this about you and swords and the practice yard? I never thought I would see the day."

"Oh, well, after watching Corwin this morning I realized how truly lacking my skills are. He graciously conceded to helping me improve them."

"You could learn from no better."

"That was my thought. I fear, however, that he may not have much time for me. The soldiers who escorted us in this morning have spread the tale of his expertise with a sword. Before you know it every one of them will want a lesson."

"Good. Just by watching him instruct you they will all

learn a thing or two—and they need it. Corwin may turn this assemblage of men into a fighting force yet.''

Judith tried to ignore the implications, but how could she? Thurkill was right. If Corwin put his mind to it, he could train these troops, show them how to win.

Had she been the fool, trusting Corwin too easily? Had she given him her heart only to have him break it, to have him use her for the same purpose as Ruford intended? Had he seductively kissed not Judith, the woman, but Judith Canmore, the royal heiress?

Chapter Fourteen

Corwin looked better than any man had a right to look, in chain mail or dalmatic, clothed or not, bearded or no. Judith again felt the warmth of his garment, the softness of the fabric—detected the scent of him woven among the strands—though they were the length of the great hall apart.

She drank too much wine and blamed her lapse on Ruford. He refilled her goblet and she continued to drink. She'd stopped tasting the sweet, hardy beverage a while ago, and knew she should stop. But the wine slid down easily and muddled her disturbing thoughts, the wine also made Ruford's attentions seem less bothersome.

Corwin's dalmatic, which had hung loosely on her, clung to his form in perfect fashion—well fitted across his broad shoulders and chest, cinched to his trim waist by the leather girdle. Embroidered trim at the cuff and hem caught the light of the torches burning in their sconces, and sent it sizzling along silken threads.

Corwin looks more the nobleman than Ruford.

He'd washed. Corwin's shoulder-length hair framed a face enhanced by his neatly trimmed beard. The beard shadowed but couldn't conceal the gracious smile on his face as he strolled about the room, seeking out first one captain, then the next. Judith couldn't overhear them, but watched in awe as the discourse almost invariably turned from somber to enjoyable.

She envisioned Corwin at a royal court, doing what he did now—singling out those whose favor he wished to gain and succeeding with ease. She hadn't a doubt he could win over the captains and do as Thurkill suggested—become their leader.

Judith put the wine aside. She shouldn't doubt Corwin, but it was hard not to. So many people had disappointed her—her parents, the abbess, even the queen—that she couldn't help wondering if Corwin would, too.

He'd promised escape, but promises were easily broken.

She leaned back in her chair and concentrated on the soothing strains of the music, provided by a woman who played a harp. For many years Judith hadn't heard a note of music beyond the chants of the Mass, nor played a harp. The sweet strains conjured memories of her childhood, when she'd foolishly believed that those she loved would see to her happiness and ensure her a future filled with laughter and music.

Instead, they'd sent her off to Romsey Abbey and had all but forgotten her, leaving her subject to being kidnapped by an upstart noble who couldn't control an army, much less the kingdom he planned to rule. Self-pity had never overtaken her so completely, and she rarely wallowed in it for long. Tonight, however, she couldn't seem to muster the effort to banish her morose musings.

Corwin eventually made his way to the dais. "Lord Ruford, my compliments on the food, the wine and the entertainment. One can see that given proper funds, your court will be a grand one."

Ruford leaned forward, his arms crossed on the table. "We have not yet talked about how to take possession of

the royal treasury. Mayhap we should seize it first. He who
controls the treasury controls the kingdom.''

''Aye,'' Corwin conceded. ''But the man who stands the
best chance of controlling the kingdom must first establish
his claim on the crown.''

''As Henry did before his brother's...death.''

Ruford had almost said ''murder.'' Many people still believed Henry had had a hand in his brother's death, though
he hadn't loosed the arrow that killed William. Upon hearing of William's demise in a hunting accident, Henry had
rushed to Westminster and seized the treasury at sword
point, even before his brother's body grew cold. Not many
weeks later, Henry had chosen Matilda, a Saxon princess,
as his queen.

Ruford was doing the thing backward. He thought he had
his queen, a Saxon woman of royal rank whose name he
would invoke to rally troops and secure his claim to the
throne. Judith Canmore, royal heiress, unwilling participant
and less willing bride.

So much for the fantasies she'd entertained about finding
her prince. Judith again grasped her goblet and took another
sip of wine.

''Henry's claim was far stronger than yours,'' Corwin
said. ''He had gained William's favor and established himself at court. Unfortunately, you cannot do so. But fear not.
With her ladyship at your side, giving you council, you
will soon win them all over.'' Corwin shifted his attention
to Judith. ''How fares our fair lady?''

Miserably, but the fair lady knew her court manners, too.

''I have been served the finest of delicacies and highly
palatable wine. My doting host has been most amusing.
What more could a lady hope for, pray tell?''

Ruford fairly preened at the false compliment, and Corwin's smile slipped slightly. ''I noticed the potency of the

brew,'' he commented. ''A French wine, perhaps? It does slide down easily, does it not?''

Thought she'd had too much to drink, did he? Well, she had, but not overly much. She still sat straight, though she acknowledged that walking might be a problem.

Ruford waved a hand in the air. ''I know not. 'Twas in Norgate's stores, so we drink it. French, you say? Have you a knowledge of wines?''

''Some. Wilmont's stores abound with fine wines. A few possess the quality to bend a person's mind and loosen his tongue too quickly. One finds oneself babbling on without realizing what one is saying until far too late to undo the damage.''

The knave! Did he think her so far gone she would tell Ruford of his intentions to escape Norgate, taking her with him? Did Corwin still plan to escape?

Ruford chuckled. ''Aye, one must always beware the wine. I see you have quit it. 'Tis good you keep a clear head. Mayhap I will not make you a captain, but my general.''

Corwin tilted his head. ''Does the wine speak, Ruford? Will you remember those words on the morrow?''

''If I do not, I have both you and her ladyship to remind me. You will remember, will you not, Judith?''

''Of course, Ruford,'' she said, and put the goblet back on the table. Her head might hurt on the morn, but she wouldn't forget that within the space of a day, Corwin had worked his way up from unwelcome intruder to trusted general. Had he also fallen from trusted friend to treacherous enemy?

Ruford raised an arm and put his chin in his hand. ''The music stops. I fear our entertainment about to end. Would I could offer you more, my lady, but no one else in the hall can play.''

Corwin tilted his head, looked at her speculatively. She mistrusted the mischievous gleam in his eye.

"Mayhap her ladyship can be imposed upon," he said.

"Truly?" Ruford asked. "Can you play the harp, Judith?"

Corwin was up to something, she knew. But what?

"I have not held a harp in a very long time," she said honestly. "I fear my unpracticed fingers would make errors aplenty."

"I do not suggest the harp, but a more courtly amusement," Corwin said. "If her ladyship is of a mind, I hope she might give us a verse or two of *Beowulf,* this time in English."

Judith felt a flush bloom on her cheeks, remembering what she'd been doing the last time she'd uttered lines of the poem. 'Twas bad of Corwin to remind her, and to ask her to entertain her enemies.

"Beowulf!" Ruford shouted, alerting the entire hall. "Ah, my lady, say you will do us the honor!"

Corwin's eyebrow raised in question. "Aye, my lady. Can you?"

Of course she could. Corwin, however, seemed to think her brain impaired. Now she knew his purpose. He tested her. A test she could easily pass. She would recite the poem he requested, or part of it, anyway. 'Twould take hours to do the whole. She'd give them a verse or two—not for Ruford's sake, nor to prove to Corwin her faculties remained intact.

"I shall be pleased to," she agreed. "Ruford, would you bring this chair near the stairway, so Thurkill might hear, too?"

Corwin's expression changed from one of challenge to one of pride. Ruford lifted the chair to lug it across the hall.

Judith took the arm Corwin graciously offered, and was glad of it. Her footsteps weren't as sure as they should be.

Settled in the chair, she began the heroic poem of the Swedish prince Beowulf's struggles and then conquest of the evil monster Grendel. The words came more easily in English than in Norman French, the lines sounding more lyrical.

From upstairs she heard the squeak of leather hinges—Oswuld opening the bedchamber door more fully so Thurkill could better hear.

"Her ladyship does not feel well this morn," Oswuld said.

Corwin wasn't a bit surprised. He kicked at a clod of dirt in the practice yard, trying to concentrate on giving Oswuld a lesson in sword handling. Unfortunately, Judith's performance last night competed for his attention.

She'd been utterly dazzling, and not only when she'd held the hall in thrall while reciting *Beowulf,* rendering the poem with the deft lyrical ability of a French troubadour. He'd been hard-pressed to ignore her earlier, to keep his gaze from straying toward the dais for most of the evening.

After noting the potency of the wine, he'd quit it after one goblet, as Ruford had observed. Judith hadn't stopped, but kept sipping at an ever full goblet—Ruford's doing. Had she known Ruford did it apurpose, to lower her defenses?

Ruford wanted Judith. The lust in the man's eyes had been so apparent any fool could see his desire. So far, Corwin had heard no talk of plans for a wedding. He found it curious. One would have thought, given the circumstances, that Ruford wanted vows exchanged quickly, to establish the marriage so central to his plans. Not that Corwin cared why Ruford waited for the marriage. He just hoped Ruford had no plans to precede the vows with consummation.

"And your father?" Corwin asked, grasping for a subject to banish the vision of Ruford and Judith together.

"No better, but no worse, I think," Oswuld answered.

So much for a distraction.

Corwin looked at the sword Oswuld held. It was ancient. The blade chipped in places. Definitely in need of sharpening. 'Twould do for now, and if wielded properly, would serve its purpose later if Oswuld found it necessary to defend himself.

Oswuld held the weapon awkwardly, unused to doing more with it than carrying it around. The lad wasn't a soldier, never had been and had no wish to be. One blow from another's weapon and the sword would fly from Oswuld's grasp.

Corwin grasped his sword hilt, a grip sure and firm, learned as a stripling from knights whose reputation as fighters knew no detractors. A knight of Wilmont training was a knight to be reckoned with, and few challenged one on a whim. Corwin knew he was among the best of them.

"Let us start with the very rudiments," he said, showing Oswuld how to grip the sword and make the weapon an extension of his arm.

A crowd began to gather. Corwin ignored them, accustomed to the attention he received at Wilmont when in the practice yard. Oswuld, however, grew nervous.

"What if they know?" Oswuld said.

"They see only two men with swords," Corwin assured him. "They know not why you take instruction."

"I shall look the veriest novice."

"Everyone must start somewhere. Besides, they come not to see you, but me. They wish to know if I am as skilled as rumor has it."

Oswuld relaxed some, even smiled slightly. "You are."

Corwin winked at Oswuld. "I know. Now for your stance."

As Corwin continued the lesson, the crowd around them grew. Even Ruford came to watch. Corwin relaxed. If Ruford stayed within sight, he wouldn't be pressing Judith for favors.

"Now I will thrust, slowly, like so," Corwin said, demonstrating. Then he stepped back. "You will block, like so," he continued, raising his elbow and angling his sword.

And so the lesson began, step by step, in careful movements—thrust and parry, attack and defend. Steps Corwin could do in his sleep.

His mind wandered, but not far, only to the surrounding area and the men who stood there.

This morning, he'd been all over the encampment on the pretext of inspecting the troops. A few of the captains had bid him welcome; the others begrudgingly allowed him a look around.

He hadn't found a way out of the keep and through the encampment, or at least not a route where he wouldn't be easily detected. Alone, he could make a dash for the road and beyond. With Judith riding with him, 'twould be risky.

Oswuld said he knew how to get his father out, but Oswuld wouldn't be leaving until Thurkill died, which could be within the hour or days from now. Judith would be loathe to leave before that happened, too, but if Ruford made too strong a move toward her, she'd reconsider— Corwin hoped.

He still pondered the wisdom of taking Oswuld into his confidence about his plans to escape. The lad seemed trustworthy enough, but Judith's safety must come before all other considerations.

Corwin knew now he shouldn't have brought her here,

but he hadn't thought the rebel army would be this big. Or the leader lodged in a keep designed to not only keep intruders out, but inhabitants in.

"Ready to try the exercise a bit faster?" he asked Oswuld.

"Probably not, but let us do so anyway."

It didn't go well. Oswuld's sword soon hit the ground, with little effort on Corwin's part.

Several men in the crowd snickered, and Corwin singled out one who'd snickered the loudest. A mercenary.

"Can you do better?" he asked.

"Anyone can," the man called out.

"Then come show me."

Though his fellows cheered him on, the man had enough sense to hold up his hands. "I like living," he said.

"I will not run you through," Corwin promised with a smile that made a lie of his words.

The mercenary shook his head.

"Anyone else?" Corwin called to the crowd.

Interest flickered across several faces, including Ruford's.

He could end it all now, Corwin realized. Call Ruford out and arrange the man's demise. Without him, there would be no Saxon noble to give legitimacy to the rebellion.

Rebellion within rebellion.

Corwin shook off the temptation. He'd never before been a man's sole judge and executioner. He'd killed, but in the heat of battle, never in deliberate fashion. But if the man laid a hand on Judith, 'twould not be at all hard to run Ruford through.

Before anyone could take up his challenge, Corwin turned back to Oswuld, who'd picked up his sword. "There, you see, Oswuld? You are a braver man than any of them for merely standing within my reach. Now come, put your sword back up and let us try it again.''

Once more, Oswuld blocked a thrust, and another. He held on through blow after blow, and even took the offensive a time or two. This time around no one in the crowd jeered, but cheered each successful move.

The lesson ended with Oswuld feeling more sure of himself and Corwin confident the lad could better defend himself. With the session over, the crowd dispersed. Ruford lingered to talk to one of his captains.

Oswuld wiped his brow with the sleeve of his tunic. ''My thanks.''

''Mayhap we can do it again on the morn.''

''If I am here on the morn.''

Keeping one eye on Ruford, Corwin slid home his sword, and made the decision he'd been putting off—to tell Oswuld of his own plan to leave the encampment. Oswuld wasn't devoted to the rebellion. Indeed, he planned to desert as soon as Thurkill died. Oswuld certainly wouldn't feel duty or honor bound to inform Ruford or one of the captain's of Corwin's intentions.

Too, if they were all leaving, 'twas best done together. Once Oswuld's escape route was put to use, and likely then discovered, 'twould be dangerous or impossible to use it again. Best he and Judith leave when Oswuld left, though Corwin wasn't quite ready to tell Oswuld that he'd have company during his escape.

He spoke softly. ''Oswuld, I have been thinking about what you said, about leaving to take your father home. I ask no details about where you go, but would like to know how you plan to achieve the feat.''

Oswuld's guard went up. ''I should tell you no tales, Corwin. If you intend to take Ruford's place—''

''Nay, not I. Your father presents a good case. I have no

wish to be a king. In fact, I am no longer sure I want any more part of this rebellion than you do.''

"You find the army lacking."

"I find many things that disturb me more than the lack of discipline and training among the men. The captains are divided, and so then are the men. 'Twould take more than the time Ruford allows to pull them into a unified army.''

After a pause, Oswuld said, "Father will be disappointed.''

Corwin clasped the lad on the shoulder. "Then we will not tell him. Do you need help? I assume you will need someone to ready the horses for you at a moment's notice.''

Oswuld looked around for ears that might hear. "You may as well know there are others at Norgate who feel as I do about the rebellion. I do not act alone.''

Corwin showed no surprise. Indeed, whenever any army sat idle for too long men became discouraged and disinterested. Desertion followed.

Dragging information out of Oswuld was proving hard. But there was really only one thing Corwin needed to know—the escape route.

"Should I decide to abandon this rebellion, I would prefer to take the easiest path. Since you have already scouted it out, will you show me?''

"If you wish, but 'tis really quite simple. Behind the tapestry in the master bedchamber is a stairway that leads down to the lowest level of the keep. Naturally, there is a doorway at the bottom.''

Not a rare thing—a hidden stairway by which a lord might escape if disaster seemed imminent.

"How did you learn of it?''

"Quite by accident. I shall have to be sure Ruford is not abed when I leave or things may become awkward.''

"True," Corwin agreed. "And once out the doorway?''

"The stable is but a few yards away, so getting to the horses without being noticed is rather easy. After that, one must depend upon speed and stealth." Oswuld looked toward the stable and the earthen berm beyond—a barrier easily ridden over, but one patrolled by guards. "Far fewer men are camped in that direction than near the front gate of the keep. Too, the woodland is closer. If done at night, and timed rightly, few will notice."

By using the stairway, Oswuld come remove his father's body from the keep without passing through a crowd of people in the great hall. He could also get to the stables without crossing the expanse of the bailey, thus avoiding curious attention he didn't want. Once on horseback, Oswuld would depend upon speed and stealth to cross over the berm and the field beyond to reach the woodland, and a measure of safety.

Corwin thought it a decent plan.

Ruford hadn't yet left the yard. And if anyone questioned Corwin's presence on the keep's upper floor, he could claim he went up to visit Thurkill.

"Oswuld, I want a look at this stairway."

The bedchamber was dark. The shutters were closed, allowing little light to seep through the cracks. Corwin shut the door behind him and stood still a moment, letting his eyes adjust.

He was tempted to search the room, to find any papers or other proof of his suspicions of which lords backed Ruford. Rolled parchments crowded a table. Two chests hugged the far wall. Both tempted him to take a closer look.

Corwin took a deep breath and set his resolve. Maybe he would look, but not until he'd found the door and explored the passageway. 'Twould do him no good to learn who aided Ruford if he couldn't escape to tell the tale.

As in the room given Judith, a tapestry covered the wall behind an ornate bed. According to Oswuld, the door was behind the tapestry in the far corner. Corwin crossed the room with short steps, holding his sword hilt so it wouldn't clang against his chain mail. No one knew he'd entered the chamber but Oswuld, and Corwin preferred to keep it that way.

He pushed aside the tapestry, and as Oswuld had said, there was the door. He grabbed the latch and pushed downward. It didn't move far enough to unlatch. He tried the opposite direction with the same result.

Locked.

Corwin eased his hand along the edges and top of the door, but didn't find a key.

He opened the shutters a crack for light, inspecting them while he did so. Not there.

Corwin put his hands on his hips, glanced around the room and whispered, "If I wanted to hide a key…"

Carefully, he rummaged about in Ruford's trunks. Clothing, shoes, a dagger—but no key.

He crossed to the table and cautiously searched among the various papers and rolled parchments. He couldn't help reading a few of them, but one in particular caught his interest. A list of names.

Ruford's allies?

Nay, more likely those who Ruford intended to attack first, for at the top of the list was Clovis, Lord of Norgate. Corwin was now standing in that man's bedchamber. He noted that Wilmont wasn't on the list, then set it aside.

He'd decided to search the bed next when he heard footsteps on the stairway. Quickly, he closed the shutters. As he was deciding whether or not to dive under the bed, the footsteps stopped outside of the other chamber door. He heard a knock, then Ruford's voice asking for admittance. Then Judith's voice, bidding him enter.

True, the exchange caught Corwin unprepared. Judith admitted Ruford into her chamber only to see Thurkill. Even knowing that Thurkill occupied the bed and that several other people were also visiting the chamber, Corwin intensely disliked having Ruford so close to Judith.

Soon, he vowed, he'd have Judith out of Norgate and far from Ruford Clark.

Corwin decided he'd best leave Ruford's chamber before getting caught, perhaps come back when he knew the man was occupied elsewhere.

Unfortunately, another search would probably prove just as fruitless. Likely the man who now called this bedchamber his own, who would use the stairway if his rebellion was discovered and he was forced to abandon the keep, had the key on him.

Chapter Fifteen

Judith tilted her face toward the sunshine, thinking maybe Ruford had the right of it—that she needed a walk and fresh air. She hadn't been out of the keep since her arrival at Norgate. Unfortunately, she also remembered that her desire to escape the gloom of close confines had gotten her into this muddle in the first place. If she'd stayed within the abbey, she might not be here.

Ruford walked at her side in quiet contemplation. If not for his mood, she might enjoy the outing. He had more on his mind than her health, and she doubted she would like whatever subject he was working up the courage to broach. He'd come up to the bedchamber and suggested this walk. Refusing would have been easy had not both Thurkill and Oswuld urged her to go. Oswuld especially. For some reason he'd been supportive of Ruford's plan. Enthusiastic, one might say.

Judith had to smile at Oswuld's obvious pride at how well he'd done in the practice yard. She'd watched the greater part of his session with Corwin from the window, giving Thurkill reports on his son's progress while admiring Corwin's methods. Patiently, methodically, he'd taken

Oswuld through the most fundamental of moves, then allowed his pupil to set the pace in the rest of the session.

Corwin could have badly embarrassed Oswuld with a show of superior skills before a rapt audience. Instead, he'd placed Oswuld's needs first. Standing at the window, with an aching head and unsettled stomach, she'd realized how terribly foolish she'd been to doubt him last eve. During their entire journey, Corwin had always put others' needs before his own, with the possible exception of refusing to enter the encampment with covered eyes.

Corwin could have pushed Thurkill to an even earlier grave, but had allowed the old man to make the journey at his own pace. And with her, well, she could recount each time he'd eased her fears, bolstered her resolve or made her smile. Aye, he'd made her angry, too, as he had last eve by goading her into reciting *Beowulf*. Even that he'd done to protect her as best he could.

She'd drank too much wine. So had Ruford. The results could have been disastrous.

Corwin's goal then, as now, was to save England from the ravages of a war, to defend the crown in the best way he knew how.

Thurkill may have asked Corwin to usurp Ruford's place within the rebellion, but Corwin wouldn't do it. Even now he must be off somewhere either gathering information or planning their escape. He'd come into the keep with Oswuld, but not up to the bedchamber. She hadn't seen him in the hall when she'd passed through on her way out-of-doors, either.

Escape couldn't come soon enough to suit her. Leaving Thurkill would be hard. Oswuld, too. Duncan she wouldn't miss in the least, nor Ruford. She wished she could help Corwin. Somehow, merely staying close to Thurkill, as

Corwin had told her to do, didn't seem like enough. But if that's what he expected of her, she should get back to it.

They'd wandered across the bailey toward the stables.

"Ruford, is my mare in here?" she asked.

"What? Oh, aye. Care to have a look?"

Judith needed no more encouragement. She entered the stables and found the mare easily, ensconced in a stall between Corwin's destrier and Thurkill's steed. Oswuld's horse stood beyond Thurkill's.

"Ah, my Beauty. Have they been treating you well? I fear I have not had the time to look in on you as I should," she said, warning the mare of her approach. Judith squeezed into the stall between the wooden half wall and the horse, and stroked the mare's neck. "I should have brought a treat for you. An apple, perhaps. Mayhap next time I come."

And maybe next time they could go for a ride—a very long ride, far away from Norgate.

"A fine horse. From where did she come?" Ruford asked.

Not an odd question, but one asked in an odd tone. She knew from which estate Corwin had bought her, but unsure of Ruford's purpose, merely shrugged a shoulder.

"I forget the name. I was so delighted to have a horse to myself that I paid little heed to much else. Is it important?"

"Not for the moment, but might be later if we have need of horses," he said. "This one comes from excellent stock. I may wish to call upon the owner."

Call upon the owner, indeed. Ruford thought to raid Aimsley for its herd of horses. She would have to warn Corwin to have a care with the estate's name.

A snuffle from the next stall brought back her good mood.

"Think you deserve a pat, too, do you?" she chided

Corwin's destrier, daring to raise a hand to the warhorse's nose. He accepted her touch, even leaned closer. For an animal trained for aggression, to kill an enemy if need be, he seemed to crave an affectionate pat.

"Now this one I know comes from Wilmont," she told Ruford. "Mayhap you should call upon Baron Gerard and purchase several of his horses."

"When I am king, I shall simply demand them."

"Ah, but if you become king, then Corwin will be Wilmont's baron. You did grant Corwin his prize of Wilmont, did you not?" Ruford's nod was hesitant. "'Twould not be politic to demand so high a price from a man who helped you obtain the throne."

He crossed his arms. "Yet it is politic of Corwin to demand the high price of Wilmont from his king?"

"You are not yet king, Ruford. Do not assume yourself victorious before the final battle is won."

"You do not yet believe I shall win, do you?"

She didn't want to argue this with Ruford. She'd given him her views on the matter yesterday, and would soon be gone.

"Mayhap, with Corwin's help."

Which he wouldn't have, because Corwin wouldn't be here, either.

"The men will fight when I tell them to. I need you more than I need Corwin. 'Tis time we set a date for our wedding."

Ah, yes. The infamous marriage. That's why he'd brought her out here. Ruford could set almost any date he wished. His intended bride wouldn't be participating.

Judith gave the destrier's nose a final pat and turned to look at Ruford. "What date did you have in mind?"

"Tomorrow."

Stunned, she blurted, "Impossible!"

"Why so? I see no reason to wait."

Judith did, but few she could give him.

"Thurkill lies dying in my chamber. Surely 'twould be an affront to all decency to…celebrate before a proper mourning period is over."

Ruford shook his head. "Judith, he could die tonight, or three days from now. I truly do not care when, though I wish he would hurry about the business. Besides, would you not prefer to marry while he still lives, so he might see you happily wed?"

She searched for more reasons. "'Tis impossible to have a proper wedding on such short notice. There are invitations to send, a feast to organize." She held out the skirt of her amber gown. "I need a proper gown. Truly, Ruford, I need time—"

He brushed her objections away with the wave of a hand. "We will send no invitations. I fear your idea of a proper wedding must wait until after we are in a position to invite guests. In the meantime, a priest and a wedding feast must suffice, both easily arranged." He looked her over, a wicked smile crossing his face. "As for what you wear, I care not, for after the feast I will have it off you. 'Tis a task I look forward to completing. Come out of there, my love, and we shall have a taste of future delight."

Judith couldn't think of anything that repelled her more.

Ruford stretched his hand toward her and she reacted instinctively. She retreated, backing into the solid wall of the stable. Oh, she'd done it now. The only way out of the stall was past a man who looked at her as if she were a tasty morsel.

He chuckled. "Your innocence betrays you. 'Tis endearing, if not taken to extreme. What harm a kiss or two?"

She wasn't all that innocent. She'd kissed Corwin and

would do so again in a trice if he beckoned. Now, if only Corwin would happen to come into the stable…

"What if someone should see?" she protested.

"We are to be wed, Judith. No one would think odd a show of affection between lovers. Besides, there is no one around to bear witness."

"No one?"

"Not a soul. I could toss up your skirts and have you in the straw and no one would be the wiser."

His expression changed. Mercy, he was contemplating his threat.

"I will not have it," she said, crossing her arms. "I will not be treated like some trollop. Truly, Ruford, 'tis shameful of you to tease me so."

"Tease? Look who teases! Do you know, when you cross your arms thus, you lift your breasts, inviting a man to touch them?"

Immediately, she lowered her arms. "I do no such thing."

Her words had no effect; he continued to stare at her bosom. Then he lunged for her.

Judith's shriek mingled with the angry cry of Corwin's destrier. Her mare echoed the destrier's cry and shifted, her backside pinning Ruford against the side of the stall.

The destrier snorted and kicked at the wall twice, then a third time for good measure.

Fully sobered, Ruford shoved at the mare's rump and made his escape before the destrier's hoof drove through the plank, sending shards of wood everywhere.

People flooded into the stable at the commotion. Stable boys, maids, soldiers—and Corwin. Relieved, and feeling rather foolish, Judith leaned her head against her mare's neck and stayed put.

Corwin gave her a quick glance, then calmed his horse.

Ruford angrily brushed at the sleeves of his tunic. "That beast of yours is dangerous," he grumbled.

After a brief burst of disbelieving laughter, Corwin said, "He is a warhorse, Ruford, and is trained to be dangerous. Surely you should have known better than to annoy him. What happened?"

Judith was sure Corwin knew very well what had happened, and she would likely receive another warning about being alone with Ruford.

"Nothing," Ruford stated. "I merely extended a hand to aid Judith out of the mare's stall and your horse took offense."

"Ah, well, that explains it then. He does have a good eye for a pretty mare. Mayhap he thought you were about to take Beauty away and made his objection clear."

Judith knew better. The destrier had picked up on her fear and anger, as most horses could. Unlike others, however, the destrier had been trained to react to what he perceived as danger. Corwin knew it. Ruford surely did, too, but accepted Corwin's offer of a gracious explanation.

Ruford waved a beckoning hand. "Judith, come out of there, carefully, before this beast goes berserk again."

"Aye, my lady," Corwin said, reaching into the stall. "Have a care for the sharp wood, and *do* ware the beast."

She took Corwin's hand, very aware that Ruford watched and disapproved, but she didn't care. All she wanted to do was run back to the keep, up to the bedchamber, and stay there until Corwin came for her.

Emma, skirts flying behind her, ran into the stable and aided Judith's cause, though not in a way she might have liked. "My lady, Oswuld requests you come quickly," she said. "'Tis Thurkill, he…fades."

Judith opened the bedchamber door, fearing the worst. Oswuld sat in the chair that had become a permanent fixture by Thurkill's bedside and was rarely unoccupied. With a resigned smile, he looked down at his father. Thurkill's eyes were open.

Pale and gaunt, the old man watched her close the door behind her.

"Ah, my lady," he said breathlessly, as though a heavy weight bore down on his chest. "Good…you came."

Thurkill tried to lift a hand, but the effort proved too much. Determined to get through whatever was to come with some dignity, Judith plastered a smile on her face and perched on the edge of the bed.

"Where else would I go, pray tell? You did urge me to go for a walk, but knew I would come right back. We ended our walk at the stable. I saw my mare. She stands next to your horse, quite snug in her stall. I think she expects us to come for them all at any moment and be off on our journey again."

Her babbling embarrassed her but amused Thurkill.

"Journey…not so…bad."

"I beg to differ. I should not care to repeat such a trip anytime soon. My backside is still bruised, though the calluses on my fingers begin to soften."

"Must give…thanks."

"For what? My softening calluses?"

"*Beowulf.*" He said the word as if in prayer.

"He heard every word, my lady," Oswuld said. "Father even said some of the lines with you. I did not know that he knew the poem."

"Learn much…serving ale."

"Too much," Oswuld rejoined. "If you had not overheard those mercenaries discussing this rebellion…ah, no matter. What is done is done."

Thurkill's expression turned earnest. "Not done. Judith...Corwin...finish."

"Aye, Corwin will finish it," Oswuld said. "That is all you ever wanted, was it not—to see a Saxon sit on the throne?" Thurkill nodded then closed his eyes. Oswuld continued, "You have worked very hard for it, given everything a man has to give. 'Twould be glorious if—"

Thurkill's face eased into peaceful repose, but not into sleep. Oswuld put his hand on his father's chest. It didn't move.

Judith looked away and pressed her lips together so hard they hurt. Oswuld held his emotions back with a shaky grip. She'd not be the one to break his hold.

The young man took a deep breath. "—if your dream came true. But 'tis not to be, I fear. Even now, Corwin talks of leaving, as we are." With those words, Oswuld rose from the chair.

Judith marveled at his calm. Something within her screamed for Thurkill to come back for another hour, a day, a little more time. She couldn't imagine what agony Oswuld must suffer.

He ran a hand through his hair. "My lady, I ask you to tell no one just yet. I have...arrangements to make first."

Judith got to her feet. "Where are you going?" she managed to ask.

"To find Corwin, then to the stable. And then I am taking my father home."

Oswuld turned and left, slamming the door behind him. She hoped he would find Corwin quickly, before he fell apart. Corwin would help Oswuld with whatever needed doing.

As for Thurkill, he had passed beyond all pain and need. For so many days she'd nursed him—talked to him, fed him, changed bedding. Her chores had come to an end with his final breath.

Judith gave a brief thought to leaving the room, but if she went down to the hall or out into the bailey, people would think it strange that both she and Oswuld left Thurkill alone. Emma had surely spread the news of Thurkill's downward turn, and someone would ask how Thurkill fared. To keep Oswuld's secret, she should stay and wait for him to return.

But she couldn't just sit here, her mind idle, or she would fall apart.

Judith threw the bolt on the door. No one could come in and discover what Oswuld wanted kept secret. And no one would come in and think she'd gone completely daft.

She sat in the bedside chair. Thurkill's body lay in the bed, but his soul had been released. Perhaps, if Thurkill wasn't too busy convincing the guardians of heaven's gates that he deserved admittance, he would hear.

Judith remembered where she'd left off in the poem last eve, and in a voice as steady as she could muster, continued the story of *Beowulf.*

"He is gone. I leave tonight," Oswuld said without any preamble or emotion.

Corwin perused the bailey, allowing a brief moment of sorrow for an old man who'd given his life for a dream— as misguided and hopeless as that dream might be.

Time had run out, both for dreams and secrets. He hadn't found the key, or the hidden door. With the escape route blocked, Oswuld wouldn't be able to sneak out of the keep to take Thurkill home.

"Oswuld, I found the door in Ruford's bedchamber locked," he murmured. "Do you know where the key might be?"

"Nay, I...nay," he said, crestfallen at the news. "'Twas not locked when I discovered it. Did you search the chamber?"

"A bit, but without success. The key might be in the chamber, but I suspect Ruford has it on him. Is there another way out of Norgate?"

Oswuld shook his head. "Not without being readily seen. Damn! I had it all planned. I thought I could—"

Fearing a loud outburst, Corwin put his hands on Oswuld's shoulders. "Steady, Oswuld. Do not despair yet. We will find a way."

"Before nightfall? We cannot keep Father's death secret for long, even with Lady Judith's help."

Corwin glanced at the unshuttered window on the top floor of the keep, where Thurkill lay dead. Had Judith reached Thurkill before he died or arrived after? Either way, she would be grieving.

"Where is Judith now?"

"Still in the bedchamber. I asked her to keep mum about Father, then left to find you."

"Does she know why?"

"She knows I intend to take my father home, but not how. I thought it best, for her sake, that she not know. But if there is no way out, the deception is pointless."

"We will find a way." Corwin repeated his earlier words a bit more forcefully than before.

"How?"

How, indeed? Unless they used the secret passageway, they risked discovery by too many people.

"Oswuld, where is the outside door? I saw no sign of it."

Corwin shook his head at Oswuld's directions. He'd passed by the spot twice and not seen it. "I am going to try to force the bedchamber door open from the passageway. If that doesn't work, we will try something else. If we have to, we will get the key from Ruford, somehow.''

Oswuld's brow furrowed. ''If you are discovered helping me, you will not be able to stay.''

''Nay, but that bothers me not. How trustworthy is the man who aids you with the horses? Can he hold his tongue?''

''I believe so. Why?''

Corwin braced for Oswuld's reaction. ''I am leaving with you tonight. When you ask him to prepare the horses, have him ready mine and Judith's, too.''

''Judith's?''

''She has been after me to rescue her ever since that first night. Now seems the perfect time to do so, would you not say?''

Oswuld's initial shock faded to acceptance. Then his eyes went wide. ''Good God, Corwin! Ruford will call out the entire army to search for the two of you.''

''While they search for us, you will have time to slip away.''

''Dangerous for Judith.''

''She can handle a horse and will be fine. When you are finished, meet me back in Judith's bedchamber. We have only a few hours until nightfall.''

By the time Corwin made it to the bedchamber, he was sweaty, dirty and frustrated. He'd found the outside door, bumped and stumbled his way up the dark stairway—all for naught. The door at the top that opened into Ruford's bedchamber refused to budge.

Hope for a secret, quiet slip into the night was fading along with the day. The evening meal would be served soon. Corwin tapped lightly on Judith's door and said his name softly at her request for identification. She slid the bolt and opened the door.

He stepped into the bedchamber, she closed the door— and was in his arms. Corwin knew Oswuld stood by the window, saw the body wrapped in a blanket upon the bed, but gave into the sweet glory of Judith pressed against him.

"Oswuld says we are all leaving tonight—hopefully," she said.

"Aye," he answered, breathing in the scent of her hair, wishing they were already well away from Norgate. Though he knew she could withstand it, the ride would be hard and the danger high. Would that it were over instead of just beginning.

"Any luck with the door?" Oswuld asked.

Corwin kept his arms around Judith as he looked at Oswuld, though he needn't hold tight. Judith didn't seem inclined to move anytime soon.

"Still locked. We shall need the key."

"Is Ruford in the hall?"

"I did not see him. I do not know where he is."

Oswuld pushed away from the window. "I am going down the hall and knock on his door. If he is not within, I will search for the key."

"And if he is within?"

"Then I will simply thank Ruford for his kindness in allowing father the comfort of her ladyship's bed, beg his indulgence a while longer, and come back here. Listen for footsteps on the stairs, if you will."

Corwin didn't stop Oswuld from going. They needed the key, and Oswuld needed something to do. He might even find the key.

"What if he does not find it?" Judith asked.

"Then we shall have to lure Ruford up to his room and demand it from him. I would rather not, but if we leave him tied and muzzled, we should be able to escape before anyone finds him.''

''When do you want him there?''

''The best time, I imagine, is right after the evening meal. 'Twill be dusk then.''

''All right.''

Corwin didn't like the sound of that. With hands on her cheeks, he tilted her face upward. She closed her eyes, expecting—hoping for?—a kiss. He just might give her one, but not yet. ''All right?''

''I shall lure Ruford up to his bedchamber right after the evening meal.''

That's what he'd feared she meant.

''Oh, no, you will not.''

She sighed and opened her eyes. '''Tis easiest for me to do it. I shall go down to table and send food up for you and Oswuld, telling Ruford the two of you keep vigil with Thurkill. After we have eaten, I will ask Ruford to speak privately—mayhap about the wedding he thinks he is having tomorrow.''

Corwin wound his fingers into her hair. ''There will be no wedding. And I will not have you inviting Ruford into the privacy of his own bedchamber. The man will think you mean to do more than talk.''

She smiled. ''I know. He will be so beside himself he will not guess anything is amiss. Is it not a grand plan?''

''Nay. I do not want you alone with him. Remember the stable?''

''I remember you and your horse coming to my rescue. Think you can do so again?'' Her smile faded. ''Please, Corwin. I promise to have a care, truly. 'Tis the one way I can be of help to you and Oswuld. And…and I need to leave this room for a time. I can no longer look at the bed.''

Corwin relented. Just as Oswuld needed something to do,

so did Judith. Both of them had been secluded far too long up here, both before Thurkill's death and especially after.

"All right. If Oswuld does not find the key, 'tis your duty to bring Ruford up the stairs."

Chapter Sixteen

Judith ate because her next decent meal might be days away.

Bubbling excitement over Corwin's decision to leave tonight clashed with her grief over Thurkill's passing. The war of her emotions made sitting here, remaining calm in Ruford's company, difficult.

Oswuld and Corwin should be finished with the meal she'd asked Emma to leave outside the bedchamber door. Then Corwin would make his way to Ruford's chamber and be waiting there when she arrived. Getting Ruford upstairs would be easy. Waiting until the evening shadows dimmed the hall, however, was proving a strain.

Judith glanced about the hall, at the men sitting at the long line of trestle tables that stretched down the room, and the women who bustled to serve their meals. The captains, whose names she'd been told but didn't remember, sat at the high end, closest to the dais, talking among themselves as they emptied their trenchers and cups of ale. Everything seemed so normal on an evening so abnormal.

Except Duncan hadn't yet made an appearance. His absence concerned her, not because she wanted to see his scowling face, but because she didn't know where he was.

Duncan had always been suspicious of Corwin and usually lurked nearby. Desertion of his self-appointed duty struck her as a bad omen. Or did her heightened tension look for trouble where none existed?

Corwin and Oswuld seemed to have the escape well planned. With the exception of one locked door, to which they would soon have the key, they foresaw no problems in leaving Norgate. Still, if Duncan didn't appear in the hall before she left, she would mention the unusual occurrence to Corwin.

Judith picked up her wine goblet and took a very small sip, mindful not to repeat her mistake of last eve.

"You have been very quiet tonight, my dear," Ruford said.

"I have much on my mind. Truly, I would welcome a diversion of some sort. Music, perhaps?"

"You are in need of a diversion from having spent too much time in seclusion with Thurkill."

Judith bristled at the reprimand, but remained composed. Within a short time she'd no longer have to placate Ruford. "'Twill be over soon."

"By the morrow?"

"Likely sooner."

"Then we can be wed on the morrow."

Judith shuddered at the thought of being wed to Ruford, at his complete lack of human decency.

"A burial and a wedding on the same day? Truly, I think the one would cast ill luck on the other."

His brow furrowed. "Then you are not so opposed to the wedding as to the timing of it?"

"I am as opposed as I have always been, but as you made evident this morning, my opposition will not matter in the end. I have decided to make the best of it, as I did while in the abbey. If one cannot have from this life what one wishes, one makes do with what one has.''

She fought to stay still as he leaned toward her. ''Very practical of you,'' he said.

''I am nothing if not practical.''

''An excellent trait in a queen and a wife. Are you saying you will be both—willingly?''

''I shall endure,'' she said, promising herself that she would most certainly endure the evening, hoping she must never set eyes on this man again.

''Endure? Sounds like a notion of the nuns, or an unhappy wife. You will enjoy your wifely duties, I can promise you.''

She might with the right man, with Corwin.

Judith glanced around the hall, measuring shadows. 'Twas time, or near enough.

''So you hinted earlier. This topic is highly improper at the table. Mayhap we should retire to someplace private to continue our discussion. Your...bedchamber, perhaps.''

Corwin sifted through the papers on Ruford's table. He tucked away the list of names he'd found earlier, along with a sheet of scribbled sums, and yet another list of supplies. Perhaps, once studied, the writings might reveal clues to the depth and breadth of the rebellion. He also took one of the rolled parchments—a map of central and northern England.

Where is she?

He'd been in the bedchamber longer than necessary, coming early to ensure he would be here when Judith arrived with Ruford. Too much time to think of how Ruford would surely react, of what might happen if he didn't have the key on him, of all that could go wrong. Of the danger to Judith.

Oswuld had assured him the horses would be saddled and packed, waiting for them in the stable. Few people would be wandering about the bailey, being inside the hall finishing their meal. Judith foresaw no problem in getting Ruford to come up to the bedchamber—and Corwin agreed, though he didn't like what Ruford would be planning on doing when he got Judith into the chamber.

Corwin opened the shutters fully, doubting Ruford would notice. The man's focus would be elsewhere, on Judith.

Finally, he heard footsteps in the passageway. Corwin drew his sword and pressed up against the wall near the door, where he wouldn't be seen until the door closed.

The latch clicked and the door opened. Judith entered the chamber and walked across the room to the window, as he'd told her to do. Ruford, following her, grabbed the edge of the door and let it swing closed behind him.

"Good eve, Ruford," Corwin said softly.

Ruford spun around, his shock quickly replaced by anger.

Before he could speak, Corwin warned, "Move or call out and I shall change my mind about letting you live."

"What are you about?"

"I have decided to grant her ladyship's request for rescue. Judith, fetch your cloak."

Smart lady that she was, Judith walked around the edge of the room so she wouldn't get close to Ruford.

"Are you all right?" Corwin asked, knowing she was, but having to make sure.

"I am fine now," she said, giving Ruford a scathing glance. "I know not if it holds import, but Duncan did not come into the hall for the evening meal." And with that, she hurried out of the room, closing the door behind her.

Ruford crossed his arms. "If you think you can use me

as a shield to get you through the hall, you are mistaken. My soldiers will have you surrounded within moments.''

''I do not need you, Ruford. Only the key you likely have hanging round your neck for the door behind the tapestry. You can either give over or I can take it. One means you continue to live, the other permanent silence.''

Ruford's face twisted with fury. ''When I am king, you will be the first I punish severely.''

''Then I have naught to worry over, for even if this rebellion had any hope of success, you would not be king. Truly, Ruford, I am amazed you thought the lords with whom you plot treason would allow you to wear the crown.''

Ruford's eyebrows rose in surprise. At his silence, Corwin continued. ''They will let you do the fighting and take the risks. When all is done, they will pat you on the head and give you some token reward—if they let you live. The most high ranking of the lords will wear the crown, not the second son of a lowland laird.''

''Judith is royal. Her rank—''

''Would not have helped you. Your allies do not know about Judith, do they? Kidnapping her was your idea, to give your claim strength. Unfortunately for you, the lady strongly objects to your villainy.''

''Whatever reward Judith offers you, I can offer you more. Wilmont and...name your price.''

Ruford would never understand personal honor and loyalty that couldn't be bought. 'Twould be a waste of breath to try to explain.

Corwin held out his hand. ''My price is already met. The key, Ruford.''

''She let you have her, did she not? All those hours she pretended to nurse Thurkill, she was beneath you.''

Fury flared hot and bright. With one step forward and a

flash of his sword, Corwin nicked Ruford's ear. Ruford clapped a hand to his head and fell to his knees.

Corwin took a long breath, amazed at his action. He'd never attacked an unarmed person in anger before, but he couldn't bring himself to feel remorse. "The next time I will take your head. The key!"

Ruford reached beneath the neck of his tunic and pulled it out. With a furious tug, he broke the ribbon and sent the key flying beneath the table.

The door's latch clicked. On the edge of his vision, Corwin watched Judith tentatively enter the chamber. A hooded, woolen cloak of deep brown covered her amber gown. Oswuld, with his blanket-wrapped bundle over his shoulder, stood behind her.

"You bitch!" Ruford spat out. "All the while you played the innocent maiden with me, you were rutting—"

Corwin put his boot to Ruford's shoulder and shoved hard. His victim toppled from his knees and sprawled on the floor. Killing Ruford would be so easy, but if Corwin committed murder outright, he'd be no better man than the villain he slew.

He reined in his temper. "Judith, the door is behind the tapestry in the far corner. The key is under the table. Try the lock. Oswuld, let us tie and silence this wretch before he gives me more cause to run him through."

As Oswuld gently laid his father's body on the bed, Judith found the key, beginning to understand what Ruford had accused her of that had sent Corwin into a rage.

"I will hunt you all down," Ruford threatened. "If it takes me the rest of my life, I will—"

Judith shuddered at the confidence in his voice, grateful Corwin silenced further threats with a towel. Her hands shook as she pushed aside the tapestry and fumbled with the key. Freedom lay just beyond the door. The thought steadied her hand, and the lock snicked open.

"It worked," she said, and opened the door to an un-lighted passageway. "We will need a candle or torch."

"No time," Corwin said. "Oswuld, go ahead of Judith. I shall finish trussing our goose and be right behind you."

Judith peered down the dark, narrow passageway, seeing not freedom but terror. If one of them should misstep…

Oswuld joined her behind the tapestry. "Come carefully, my lady. The stairs are but a few feet ahead and steep. Hold on to the walls for balance."

She took his advice and followed Oswuld into the abyss. She'd taken two stairs downward when Corwin closed the door behind him, snuffing out what little light had come from the room above. 'Twas like being suddenly blinded in a room with no air.

"Corwin?" His name almost caught in her throat.

"I am right behind you, Judith," he said, his voice sooth-ing and reassuring. "The stairs bend to your right. Listen for Oswuld's steps. Take one at a time. You do fine."

One stair at a time. Judith set her resolve and moved her foot. One stair. Another. Corwin followed close behind, not more than two steps away. A bend to the right. Ever down-ward.

"There, see the light at the bottom from under the door?" Corwin asked. "Only a little way now and we will be out. Have a care on the last step. 'Tis steeper than the others."

"Hold a moment, my lady," Oswuld said, then opened the door a crack.

Light, blessed light. She took the last few stairs with haste. So did Corwin. He brushed past her to open the door farther and peer out.

"Seems peaceful enough," he said. "Wait here while I fetch the horses."

She wasn't waiting anywhere. "I will help. 'Twill go faster if we both go."

"Judith," he said.

She waved away the argument he was about to give her. "I know. 'Tis dangerous. I am coming with you anyway. We waste light. Let us go."

He studied her for a moment, then told Oswuld, "We will be right back."

Judith kept up with the brisk pace Corwin set, glancing around the bailey. She saw only two people, both near the keep's stairway. No one walked the earthworks.

"No guards?" she said.

"Ruford does not fear an attack, so sets no guard. I might feel confident, too, with an army camped outside my front steps."

They entered the stable without mishap. Judith lifted her skirt and fairly ran toward her mare. She stopped abruptly when Duncan came out of one of the stalls, his sword in his hand.

"In a hurry, Princess?"

Corwin answered for her. "Aye, she is. Let her pass," he said, his words accompanied by the slide of his sword from its scabbard.

"I went through too much trouble to fetch her to let her go," Duncan said. "She stays."

"Move aside, Judith," Corwin said.

She slipped into the stall with Oswuld's horse, knowing what would happen next, confident Corwin would make short work of disarming Duncan. Still, Duncan's smile unnerved her.

"You will not find me an easy opponent this time," he

said. "I watched you with Oswuld. You teach well, and I learn quickly."

Duncan made good on his statement. This time he didn't lunge at Corwin, but attacked with more finesse. Their blades clashed, steel ringing upon steel in a burst of swift strokes, Corwin taking the defense, no discernible expression on his face. She wished he would just end the thing, do one of those awe-inspiring moves she'd witnessed, and send Duncan's sword flying so they could leave.

But he didn't, and the longer the two fought, the more she realized something was very wrong with Corwin. He held his own, but that was all. Then he grimaced, clutched his stomach and staggered back a step. He regained his footing, but lost all advantage.

Had he been wounded? Even as she wondered how it could have happened, she looked about for a weapon. There wasn't one, and even had there been, she wouldn't know the first thing about how to wield it. She'd get herself killed, and maybe Corwin, if she tried to interfere.

But there was one who could interfere.

Judith slid slowly down the row of stalls to Corwin's destrier.

The huge warhorse was nervous, his muscles twitching with each clash of steel. Being very careful of his rear hooves, she made a warning, shushing noise, then eased in beside him. Mercy, if he moved at all, the mere bulk of him would crush her against the side of the stall. She ran her hand over his hide as she eased forward. He tossed his head, but held still.

"All right, you big beast," she whispered, reaching for the bridle that bound him to the stall. "Let us see how well you can protect your master."

With the bridle untied, the destrier needed little urging to back out of the stall. Once out, he turned toward the sound of battle. He snorted and pawed at the dirt, but held his ground.

"Shoo. Go. Do something!" she urged the horse, while peering around the edge of the stall. Corwin still took the defensive, losing ground.

She screamed when Corwin yelled, dropped to the ground and rolled. The horse echoed her scream, then charged. Duncan had only time to turn and face death with wide-eyed horror before being tossed into the air, flying high before returning to earth with a heavy thud. The destrier reared, hooves high off the ground. Judith turned away, unable to watch the destructive power of the weapon she'd wielded.

Then there was silence. She leaned against the side of the stall, her eyes closed, her stomach in a tangle, fighting tears of anger and fear and sorrow. She couldn't let go now. They had yet to make good their escape. If Corwin was able.

Judith heard him coming and opened her eyes as he cradled her cheeks in his hands.

"I do not know whether to thank you or give you a severe tongue-lashing. He could have as easily killed you as Duncan."

She didn't trust her voice, so she whispered, "I knew not what else to do. Are you wounded?"

He answered her fear with chagrin. "Nay, I am fine now. The pain is gone."

"What happened?"

"Truth to tell, I am not completely sure. In her letters, has Ardith ever mentioned anything...unusual about our being twins?"

The completely unexpected change of subject caught Judith off guard. How could one event possibly have anything to do with the other? "Beyond her belief the two of you are closer than other siblings might be, nay, not really."

"Then explanations are best left for later. Come, let us get the horses and leave before we lose the light."

The sun had set hours ago, giving over to pale moonlight. Judith guided her mare among the trees, keeping close to the horse that bore Thurkill. Oswuld led the way; Corwin followed behind her, listening for pursuers. There had been none so far.

They broke out of the woodland onto a road, and Judith braced for what she hoped would be the last nerve-rending upheaval tonight—saying farewell to Oswuld. Corwin rode up beside her as Oswuld turned to face them.

"This is where I leave you," he said, then glanced south. "This road will take you into Durham, and beyond."

"Where do you go?" she asked.

"First to Sunderland. We buried my mother there when I was a child. Hopefully, I can lay Father to rest beside her. From there?" He shrugged and grinned. "I suppose that will depend on whether or not Ruford yet seeks my hide."

Corwin grinned back. "You need not worry too much over Ruford. I assure you, he is making plans to seek my hide first."

"Probably. Have a care he does not find you." Oswuld then turned to Judith. "It has been a privilege, my lady. You have a care, too."

"And you," she managed to answer. "I hate parting, not knowing whether you will be safe."

"All will work out, my lady. And if you should ever need me, ask after me at White Swan Inn, south of Coventry. My brother will know where to find me."

Corwin reached out and grasped Oswuld's hand. "Should you ever need help, or find yourself in need of a living, go to Bury Saint Edmunds. Most anyone there can direct you to Wilmont, or Lenvil.''

"I may have to take you up on that offer, my lord. Fare thee well," he said, then turned his horse north, bearing his father's body behind him.

Corwin turned south. Judith followed.

"I had thought to make Durham tonight," he said. "But if you are as bone weary as I, what say we find a decent spot to halt and lay our heads until sunrise?"

Not only bone weary but nerve wrought, she welcomed the suggestion. "Oh, please, aye."

Corwin led her back into the woodland, and stopped at a spot not far off the road. They tied the horses to a low tree branch. As they pulled off the saddles, Judith glanced over at Corwin. He showed no sign of weakness, or of being in pain.

"What happened to you in the stable?" she asked.

Corwin carried his saddle to the edge of a patch of long grass, wondering how much to tell Judith. Warnings for silence remembered from his childhood urged caution.

He took Judith's saddle from her hands and placed it within the nest of grass. He wanted her close, but not too close. Of course, given what he was about to tell her, she might put further distance between them. Would Judith turn from him in horror, or try to understand, as Gerard had for Ardith's sake?

"When Ardith and I were children, we discovered we shared a rare accord with each other. In times of great danger, or great pain, a…link between us flares." Though he could give many examples, some of which he was far from proud of, he gave the easiest to understand. "For instance, when we were children, I fell out of a large tree. Ardith was not with me, but knew I had fallen and broken my arm. She felt the pain of it."

Judith looked at him quizzically, then asked, "She *felt* your pain?"

"Aye. The same is also true when Ardith is in great pain. I feel it, as I did today."

"You are saying that, in the stable—"

"Ardith could not have chosen a worse time to give birth."

Judith's face went blank, then her eyes went wide, her mouth opening in a silent intake of breath. "Oh, my."

"Now, before you get the wrong idea—nay, I do not know what giving birth feels like. 'Twas more an awareness of something amiss, then a shot of pain." He ran a hand through his hair. "Unfortunately, I thought myself too far away from her to feel anything, and it took me by surprise. The shock threw me back to when her firstborn arrived. She was at Wilmont, I at Lenvil, yet I spent an hour unable to do much but sit. This time, it caught me short and hard in the middle of a sword fight."

"You are both—all right."

"I believe so," he said, hoping Ardith was fine. "I had planned to go to London straightaway, but if you have no objection, I think we will stop at Wilmont first. I need to check on Ardith, and talk to Gerard before facing Henry."

"I have no objection." She rubbed her face with her hands. "Truly, a visit with Ardith might be most welcome."

Judith looked ready to fall over. She'd been through much today.

"I am rather proud of you, you know."

She managed a smile. "I thought you were still angry with me for loosing your horse."

He shook his head. "You probably saved my life, though I admit you scared me when you risked your own."

"You risked yours for me."

"'Twas a duty I took on when I set out on this venture. I asked you to go along with it, vowing no harm would come to you. I keep my vows."

She took a deep breath and looked away. "Of course, your duty comes before all, does it not?"

It should, but right now duty seemed a lonely thing.

"I vowed to protect the Canmore heiress. But it is Judith—a woman rare and precious—for whom I would give all without a fight should she ask the sacrifice of me."

He hadn't meant to start her tears flowing, truly had no idea for which reason she cried—she had several. Faced with her tears, he couldn't do anything else but take her in his arms until the sobs subsided.

Longing, deep and intense, washed through him like an ocean wave, threatening to pull him under. He couldn't succumb. Judith was far too upset, too vulnerable. Even knowing it, he wanted to kiss her tears away, take her to another place where no pain existed, only ecstasy. Duty battled with desire. His wish to comfort argued with selfish need.

"I truly hate your chain mail," she said. "You keep yourself encased in cold metal."

"Right now you should be thankful for it. 'Tis all that keeps you safe from me."

"What if I do not wish to be safe from you?"

"Judith—"

She put her fingertips to his mouth. "I know of every reason you are about to give me for holding to duty. You have yours, and I mine. Nothing will change that. But Corwin, from now until we reach Wilmont, could we not forget?"

Her eyes had dried. Her words, delivered in a steady voice, reverberated through him, strumming cords of desire already tightly strung. Corwin struggled to save them both from sure disaster.

"There will be regrets," he said.

"Not on my part. I love you, Corwin. If all I can have of you is a few days, then I want all of it."

Judith loves me. His heart rejoiced even as it broke.

Corwin lost the battle. "Two days, three nights, and most of it spent riding hard. 'Tis all we have."

Judith reached around his neck and began unfastening his chain mail.

Chapter Seventeen

Corwin pulled at the ties of her cloak. Judith felt it slip from her shoulders, but concentrated on ridding Corwin of the metal rings encasing him. Her focus wavered whenever Corwin's hands moved—down her arms, around her waist, along her ribs and near her breasts.

Frustrated at her lack of progress, she finally said, "Help me."

While he unfastened his sword and tugged off his chain mail, Judith picked up the cloak and spread it over the spot he'd chosen for their bed. When she turned back, she found he'd also made quick work of removing his gambeson and the linen sherte beneath as well.

She'd seen him stripped thus before, down to his breeches. Now as then, she marveled at the sculptured perfection of Corwin's upper body. When he reached for her, she slid into his arms and pressed against him. Her cheek to his chest, her palms to his back, Judith gave up a sigh when he closed his arms around her and squeezed tightly.

His kisses were as potent as wine. With each, she became ever more aware of the brush of his soft beard against her chin. Of the cool breeze wafting across her skin as he removed her gown, then her shift. He eased her down on the cloak, then knelt near her feet.

He picked up her foot and slowly removed her boot and short hose, while his gaze traveled the length of her. She grew warm where his gaze paused—on her breasts, at the juncture of her thighs. She squirmed at the intensity of his perusal, hungry and dangerous, but also rather liked the thrill of his eyes on her—evaluating. And if she read his expression aright, appreciative.

"Well?" she asked as he removed her second boot, flushing at her unsubtle appeal for praise.

"You are lovely, Judith," he said. "From those wondrous silver eyes of yours to the tips of your toes."

Her flush deepened. He smiled as he tossed the footwear aside, then slid a hand up her calf. "On the day we met, I took one look at you and fantasized about the treasure a man might find beneath your unrevealing robe."

"Did you?" she managed to say despite her delighted shiver.

"I did, and I am happy to say my fantasies are well met—nay, exceeded. A Greek goddess come to earth in human form."

"Corwin, stop," she said, lightly protesting his overdone glorification of her attributes.

"I fear I cannot, my lady," he said, shifting to remove his own boots. "I am compelled to utter poetic praise to thy beauty and grace."

"You have gone daft, then."

He tossed his boots next to hers.

"Mayhap I have," he said, turning serious. His azure eyes heated. "Mayhap you should put your clothes back on, wait for some other man who can give you—"

"Nay!" she said, rising to face him. "As you once noticed me, so I noticed you. I, too, suffered fantasies." Judith ran a finger along his prominent collarbone. "My nighttime visions of you fell short. You are magnificent to look upon. I want no other man, Corwin. Only you. All of you."

She leaned forward for a kiss. He granted her wish thoroughly, then pulled her into his arms and onto his lap. His hands roamed. Judith leaned into the caresses and kisses. Her own hands weren't still. She touched him where she could reach, and basked in a moment of triumph when his muscles twitched beneath her fingertips. 'Twas a heady revelation—that her touch affected him as his did her.

He fell backward, down onto the cloak, taking her with him. He tugged the tie from her braid to free her hair, separating the long strands with his fingers.

"There, one of my fantasies come true," he said.

"Have you others?"

"Oh, aye."

"Show me."

He rolled her over, leaned above her and assaulted her senses. This was what she'd yearned for—Corwin's loving. She thrilled to each arousing caress, thought she might melt when those caresses became increasingly intimate.

Once more Corwin drew away from her. He shucked his breeches, revealing the whole imposing length of him, laying open to her view the truly magnificent physical proof of his male need.

Her body responded with a shocking flash of raw hunger, an urgent desire to mate.

Corwin sat still, allowing Judith to look her fill. He knew he would be her first, and wanted to go slowly. But she responded to him with such eagerness that his resolve had begun to wane. Now, she stared at his arousal as though ready to pounce on it. Instead, her delicate hand reached out to touch him, gently but firmly, caressing him along the sensitive underside. Ache and longing became pain.

Control all but vanished. Her innocent exploration fired him from raw steel to tempered blade.

He wanted to dive into her, to lose himself within the softness of Judith's sweet body. Perversely, he wanted a hard and fast coupling, but one that lasted the whole night long.

He wouldn't last that long, not in the state he was in. A few strokes and he'd be gone. So Judith had to be ready for him. He pressed his hand to the juncture of her thighs. She hissed and rose up. Hot and wet, she offered him a gift no man could refuse, least of all the man she claimed to love.

No woman had ever told him she loved him, not even in the throes of passion. In truth, there had never been another woman he'd wanted to hear words of love from, and Corwin hadn't realized how badly he'd wanted them from Judith until she'd said them.

He covered her, nuzzling in the valley of her breasts, giving himself—and her—a bit more time. Too, he wanted to be sure there would be no surprises on her part.

"Judith, do you know what we are about to do?"

She ran her fingers through his hair. "Only that you will join with me and we will be one. I assume it will be as pleasurable as the rest."

He dearly hoped so. "There may be some pain, but I will ease it, I swear to you."

"Then I shall not worry, for you always keep your vows."

Not always. He broke one tonight—having more than touched the woman he swore to protect, even from himself. He was about to bury himself deep within Judith and take her virginity, and couldn't come up with a dram of remorse.

Corwin rolled off of her and propped himself up on an arm, and Judith once more admired the power of the man.

Sheer male animal in the guise of Corwin of Lenvil. Fierce knight and tender lover. Her lover.

He put his hand between her thighs. "Spread your legs for me, love," he said softly.

Whatever Corwin wanted her to do, Judith swore she would, for she could do nothing else. Her body screamed for his, for the completion of an act that would make her a woman in every way. Corwin's woman.

She closed her eyes as he touched her again in that place wet and aching, waiting for him. He caressed her until she thought she might die from the pleasure of it. Then his hand came away, and he rose above her. He gripped her hips, and ever so slowly slid the tip of his male sword into her female sheath—then plunged to the hilt. Only on the edge of awareness did she feel a brief shot of pain. Her body convulsed upward, meeting his, feeling full and alive and on the verge of shattering.

The deed done, Corwin lowered himself to his elbows and kissed Judith's face and neck until she relaxed somewhat. Only her short-lived grimace had confirmed her pain. From now on, for as long as he could manage, he would give her only pleasure.

With slow, strong strokes he loved her. He held his own need at tight rein, ensuring Judith's pleasure came first and with splendor. 'Twas not easy.

She clutched his shoulders and breathed in soft little pants, driving him wild. Her face twisted with the sweet agony of a woman about to come apart, feeding his need for release. And still he hung on, thrusting her ever upward—and then over.

She reached ecstasy with a gasp of surprise, and then a long, heartfelt moan of pleasure. Not a moment too soon. He lay atop her, his body pounding with a fierce release, his heart and soul soaring in perfect satisfaction.

Her silver eyes opened, sparkling. "I did not know," she said softly.

Nor did I. Not like this. Not with such mind-numbing awe or so complete a physical drain. Moving seemed impossible, but move he must to allow her to breathe. Unwilling to separate from her, when he rolled to his back he took her with him.

She snuggled atop him and nuzzled her face into his neck. Content, or so he thought.

"Can we do it again?" she whispered.

To his amazement, his body answered instantly that they could. So they did. With Judith atop. Harder and faster. With no less glorious results.

She slept afterward, curled into his side, using his shoulder as her pillow.

Corwin lay awake, listening to the night sounds, wanting badly to hold back the dawn. It would come, as would the days after. Two days, two more nights. Not enough time. He craved more—a lifetime. One could not cram an entire lifetime into the hours left until they reached Wilmont.

He kissed Judith's forehead, making her the silent vow he'd made to himself amid the bouts of mindless passion, and meant no less now.

If there were some way for them to be together, to wed and build a life together, he would find it—no matter who he must placate or defy. Judith was his, and he wouldn't give her up without one hell of a fight.

Judith had always wanted to visit Wilmont, to see the castle where Ardith lived so happily with Gerard, and get to know the boys mentioned so frequently in her newsy letters. Nearing Wilmont's gate, Judith wished she were as far away from the place as she could get. But knowing Corwin wouldn't go with her, she rode on.

The days had been long and hard, riding as fast and far as the horses could bear. The nights had fled by, spent loving and sleeping curled in each other's embrace. Each dawn meant the passing of another night together, and even so, Corwin had been up and about at the break of each, readying the horses and cajoling her into rising. This dawn, their very last, had been no exception.

Corwin was in a hurry to reach Wilmont. She knew his reasons. They'd talked more about his unusual link with his sister, one Judith didn't understand fully. But she acknowledged his need to see Ardith and her new child. And there was still the rebellion to deal with. Corwin felt sure Gerard would not only want to hear about it, but might know what to make of information Corwin had stolen from Ruford's chamber.

Still, he could be a little more upset about the end of their too brief affair.

From atop Wilmont's palisade she heard a shout. A guard near the gate waved his lance, calling out, pointing down at them. Others soon joined him. From her side, Corwin laughed and then waved. A cheer went up.

"Ah, 'tis good to be back," Corwin said, and urged his horse to a faster pace. She followed him through the gate into the sprawling, busy bailey. People made way for them, smiling up at Corwin, some shouting a welcome. As they rode up to the castle's stairway, young men rushed forward to take the horses. Corwin bounded out of his saddle, then reached up to help her down. Once on her feet, Judith had little time to either look about or gain some manner of composure. Corwin grabbed her hand and rushed her up the stairs.

He pushed open the huge oak doors, and they entered the great hall of Wilmont. Judith gasped at its splendor. Columns of glimmering marble supported the high, ornate oak rafters. All manner of ancient weapons hung on the whitened stone walls, the trappings of soldiers interspersed with large, colorful banners.

Dogs lounged in the warmth of a huge hearth, where women worked with distaff and spindle. On the dais stood a table covered with pearl-white linen, presided over by several dark, high-backed chairs. Beyond the dais, hawks and falcons preened on their perches.

For all its expanse and show of wealth, 'twas still a warm, homey room, made so by Ardith—who rose from her hearth-side chair, squealed Corwin's name and came running across the room. She fairly leaped into her brother's arms. Corwin spun Ardith around once before putting her back on her feet.

"Thank God," Corwin said, relief strong in his voice. "From the force of your pain, I did not expect you to be on your feet this soon."

"Truly? 'Twas not as bad this time as last." Ardith touched the hair on his face. "A beard?"

"What think you?"

"It makes you look…changed, somehow. For the good, I think."

Ardith then turned and opened her arms. Judith stepped into her friend's hug and returned it with equal fervor.

"I am so glad to see you both," Ardith said. "We have all been so worried. Your aunt Matilda is near frantic."

"She need not have been. Corwin has kept me safe these many weeks."

Ardith sent a questioning glance Corwin's way. "Did he, now? I sense a story here."

"Aye, and a long one," Corwin said. "If you would see to Judith, I need to talk to Gerard. Upstairs?"

At her nod, he requested ale be sent up, then hurried off.

Ardith grasped Judith's hands. "You look done in.

Come, sit by the hearth. We will get you some wine and you can tell me this long story.''

She would rather put it off, let Corwin do the telling, but knowing Ardith's tenacious ways, she might as well begin. ''I shall trade you a story for a look at the new baby.''

''Done,'' Ardith said. ''Come meet Matthew.''

The door to Gerard's counting chamber stood open. Gerard sat behind a table stacked with parchments. He looked up, his eyes narrowing, as Corwin entered.

''Corwin?''

''Aye, 'tis me, and aye, I grew a beard.'' Corwin sank down into the chair opposite Gerard, wishing he'd shaved the beard to spare himself the strange looks he was getting.

''Did you find her?'' Gerard asked, diving right to the heart of the matter.

''I did. Judith Canmore is in the hall, in Ardith's care.''

''Well done, though it took you long enough. You do realize that authorities from two kingdoms are looking for both of you?''

''I suspected as much. 'Twas a constant worry that someone might actually find us.''

Before Gerard could express the surprise on his face, the ale arrived—a large bucket full to the brim with frothy brew, accompanied by two goblets. The obliging servant closed the door behind her when she left.

With goblets filled, Corwin said, ''I imagine William sent you a report on how this whole thing got started.''

''I have also heard from others. William said the last he saw you, you were riding west and had planned to return to Romsey Abbey before nightfall. I have also heard from the sheriff of Hampshire, who feared you might have fallen victim to Judith's kidnappers because you did not return to Romsey as you told him you would do.''

Corwin recognized the signs of an upcoming lecture, but didn't dodge it, wanting to hear what Gerard knew.

Gerard rummaged among the parchments on his table and came up with what he looked for. "Three days ago, this arrived. 'Tis a request for payment for a mare you borrowed but did not return. She must be coated in gold for the price de Saville asks." He tossed the paper aside, his ire rising. "It badly upset Ardith on a day she did not need upset. She had been able to brush aside the sheriff's concerns about you until this came."

Corwin voiced his sudden insight. "That is why I felt her pain so acutely. Her thoughts must have been focused on me."

"I hope it hurt."

"Oh, it did. She caught me in the midst of a sword fight. Imagine being hit in the gut with a plank while blocking a downstroke."

Gerard winced, then asked, "Where were you?"

"Norgate. We were making our escape when—"

"What the devil were you doing clear up there?"

Corwin smiled. "Saving England."

Gerard picked up his goblet and dipped it in the bucket. "I think you had best start from the beginning."

Corwin picked up the story where William had left off, telling Gerard of finding Judith's kidnappers, learning of the rebellion and deciding on a plan of action.

The story poured out as the ale went down. Gerard sat back in his chair, listening, asking few questions, looking over the papers Corwin gave him. Soon Corwin found himself back in the stable, facing Duncan.

"Oswuld was waiting for us to get the horses. Judith ran toward her mare and Duncan popped out of a stall with his sword drawn. I no more than drew mine when I felt Ardith."

Corwin checked the ale bucket. Empty.

"You managed to overcome Duncan, I gather."

"Nay. I managed to hold him at bay until Judith rescued *me*. She backed my destrier out of his stall and I used his training against Duncan. Woman could have gotten herself killed."

"You could have all died."

"But we did not. We need more ale."

Gerard tossed Ruford's papers on the table. "You need food, then sleep. I will send a fast messenger to London, to tell Matilda her niece is here, and inform Henry that I send knights and foot soldiers to Norgate. If the rebels have not all fled, mayhap we can catch a few, especially this Ruford Clark."

"The king is back from Normandy?"

"He is." Gerard smiled. "You will be happy to learn he intends to bestow a handsome reward on whoever returns Judith safely to his care. It seems Alexander of Scotland has been hard on Henry's nerves over an apparent lack of protection for a certain Canmore heiress. When these two kings find out that you have also saved England from a rebellion and Scotland from a good deal of embarrassment, I imagine the reward will grow larger. I do believe you are about to become a rich man, Corwin."

Corwin rose from his chair and tossed his goblet into the empty bucket. "I do not want their reward."

"Now I know you have had too much ale."

Corwin shook his head. "They can keep their coin or land. I want none of it."

"Corwin, that is…witless."

Corwin picked up the list of lords' names, scanned them, wishing he'd had but one more day at Norgate. "Nay, 'tis simply a matter of refusing one reward for another. You are right. Henry is spared a war for his crown. If Alexander had imprisoned Ruford instead of banishing him, the rebellion would not have had a ready Saxon noble to rally around. Both neglected to protect Judith. I can give the kings names, not only of Ruford Clark, but his captains. I wish I knew if these lords supported the rebellion or were intended victims, but mayhap that is for Henry and Alexander to ponder. Either way, I *do* deserve a reward, a hefty one.''

''You have a reward in mind. What?''

''Judith Canmore.''

Gerard's initial surprise faded to disbelief, then to deep thought. Corwin silently watched his overlord's reactions, sure only of that, in the end, he could trust Gerard.

Gerard rose from his chair. ''Corwin, Judith Canmore is—''

''Mine. She is mine, if she will have me.''

''—an heiress. A Canmore. Her royal heritage runs thick in her blood.''

''And I love her despite it. Gerard, as you love Ardith, so I love Judith. As you once risked all—Wilmont, your very life—for my sister, so I am prepared to do for Judith.''

Gerard lowered his head, then raised it again. ''The difference being that I risked all from a position of power. I hate to say this, Corwin, but you are not a Norman baron with the power to risk the king's wrath and come out unscathed.''

Corwin smiled. ''No, I am not. Which is why I am very grateful that my brother-by-marriage is a Norman baron who can help me figure out how to get what I want. I also have another Norman brother-by-marriage who is a valued advisor of the king's. What good are the two of you if you cannot help me on occasion?''

That gave Gerard pause, but he recovered quickly, and

with a wry smile. "Now I need an ale. What makes you think Judith will accept your suit?"

She loves me.

"She loves me, she says. We have done far more these past three nights than sleep."

"Oh, that complicates matters nicely." Gerard came around the table and laid a hand on Corwin's shoulder. "Corwin, be very sure it is love Judith feels and not gratitude or mere lust. If we embark on this venture, not only will your resolve be tested severely, hers will be as well. I can assure you, Henry will not give her over easily. Now, what say we see how our women fare?"

Side by side they took the stairway down into the hall. At the bottom, Gerard called out to his steward. "Walter, I need our swiftest messenger and the captain of my guard. Now."

Corwin turned toward the hearth. Two of his sisters sat there. Bronwyn, who'd come to aid Ardith during the birthing, and whose Norman husband, Kester, could be trusted for help. And Ardith, who held her firstborn, Everart, a lad of three years. At her feet a child of six, Daymon, Gerard's illegitimate son, sprawled on his belly, his chin in his hands. Gerard's mother, Ursula, worked a spindle.

All looked entranced at Judith, who was obviously telling some story—and cradling a baby in her arms.

The sight hit him square in the heart. This was what he wanted. Judith as his wife, a child or two or ten. A family. Was it possible Judith could already be with child?

The longer he looked at her, holding Ardith's child, the more he hoped the deed done. He walked toward her, wondering if it was possible to accomplish such a feat in three nights. Three bliss-filled, incredible nights. They would have one more, at the least. Tonight. In a bed, in an upstairs chamber. On the morrow they would leave for London.

Daymon got up and ran toward him. Corwin caught the boy and lifted him up. "Corwin, did you really fight four men at one time and prevail over all?"

Apparently, Judith had been telling their tale, too, and had done so in Norman French for the benefit of Gerard's mother, who understood not a word of English. The others in the small group who'd been listening to Judith understood and used both.

Corwin easily slipped into the language of the nobility. He leaned close to Daymon's ear and whispered, "Truly, only three. I had already vanquished one when the others attacked. But let us keep the secret and not ruin her ladyship's tale."

Daymon nodded. A lock of golden blond hair that matched his father's and half brother's fell into his eyes. "'Twould be rude to ruin her tale."

"That it would," Corwin said, giving the boy a hug and putting him down, only to find Bronwyn standing before him, tears in her eyes.

Unlike Ardith, who'd nearly knocked him over with a greeting, Bronwyn gave him a modest hug and quick kiss on the cheek. Also unlike Ardith, who preferred simplicity in manner and dress, upon her marriage to a wealthy Norman, Bronwyn had reveled in her life at court and newfound wealth. Corwin couldn't help but wonder at the cost of her emerald silk gown, heavily decorated with gold thread.

Though Bronwyn loved her family and truly adored her husband, Corwin knew her tears weren't for him. She wouldn't have fretted over the safety of her younger brother as deeply as Ardith had worried over her twin. He brushed away the tear that escaped her eye. "What is this?" he asked, suspicious.

"Do you know, Corwin, how affective a tale Lady Judith

tells? I suspect she embellishes, for the boy's sake. Still, she makes you sound almost...heroic.''

He leaned toward her, his eyes narrowed. ''Are you saying I cannot be heroic?''

She smiled, wide and brilliantly. ''Nay, silly. I know you have dash with a sword and a devotion to duty. 'Tis not so much the tale she tells as how she tells it. Most entertaining and moving. I am so glad you brought her here before going on to London. I can now tell everyone I heard the tale first. My thanks, little brother.''

He'd given her something to brag about at court, the reason for her gratitude. ''Happy to oblige.''

Still beaming, she turned and flounced back toward the hearth. As they followed her, Gerard rolled his eyes and shook his head. Corwin held back his laughter.

After a quick greeting to Gerard's mother, and chucking little Everart under the chin, Corwin leaned over the newest member of the family, still firmly cradled in Judith's arms.

''Who have we here?'' he said, tugging the blanket aside to get a better view.

''This is Matthew,'' Judith said, gazing down. ''Is he not the most adorable baby ever?''

Was it wistfulness he heard in her voice, or did all women grow emotional over babies? On closer inspection, he decided Judith had a point.

''Well, Ardith, you did it right this time. Brown hair. Blue eyes. He looks like us. Well done!''

Through the round of laughter, Corwin heard the sound of booted feet hurrying across the plank floor. Gerard's messenger and captain had arrived with far more haste than Ruford's men had when summoned, yanking Corwin back to the business at hand.

''Ardith, have you a chamber ready for Judith?''

Her eyes went wide with horror. "Oh, dear! I was so busy listening to her story I forgot."

Ardith made to get up, but Bronwyn pushed her back down. "You are not running away from me again. Lady Judith may have the chamber I was using until I took a pallet in the nursery. My trunks are in there, but the chamber is clean and the bed linens fresh. I will get a maid or two to show her up."

"I will do it," Corwin said. "Which chamber?"

Bronwyn's eyes narrowed. "The one you normally use when in residence. But Corwin—"

He interrupted the upcoming protest regarding propriety. "As you have heard, the lady and I have had a long journey, and we have much to discuss on how to proceed from here. When we are finished, I will send for maids."

Judith rose from her chair. "He is right, Lady Bronwyn," she said, and handed the baby over to Bronwyn's care. "Our tale is not yet finished. We have much to discuss and I would prefer to do so privately."

Bronwyn bowed her head. "As my lady wishes."

Bronwyn relented, Corwin knew, not because she wanted to, but because of Judith's royalty. Of everyone here, Bronwyn knew her place within the strict confines of the classes. His sister's quick acquiescence and deference brought home just how difficult getting his reward might be.

Provided Judith wanted it, too, and was willing to stay the course. She'd said she loved him, had taken him as her lover. But was she willing to accept the censure of two kings, give up a life of privilege, to be the wife of a not-even-noble Saxon knight?

Chapter Eighteen

Judith entered the bedchamber, noting how the same cozy feeling prevailed in this room as in the hall below. Open shutters admitted light. A huge, drapery-enclosed bed dominated the room. A small table near the bed held a basin and towel. A high-backed chair stood in the corner near a brazier.

Three enormous trunks lined the far wall. Bronwyn's trunks. Likely filled with gowns of the same splendor as the emerald silk she wore this morn. One would think Bronwyn intended to live at Wilmont forever and beyond instead of merely visiting to help Ardith with the new baby.

A precious baby. A tiny new life made more dear because he so resembled his mother, and thus Corwin.

Judith didn't need to look back to know Corwin had followed her into the chamber and closed the door. She felt him there, her awareness of him heightened by knowing he sometimes used this chamber as his own.

Judith ignored the bed as best she could while walking over to the window. The view without included the portion of the bailey where merchants' shops lined the high palisade that surrounded Wilmont. Beyond the palisade she could make out only the tops of trees from the nearby woodland.

How many times had she looked out a high window of Romsey Abbey, wishing she were free to go roam among the trees? She'd done so the morning of her kidnapping, and then convinced Sister Mary Margaret and others to escape with her.

"'Tis nearly over, is it not, our adventure?" she said, perversely wishing it wasn't.

"Almost," Corwin answered. He came to stand beside her and share the view out the window.

"What happens now?"

Corwin pointed toward Wilmont's gate, where soldiers and horses were gathering. "Gerard sends men to Norgate, to rout any of the rebels who may still be there. I have a feeling 'tis a useless venture. Ruford knows we will tell authorities of his stronghold and his purpose. I imagine the troops have moved from Norgate, if not scattered throughout the kingdom."

Judith didn't care what happened to the troops, only to the man who'd vowed to hunt them all down and take his revenge.

"And Ruford?"

Corwin shrugged a shoulder. "If he stays in England or Scotland, he will be captured eventually. Gerard also sends a messenger to London, who will inform the king that you are here and safe, and give him the information we have on the rebellion. Henry will not only increase the palace guards but send word to a number of his trusted vassals and have the seaports watched closely. What the king wants, the king usually gets, and he will want Ruford Clark with a passion."

Just as she wanted Corwin.

She'd always known this time would come. Letting Corwin go to get on with his life was the hardest thing she would ever do. He would come to London with her, for King Henry would want to question him extensively on the rebellion. There was likely a reward waiting for him to collect. He certainly deserved a reward for all he'd done. Then Corwin would leave London, and she might never see him again.

She didn't want to think about the reward Henry likely had waiting for her. Marriage, to some high-born, wealthy noble. A man who would lock her up within a strong castle and keep her there so Henry needn't worry about her anymore. Corwin had the right of it. What the king wanted, the king usually got, and Henry would marry her off where he thought it would bring him the most benefit.

"I imagine we leave here soon," she said.

"On the morn."

"We will not be alone this time."

He gave a short burst of laughter. "Nay. Gerard will provide an escort worthy of your rank, I can assure you. Nor will the earth be your bed any longer. We will spend tomorrow night at an abbey halfway between Wilmont and London. The abbot will give you the best bed to be had in the ladies' court. The day after, we will go to Westminster."

She'd rather sleep on the ground, in a patch of long grass, with Corwin beside her—loving her so thoroughly she couldn't help but fall into a contented sleep when done.

She edged closer to him, to the man she already missed with all her heart. Her ire rose against the unfairness of having to give up the one man she would ever love. What good did her royal blood do her when it made happiness impossible?

Corwin put his arm around her shoulders and continued to stare out the window. He would miss her, too, she knew, at least for a while. Until some other woman took her place in his bed, maybe even engaged his affections. Became his wife.

She shoved the future to where it belonged, beyond her ability to change. For now, *she* belonged beside Corwin, and a huge, drapery-enclosed bed stood only a few feet away. Mercy, she'd become a wanton in a short time, ready to tear the chain mail off Corwin with the slightest encouragement.

"I have given a great deal of thought to what form the king's reward will take," he said.

"Land and coin," she said immediately. "'Tis the norm. The only question is where and how much."

He nodded. "All I have is one small manor, Lenvil. The demesne is not large but serves my needs. It boasts a village and church. The people are hardworking and friendly, and pay their rents on time. 'Tis not much, but more than many have."

"Now you will have more. If one of the holdings within the reward suits you, you can make another manor your home."

He shook his head. "Lenvil will ever be my home, so long as Gerard sees fit to let me keep it. I truly do not wish for another. I have no need for the king's land or coin."

'Twas the first she'd ever heard of a man who had no wish for money or land. In wealth and property were power, and those who owned it ruled.

"What will you do with the reward then?"

"I am thinking of refusing it."

Shocked, she blurted out, "Refuse? Corwin, that is…"

The corner of his mouth quirked with amusement. "Gerard called me witless."

'Twas as good a word as any. "All right then, witless.

You deserve a reward, and must take what is offered or you insult the king.''

"Oh, I deserve a reward. So do you. I am hoping we might agree on what form the reward might take.''

Confused, she tossed up her hands. "I will have no say, nor will you. 'Tis for the king to decide.''

"What if I asked for something in particular, something I want above everything? Might he listen and consider it?''

"Mayhap, if what you ask for is within his power to grant.''

"He is the only one who can.'' Corwin ran a hand through his hair. "I know I do this badly, but I fear to...ah, hell. I have no right to ask for what I want, and at a word from you will take what Henry offers and go my way.'' He turned slightly and gripped her shoulders. "I have no place within your world. You move in circles I am only permitted to view from a respectable distance. I am not of royal blood or even noble, merely a landed knight.''

Corwin took a deep breath. Judith held hers, hardly daring to hope where his words and upset seemed to be leading.

He cupped her face in his large, warm hands and said softly, "I love you, Judith, and want you as my wife. I intend to turn down whatever reward Henry offers and ask for you. I swear, if you agree, I will fight heaven and hell and Henry to make it happen.''

Judith's heart swelled to beyond bearable. "Say it again, Corwin, just so I am sure I heard you aright.''

"I love you, Judith.''

She grabbed hold of his chain mail, tugged him down and kissed him hard. "I love you, too.''

"Be my wife.''

"Find a priest.''

He wrapped her in his arms, held her close. "Ah, my

love, if I thought for one moment that Henry would not have our heads, I would. For myself, I would risk it. But I will not endanger you or Gerard.''

If they married without Henry's permission, the king would not only punish them for doing so, but punish Gerard for allowing it. Corwin would risk himself, but no one he loved.

Corwin loves me. But love rarely played a part in royal marriages. Political alliances were considered first and above all.

''Oh, Corwin, do you think it possible? I fear to hope.''

''I wish I could give you some surety, but there is none. Many besides the king will object. Right now, having done the king a great service, we are in the best position to have our petition granted. Gerard will help us, as will Bronwyn's husband, Kester. We can but ask. Much may depend upon our resolve.''

She smiled up at him. ''I can be quite stubborn when I set my mind to it. Only talk to Abbess Christina. She and I had some mighty rows over my refusal to take vows.''

''This will be different. We will face the court's censure as well as the king's disapproval. Standing firm may be harder than either of us imagines.''

Judith stood on tiptoe and wrapped her arms around Corwin's neck. ''If the prize at the end is you, I will not only stand firm but will help in any way I can.''

''Take no undue risks,'' he said, his fingers undoing the ties of her gown.

She kissed him, encouraging him, letting his comment go unanswered. She'd already taken the biggest risk of all by falling in love, by giving her heart to Corwin.

They made love on a feather-stuffed mattress. Judith soared at Corwin's touch, thrilled to his entry and shattered at his intimate thrusts just as she had on the forest floor.

Even as the last ripples of completion wafted through her, Judith thought of the days to come. Of standing before Henry awaiting a decision on their marriage. Corwin had allies in Gerard and Kester. Their influence would count for much. But Judith knew of another who might help, one closer to the king than anyone—the only ally Judith might have. Matilda, Queen of England.

His destrier wanted to run, as though sensing the stall and food awaiting him when they reached the palace. Corwin sympathized but held the horse to a pace comfortable for the foot soldiers within the escort. With London but an hour away, he had no reason to hurry except for his impatience for an audience with King Henry.

Gerard had, indeed, provided an escort suitable for a royal heiress. A mixture of knights and foot soldiers made up a small army, designed to discourage the most daring of outlaws and to impress all who saw the company.

No one could doubt the reason for this grand display. Judith rode by his side, clad in a gown of midnight blue and shimmering silver. Judith had admired the gown, and Bronwyn promptly made a gift of it over Judith's protests. She rode her mare—now truly her own. Another gift, this time from Gerard.

She'd then stopped voicing admiration for anything, for fear Corwin's family would hear royal desire in her voice and make her another gift. Judith hadn't abused her rank. Bronwyn and Gerard both had their own reasons for giving the gifts. Still, Corwin couldn't help wishing the tactic would work with Henry.

Corwin knew he'd done nearly all he could to prepare for his meeting with the king. He and Gerard had gone over all the arguments and prepared defenses for each. He'd even shucked his chain mail at today's noon respite, in favor of a deep green dalmatic most suitable for court, though he wore his sword. Still, it all came down to his lack of rank, to a mere knight who reached high for a royal heiress.

Corwin turned at the sound of a horse coming up hard behind him, unconcerned that the rider could be anyone except one of Wilmont's knights. He knew something more was amiss than a broken-down wagon as soon as he saw the man's face, which held anger and shock.

"A group of men bear down on us. I believe they mean to attack!" he said incredulously, pointing behind and to the west.

Corwin spun his horse around. From across an open field a large dust cloud rose above the heads of perhaps twenty men, coming on hard indeed. He knew who the leader must be without seeing his face. Only one man wanted him badly enough to attack a company of highly trained Wilmont soldiers, so close to London. Ruford Clark.

Corwin shook his head at the stupidity of it even as he shouted orders for the men to form battle lines across the field.

Judith's eyes grew round as she watched the soldiers array themselves for battle. Corwin didn't want her to see the fighting, nor take the chance that by some strange twist of fate she might be hurt.

He called out to four knights. "To me," he commanded. They obeyed immediately.

Corwin chose the one he trusted above all others with Judith's care. "Alain, take lady Judith to the king at Westminster. Alert the royal guard to the presence of rebels in the area. We will protect your rear. Do not stop until she is within the palace."

"Nay," Judith cried out. "Come with me. You are not prepared for battle."

He wasn't, but he was still in command. There wasn't time to say all he wanted to, only a moment for a brief reassurance. He positioned his destrier next to her mare, facing Judith, then grasped her hand and looked deep into her eyes.

"I send you ahead as a mere precaution. You are not to worry. I will follow you shortly. Understand?"

She pursed her lips and nodded slightly, but the worry didn't leave her eyes. He lifted her hand to his lips and kissed the palm hard. "Now go. See how fast your mare can run."

With two knights ahead of Judith, and two behind, Corwin felt sure she'd be safe. He watched her flight for only a moment before turning to face Ruford and his mercenaries.

Judith rode with her heart in her throat, pulsing to the speeding rhythm of her mare and the four destriers. Corwin had said not to worry, and she hoped to heaven his remaining knights would protect their unarmored commander.

Still, she'd known without being told who led the attack on the company. Only one man would dare, the man who'd vowed to hunt them down and make them pay dearly for ruining his plan to overthrow the crown and take it for himself. Judith knew in her bones that Ruford and Corwin would exchange blows.

Holding tight to the reins of her galloping mare as the leagues to London's gates flowed by, she prayed so hard for Corwin's safety she barely noticed anything around her. Judith tried not to envision the worst, of Corwin and Ruford standing toe to toe, swords drawn—Corwin unprotected save for the skill of his sword arm. She'd watched him fight thus against Duncan and three soldiers, and took some comfort in the extent of his skill.

Still, in the heat of a battle, anything could happen.

She'd obeyed Corwin's command to flee because he'd given her no choice. He'd been right not to. While he made a stand, 'twas her duty to alert the king and royal guard. Above all, they both knew their duty—preserve the crown and the man who wore it.

So she would do her part, and while she was at it, make sure Henry understood with all certainty that 'twas Corwin of Lenvil who stood firm between the crown and Ruford Clark.

Corwin drew his sword and rode up behind a line of men ready with lances and shields, wanting Ruford to see his intended prey and head straight for him.

He looked over his company. At the ten knights beside him, most of whom could fight and command as well as he could. At the thirty foot soldiers armed with lance, sword or mace, who knew what to do with few words from a commander.

As the enemy drew closer, Corwin spotted Ruford—not leading his men, but hanging toward the rear. His disdain for the man heightened. He raised his sword and pointed it at Ruford.

"The leader rides at the rear on a black stallion," he shouted to his knights. "He is mine!"

Corwin's anger rose, feeding the anticipation of the upcoming fray. He gripped his sword tightly, the metal warming to his hand, becoming an extension of his arm. He could feel the earth shake with the pounding of horses' hooves, could smell the dust, see his attackers' faces.

Ruford's men were well within range when Corwin gave his first command. Half of the lancers stood and, with deadly accuracy, loosed their weapons. Four horses went down, causing the attacking company to falter and separate. Corwin could hear Ruford shouting commands, urging his troops into a head-on attack.

Corwin unleashed the remaining lances and ordered those men to the rear. Again, Ruford's men suffered, spreading out farther, yet on they came. Corwin hoped the mercenaries had been well paid and already spent the coin. Most of them would not live through the melee to come.

The attackers hit the line of swords and maces. The line gave way in several places, trapping most of the enemy between Wilmont's foot soldiers and knights. The enemy had nowhere to go but down. Corwin waved his knights into the fray, keeping Ruford in his sights, hoping no one killed the man before Corwin could get to him.

He wanted Ruford, and wanted him alive. What better gift to give Henry than the man who'd dared to covet his crown?

Corwin edged around the outside of the circle, ignoring the din of steel striking steel and men shouting—some in triumph, some in pain. Uprooted wheat flew up and into the breeze, stinging his face and obscuring his vision. Yet he held to the sight of Ruford's blond beard, not hidden by the man's conical helmet.

Ruford raised his sword, intending to hack at a foot soldier. Corwin shouted his name. Ruford's sword halted in midstroke. His head came up.

Corwin called out his challenge. "'Tis me you want, you whoreson of a traitor. Come and get me."

With London's northern gate in sight, the knight named Alain pushed his horse to a faster speed. His sword drawn and waving high above his head, Alain shouted for those milling about to clear the way. People scattered. The guards at the gates objected to his high-flown ways, but Wilmont's knights paid them no heed.

Judith had ridden through London's narrow street many times, but not at this pace. Not behind two mail-clad knights shouting at the top of their voices, brandishing swords and clearing the way. Not with people running and screaming all around her, hugging buildings to avoid being trampled under warhorses' hooves.

Judith held on to her mare and followed, hoping no one suffered a hurt, but more concerned with completing the wild ride. They fairly flew through the town, barely slowing through the turn toward the western gate. Once out of London, the knights returned their swords to their scabbards and headed for Westminster, and the group of buildings on the bank of the Thames—Westminster Hall, flanked by the palace and abbey of the same name.

Judith knew well the ways of the court. 'Twas midafternoon. If King Henry held to his usual habits, he would be in the hall, hearing petitions. Matilda might or might not be with him, depending on her mood. Judith's talk with her aunt could wait; warning the king could not.

"Alain, to the hall!" she shouted to the leading knight, and hoped he'd heard her.

Ruford dug his spurs into his horse and charged, blood lust shining in his eyes. Corwin wheeled his destrier and led Ruford away from the battle. He wanted Ruford to himself, one to one, with no one to interfere.

He didn't go far, nor did his commander's instincts desert him. Already he could hear the sounds of the melee lessening, his knights shouting orders to back off and close ranks. Those within the circle could either lay down their arms or attack again to a certain death.

Corwin turned to face his opponent, who came on as if

the devil himself nipped at his heels. Maybe some demon did, for the fire of madness burned hot and bright on Ruford's face. Corwin secured his reins, trusting his destrier to respond to the commands of his knees. He gripped his sword with both hands and braced for the blow to come.

The swords met with a resounding ring that reverberated through the air and Corwin's arms. The momentum of Ruford's horse carried him onward, sparks flying as the blades slid across each other. Corwin turned, expecting another headlong rush. But Ruford reined in and turned slowly, tearing the helmet from his head and flinging it to the side.

"'Tis over, Corwin. You have lost," he said, a feral smile spreading across his face.

Corwin gave a quick glance toward his soldiers, who even now made prisoners of the mercenaries and gathered up the wounded or dead.

"I beg to differ. Seems to me all that is left to do is capture the leader of an already defeated band."

Ruford shook his head. "Judith Canmore will not make it to the hall in time to warn the king of my intentions, if she arrives at all. Even now my allies act. The rebellion goes on as planned, though you did force us to hurry. Nay, Corwin, I am not defeated. I will wear the crown of England."

A cold chill gripped Corwin. Had he sent Judith not to safety, but into the midst of a bigger battle than the skirmish fought here? Corwin stilled the slight tremble of his hands. Ruford was lying; he had to be.

"Your rebellion is doomed, Ruford. Judith does not carry word of the rebellion to the king. A messenger sent from Wilmont has already delivered the information to Henry. He has known for some time of your treachery."

Ruford's smile slipped. "No matter. There are others who serve our cause, lords of high rank and vision—"

Corwin interrupted, hoping to deflate Ruford further. "I fear he knows about your allies, too. You should have taken better care than to leave a list of their names on your table, Ruford. Quite careless of you."

The play of emotions flickering across Ruford's face was fascinating to watch, confirming Corwin's guess about the list of names, while raising his concern for Judith. The king had been warned of the rebellion, and told that those lords on the list could be friend or foe. Henry would take precautions. But if, as Ruford suggested, those lords were at court and making a desperate play for the throne, Judith could be endangered.

Corwin had to make quick work of capturing Ruford so he could get to Westminster.

He took the offensive. With both hands wrapped around the pommel of his sword, he charged with all the speed his warhorse could muster in that short distance. Ruford brought his sword up in defense, but the force of the blow sent his sword flying and nearly unhorsed him. Corwin wheeled his destrier in a tight circle and came up on Ruford from behind. With a mighty shove, he knocked him from his mount.

Corwin dismounted and walked over to where Ruford lay facedown in the dirt, not moving. He hoped he hadn't killed the man, just knocked him senseless. Alive, Ruford would be of more use to him.

Using the toe of his boot, Corwin nudged Ruford in the ribs. With the quickness of a striking snake, Ruford rolled to his feet, brandishing a dagger, and lunged. Corwin protected his chest, but not his arm. The dagger sliced deep through silk and skin. Though a haze of rage and flaming pain, Corwin saw a gleam of triumph in Ruford's face—and denied him.

With a war cry, Corwin raised his sword, aimed for the

dagger and swept it away—along with part of the hand that held it. Ruford fell to his knees, screaming in agony. Using every measure of his willpower, Corwin backed up, knowing that if he struck again he'd kill the vermin.

Panting hard, blood oozing through the fingers he held over his wound, Corwin glanced over his shoulder. Two of his knights stood nearby, swords drawn, ready to aid their commander if he fell. Corwin didn't want to think about how close he'd come to falling.

"Pick him up and have his wound bound tight," Corwin ordered, not trusting himself to go anywhere near Ruford. "I want him to live long enough to make a gift of him to Henry."

He slid his sword into its scabbard and walked over to where the wounded were being treated, fighting lightheadedness. A foot soldier walked toward him, a strip of linen in his hands.

Corwin took his blood-covered hand from his wounded arm.

The soldier squinted at the wound. "Needs stitching."

"Wrap it. I will have it looked at in Westminster. How fare the wounded?"

"None of our own will die."

Ruford had stopped screaming, having passed out. After the villain's damaged hand was bound, Corwin ordered him tossed over his horse. With three knights as escort, Corwin headed for Westminster. Toward Judith. Praying he hadn't sent her into the midst of a nobles-led revolt against the king.

Chapter Nineteen

Upon reaching the steps of Westminster Hall, Judith ignored all decorum and swung off her mare. Her skirts held high, she sprinted up the stairs and through the hall's huge open doors.

She got no farther. Two royal guards barred her way with lances crossed between them. She was pleased to see Henry had taken the rebels' threat seriously, but was irked by the delay.

"I am Judith Canmore, niece of Queen Matilda. I must speak with King Henry. Let me pass."

The guard looked over her shoulder, at the three Wilmont knights who'd followed at her heels.

"I am Alain, knight of Wilmont. Judith is who she claims. I will vouch for her."

The guard snickered. "And who will vouch for you?"

"I will." The lances parted for the short, pleasantly featured man who came toward her. "Alain," he said, with a nod of greeting toward the knight. Then he smiled at her. "You must have come from Wilmont, my lady. You wear one of my wife's gowns."

She returned his smile, delighted she'd found this

brother-by-marriage of Corwin's so soon. "You must be Kester, then."

"I am," he said, looking once more beyond her. "Where is Corwin? I expected him to be with you."

Unsure of how much she could say in front of the palace guards, she hedged. "He was but has suffered a delay. My lord Kester, we must see the king forthwith."

"Certes," he said, then turned to the guard. "The queen is in her palace chambers. Inform her Lady Judith has arrived."

Kester offered his arm. Judith grasped it more firmly than court manners dictated. He patted her hand as he led her toward the dais at the far end of the hall.

"The king and queen have been very worried about you," he said. "Both will be pleased to see you are safe."

"I am, but Corwin is not," she said softly. "Even now he fights a band of rebels mere leagues from London's north gate."

Kester halted. Alain came up beside her.

"'Tis true," Alain said. "A mounted band of twenty."

"Is aid needed?" Kester asked.

Alain shook his head. "With Corwin in command, and given the quality and numbers of his men-at-arms and knights, I should think the encounter won by now. By your leave, my lord, I would like to return with a wagon or two to bring in the wounded."

Judith's fears for Corwin flooded back. 'Twas disconcerting, knowing she could do nothing but remain in the hall and await Corwin's arrival, praying he was unhurt.

"Let us inform Henry of this latest development, then you shall have your wagons," Kester told Alain.

Kester quickened the pace down the long length of the hall, the sound of their footsteps ringing off the marble floor up into the vaulted rafters high above. Judith glanced at the nobles scattered about the magnificent hall. Some she recognized, some not. She would have to converse with some of them later—such were the ways of the court. But for now, she focused on her purpose and on the man who stood near his throne on the raised dais.

Judith hadn't seen King Henry in years, but couldn't mistake him, even without the golden crown that banded his high forehead and sandy-colored hair. Though he was of a scholarly disposition and had a light build, Henry's power shone in his eyes and his stiff, regal bearing—and rang out through a thunderous voice when he was angered.

"Majesty," Kester called out as they neared the dais, drawing Henry's attention. "I have the honor of returning Lady Judith Canmore to your care."

Judith refrained from stating her opinion on the quality of the king's care. When Henry stepped down from the dais and held out his hand, she let go of Kester and accepted the king's gesture, dipping into a low, nearly groveling curtsy.

"Your Majesty," she said, managing a respectful tone.

"Rise, Judith. Let us have a look at the woman who has caused so much concern of late."

She heard the irritation in his voice and chose to ignore it. Needing the king's goodwill, she shouldn't point out that she'd done nothing wrong except crave an hour beyond the abbey walls.

"Your concern is appreciated, sire, but not necessary. For all the while I was gone, Corwin of Lenvil kept me safe. Even now, as he fights a rebel band beyond London's north gate, he sends me to you to keep me from harm."

Henry looked to Alain. "Are you sure they are rebels and not outlaws?" the king asked.

"A Wilmont company has not been attacked by outlaws in many a year," Alain said. "Corwin sent us on our way before I could get a good look at the attackers, but given the nature and timing of the attack, 'twould seem Lady Judith's assumption is sound.''

Henry turned his attention back to her. "Did you recognize any of them?"

Henry truly wanted to know if Ruford Clark led the band.

"They were too far away to distinguish faces. But 'twas Ruford Clark who vowed to hunt us down. I believe he found us."

"Be on your way then, Alain," Henry said. "Kester, see he has all he needs."

The men left, leaving her alone with the king.

"Judith, I must caution you to say nothing of this rebellion. Few know, and I would keep it so until all of the knaves are captured."

"As you wish, sire. Does the queen know?"

"She does. Matilda was present when the messenger arrived from Wilmont. 'Twas most distressing for her to hear of your ordeal. She is a bit put out that Corwin did not rescue you and send you back to her immediately."

Matilda might have been put out, but not Henry—not after he'd heard of the threat to his crown. And that, she supposed, was as it should be.

She laughed lightly. "There was a time when I was a bit put out with Corwin, too," she said, bringing a rare smile to Henry's face. "But then he told me what he was about, and once I decided I could trust him, his plans made sense. Ever and always, his aim has been to thwart this rebellion, to serve the kingdom and his king in the best way he knew how. Truly, my life was never in danger, but Corwin's often was, as it is today."

"Corwin is one of Wilmont's finest knights. Many a time I have watched him wield a sword, both in the practice yard and on a battlefield. I assure you, Judith, the man is well able to defend himself.''

"I, too, have witnessed his skill. Yet I worry. If Ruford Clark leads the rebels, I have no doubt he and Corwin will come to blows. Corwin wears no chain mail. I fear he may be among the wounded.''

Or dead. But she couldn't bring herself to say it aloud.

The king chuckled and patted her hand. "Set your mind at ease. Corwin will come shortly. He knows there is a reward awaiting him and he will not pass it by, wound or no wound. Here, your aunt comes. She has waited impatiently for your arrival.''

Judith knew a dismissal when she heard one. As much as she wanted to discuss Corwin's reward, that would have to wait for Corwin. 'Twas his reward he sought to change, and his place to do the asking. She'd done all she could, for now, by ensuring Henry knew of Corwin's high sense of duty.

She dipped into another curtsy, then backed away from Henry, not turning around until having to step down from the dais. With her aunt, there was no need for formality. Matilda approached her with arms open.

Judith felt like a peacock, gowned so elaborately in contrast to the queen of England. As was her habit, Matilda wore a gown of rich fabric, but little decoration. Her simple style, plain features and earnest piety had earned her the scorn of the court. The Normans' blatant disapproval of their Saxon queen, coupled with Henry's infidelity—which many delighted to taunt her with—drove her to frequent retreats at Romsey Abbey.

Yet Matilda bore it all with quiet dignity and fortitude. She took comfort in her two small children, and in Henry's respect for her intelligence. When he left the country, he asked his wife and queen to rule in his stead—not some other noble.

Matilda's hug was long and hard, too affectionate a display for out in the open in Westminster Hall. Yet Judith couldn't complain. She needed her aunt's warmth and help now more than ever.

"I had almost despaired of ever seeing you again," Matilda said. "'Twas with a gladdened heart I learned you were at Wilmont. You do look well, if a bit overdone. A gown of Lady Bronwyn's, is it not?"

Matilda was nothing if not forthright.

"Aye. I admired the gown and she gave it to me. I could hardly insult her by not wearing it."

Besides, the amber silk gown she'd worn out of Norgate had suffered considerably on the journey to Wilmont.

"We shall have to see if we can find something more... suitable. While we do, you can tell me of your ordeal."

Matilda meant to take her up to the royal chambers in the palace. Judith meant to remain in the hall.

"If you do not mind, Majesty, I should like to remain in the hall awhile longer, at least until Corwin arrives."

Matilda raised an eyebrow. "He did not accompany you?"

Judith briefly told of the morning's events, of the attack and her swift ride through London, then added, "Corwin will surely come to the hall, to report to Henry. I wish to be here when he does."

"I see. A bench then?" Matilda asked, waving to the side of the hall.

Once they were seated, the queen sighed. "I have often reproached myself for not swiftly answering your letter those many weeks ago. Had I sent someone to fetch you to court, as you asked of me, none of this would have happened.''

"Perhaps," Judith said, remembering her anger at Matilda for ignoring the request. "But then, Corwin would not have come to rescue me, and we would not have known of the rebellion, and the throne might yet be endangered. Mayhap 'twas all for the best.''

"You have endured much in the name of duty."

And would endure more in the name of love.

"'Twas not all duty, Aunt."

"Tell me."

Judith began at the beginning, on the day Thurkill, Oswuld and Duncan came upon her while picking herbs, and the eve Corwin had again burst into her life and made her miserable. While watching the door for Corwin, Judith told her aunt most everything—from the desperate moments to the nights of bliss in Corwin's arms. From the pain of watching Thurkill die, to the joy of holding Ardith's baby. Though Matilda gasped and sometimes blushed through the telling, the queen spoke only at the end, when told of Corwin's intent to refuse Henry's reward and ask for Judith's hand instead.

"Oh, my."

Matilda's expression didn't look encouraging, either.

"I love him so much," Judith said, fighting frustration both at being born to royalty and that Corwin hadn't yet appeared. "I do not want to give him up. If Henry refuses us—"

"'Tis not entirely Henry's decision," Matilda said. "Your marriage must also be approved by King Alexander. In light of all Corwin has done, both might be willing to agree."

Judith's heart lightened until Matilda continued, "However, Henry must also deal with his nobles, and from that quarter will come a hue and cry. You must realize, my dear, with your kidnapping came much speculation on what to do with you when you returned—or your dowry if you did not. Corwin asks Henry not only to give a Saxon a great deal of wealth and power, but to deprive a Norman as well.''

''What if we gave up the dowry, too? I do not think Corwin has even considered it.''

''Impossible. Your dowry goes to whomever you marry.''

''What if I am with child?''

''Few would care. Most would take you for your name and wealth alone.''

''What if I refuse?''

Matilda's expression told Judith she should know better. She did. A marriage could be forced.

Judith sank back against the wall, not yet ready to admit defeat, but unable to see a way to win. ''Vultures, all of them. They are no better than Ruford.''

''Aye, but take heart, for Corwin does have powerful allies, and many admire the man for his accomplishments alone. Him having Gerard of Wilmont's blessing will silence a few, and this latest escapade will only add to Corwin's reputation. If he were Norman, they would hail him as a true hero of the realm.''

As if the queen's words had conjured him, Corwin came through the doorway. No guards blocked his way or questioned his identity. He strode confidently up the center of the hall, followed by two knights who dragged Ruford Clark between them. She noticed the bloody bandaging on Ruford's hand, and looked for a similar one on Corwin. She saw none.

Pride and relief brought her off the bench. His smile and outstretched hand drew her into the middle of the hall. She was nearly upon him when she saw the bandage on his arm—soaked through and bloodred against his torn green dalmatic. His face was too pale for comfort.

"You are wounded," she said as she took his hand and matched his stride toward the dais.

"A dagger scratch," he said. "'Twill be fine as soon as stitched. You are all right? Alain passed us on the road, said you encountered no problem getting here."

A scratch didn't bleed so heavily or need stitches.

"Nay, none. How were you wounded?"

"Inattention. 'Twill not happen again." His smile widened, but he forced it. "Come, I have a present for the king."

He meant Ruford, of course. Henry would be well pleased. Corwin must keep to his feet for a few more minutes, then she'd get him into a bed somewhere and have his wound attended.

"Before you talk to Henry, you should know I told all to Queen Matilda. She thinks Henry may be disposed to our request, but foresees problems with the nobles."

An inarticulate sound was his only answer before they reached the dais.

Henry had watched them approach, and now glanced down at her hand clasped in Corwin's. Though Henry's eyes narrowed, Corwin made no move to let her go, and she didn't pull away. Together they bowed to the king, though Corwin's movements were shaky.

"'Tis good to see you again, Your Majesty," Corwin said.

"We believe you in need of a physician," the king observed.

Corwin let out a burst of laughter. "Aye, Majesty, I am. But once I lie down I may not get up again for a long while, so must finish my tasks first."

Henry glanced over the group gathered before him, then at the few nobles whose curiosity had got the better of them. He motioned a guard forward.

"But for these few, clear the hall."

The guard began seeing Henry's order carried out. Queen Matilda stepped up on the dais, next to her husband. Judith felt Corwin's body tremble. She ducked under his arm to support him.

"Proceed, Corwin. With haste," Henry said.

Corwin made a backward motion with his hand. "Majesty, I give you Ruford Clark, though I fear him in worse need of a physician than I. I thought you might like to let him have a glimpse of your crown before you do whatever you choose to do with him."

The knights who held Ruford laid him on the dais at the king's feet, none too gently.

Corwin continued. "I must also tell you that Ruford all but confessed that the names on the list I sent you are those of his conspirators."

"Well done, Corwin."

"I thought so, too. Deserving of a hefty reward."

Corwin's almost giddy comment brought Judith's head up. His eyes were far too bright. She touched his neck— and found his skin far too warm.

"Fever," she said. "Your reward can wait, Corwin. You need to lie down."

He shook his head, as if to clear his thoughts. "Nay. Must be done now." He peered up at Henry. "Your Majesty, I know of the reward you offered...for Judith's return. I claim it, and give it back. If it pleases you, sire, I beg you grant...a boon."

The king's confusion showed. "Did we hear aright, Corwin? You refuse the reward?"

"Not refuse, only change. You may keep your land and coin if I may have Judith. Only Judith."

Stunned, the king bellowed, "*Only* Judith? Do you know what you ask, man?"

"I ask for the woman I love. What better prize…could a man…want?" Corwin answered, then went limp.

If the two Wilmont knights hadn't stepped forward to help her, she and Corwin would have both fallen to the floor.

"The fever affects his mind," Henry commented.

Judith left Corwin to his knights' support and stepped onto the dais. She'd never approached Henry in a familial manner, but did so now, having nothing left to lose.

"'Tis truly what he wants, Uncle, as do I."

He stared at her a moment, then said, "If we grant this request of Corwin's, we will have another rebellion on our hands."

Matilda placed a hand on Henry's arm. "Perhaps not, husband. I may have a solution if you are willing to give it consideration."

Corwin woke to the sounds of a harp and a woman humming. Judith humming?

He knew he still lived. His arm and head hurt too much to wonder otherwise. As sleep left his eyes, he realized where he was—lying naked in Gerard's bed, in Wilmont's chambers in Westminster Palace. He couldn't remember getting here. Truly, the last thing he could remember was standing before Henry, leaning hard on Judith.

Had he made his request for her hand? He thought so, and had probably done so badly—just blurted the thing out. In doing so, had he lost all chance of winning Judith?

Corwin turned his head toward the window and stared at

his love. She sat on the floor in a beam of sunlight, strumming the harp in her lap.

Sunlight? He'd brought Ruford to the king not long before the evening meal. He must have slept the night away. Had Judith stayed with him? At some point, she'd changed gowns again. Bronwyn's showy silk one had given way to a simply adorned gown of sky-blue linen. One such as the queen would wear.

If Judith did become his wife, the first thing he would do was have gowns made for her, ones she could call her very own. But no matter what she wore, Judith looked lovely, as she did now. He opened his mouth to whisper her name, then changed his mind, satisfied to look his fill.

Her hair, as always, refused to remain completely confined within her braid. Soft wisps of dark brown hung forward to caress her cheeks. Dark lashes framed silver eyes that concentrated on the harp. Long, delicate fingers plucked the strings. His Greek goddess. His lover. His life.

Judith looked up and smiled at him. A smile to die for.

"Awake at last," she said.

She put the harp aside, and with graceful movements, rose from the floor. The nearer she came to the bed, the more he wanted to pull her in with him. He didn't have to pull. Judith sat on the bed and leaned down for a kiss. Luscious, though too short, it confirmed that he lived. His loins responded instantly to the mere touch of her lips.

"I began to despair of you," she scolded. "You will promise not to scare me so again."

"I shall try," he managed to answer through dry lips.

"'Tis the most I can hope for, I guess." A knock on the outer chamber door distracted her. "Ah, food. I will return anon."

While she scurried out of the bedchamber into the sitting room beyond, Corwin ignored the pain in his arm and sat up, leaning against the bed's headboard for support. His wound had been stitched and a fresh bandage applied. He remembered nothing of that, either.

When Judith returned, she retook her seat on the bed and put the platter on his lap. "Matilda has been making sure I eat." She popped a piece of bread into her mouth. "After I refused to come down for the evening meal that first night, my aunt has been sending platters up. Here," she said, feeding him cheese, "you need this more than I."

His head was still muddled, but clearing. "There was no reason for you not to eat your meal in the hall when all I did was sleep."

She huffed. "All you did was almost die. You have been near senseless with a fever for two days. How could I leave?"

"Two days?"

"And two extremely long nights. I thought…" Her voice cracked. Her expression melted from what he now knew was false cheer into distress. "I thought, for a while, I would lose you."

Corwin set the platter aside and gathered her into his arms. "I am here, love."

She let out a long sigh. He knew she cried only by the wetness on his chest. He held her close, willing to sit here forever if she needed it to regain her poise.

Forever. Lord, how much he wanted forever. To hold her, just hold her.

She turned her head slightly and wiped at her eyes, but beyond that didn't move.

"Your knights carried you up here and helped me put you to bed," she said softly. "The physician came and stitched your arm, but you never moved. Then your fever raged so high the cold cloths grew hot nearly as soon as I applied them. 'Twas near dawn this morn when your fever finally gave over.''

He kissed the top of her head. She took another long breath.

"Alain has been wonderful. He came up several times, said to tell you when you woke that your men are all cared for and anxious to see their commander recover. Matilda has visited often, as have Kester and Bronwyn."

"Bronwyn?"

"Aye. She followed us by a day. When Gerard told her that her younger brother was about to make a splash at court, she could not stay away."

"Sounds like my sister."

Judith laughed lightly. "She is unique, and quite lovable. Oh, and Kester, bless him, had the foresight to send a messenger to Wilmont to tell Ardith why her arm pained her. I sent another this morning to let her know your fever broke."

He'd have to send yet another message to Ardith, apologizing profusely for not having his chain mail on. But then, he hadn't been expecting a battle of weapons with Ruford, only a battle of wits with Henry.

Corwin heard the strength returning to Judith's voice. He almost hated to question her, but he'd lost two days he couldn't afford to lose, not if he hoped to win her.

"What of Ruford?"

"Dead. Hanged himself in a Tower cell. Several of the lords who were involved with Ruford were here at court, Henry thinks to make a concerted move. They are now in the White Tower, and troops have been sent to fetch the others." She lifted her head. "Clovis of Norgate was a conspirator, but he began to weaken in his resolve, so they killed him and made his keep Ruford's stronghold."

"Word of the rebellion is out, then?"

''Not really. Henry has taken care to keep it secret until all of the conspirators are captured.''

Corwin brushed at a tendril of her hair. ''And what of us?''

She smiled. ''Matilda was right. Henry is inclined to approve our marriage, and has sent to King Alexander for consent. Once we have it, all we need do is placate a few of the noisier Norman nobles.''

''Easier said than done.''

''Perhaps, but Matilda thinks it possible.'' She huffed. ''These Normans are an unusual lot. Do you know, some of them do not believe you are ill? They wonder if I have not locked myself in these chambers so I can have my wicked way with you whenever I wish.''

A truly sterling notion. ''Since I am no longer sick, what say we prove them right?''

''Your arm—''

''Will heal. I need you more than I need the arm.''

''The platter.''

Corwin gave it a shove off the bed. ''What else?''

With a wicked little smile, she said, ''My gown.''

With the gown, he needed her help. The spirit was willing but the arm was weak—but only the arm. He was as randy and ready as a stud stallion by the time she lay naked next to him.

Between kisses and gentle touches, he told her, ''In this very bed, Gerard and Ardith first loved.''

''Did they?'' she said a bit breathlessly. 'Twould not take long to make Judith ready, thank goodness, and she would have to do most of the work. He didn't think she'd mind.

''Aye. Gerard moved Ardith in here with him and they rarely came out. 'Twas a shock to all at court, and many speculated on what they did all day, and all night.''

Her hand drifted down to stroke and pet him to madness. "And what did they do?"

"Made love. Talked and got to know one another well. Made love. Gerard taught Ardith how to wield a dagger. Made love."

"I know how to wield a dagger."

"Then make love to me. Come atop."

Judith obeyed swiftly, coming astride him and taking him into her in one fluid motion.

"And they are now wed, and happy beyond reason," she said, tossing her head back, giving in to the motion he guided with his hands on her hips. "'Tis a good omen, is it not?"

She lost it then, melting around him.

He didn't believe in omens, only in hard work and duty, and now love. If the ecstasy on her face was an omen, however, aye, 'twas a good one.

Corwin gave himself over to his release, hoping to God Judith was right.

Chapter Twenty

"Nearly time, Judith. Are you prepared?" Matilda asked.

Judith turned from the window to face her aunt. Ever since Corwin's fever had vanished—five interminable days ago—Queen Matilda had insisted Judith reside in the ladies' solar within the royal chambers. Corwin had agreed, although reluctantly, hoping their obedience to royal dictates might aid their cause with King Henry.

So she'd gone along with it, and wished she hadn't. She'd seen little of Corwin. Their formerly long talks had been reduced to mere greetings in passageways or short visits under the watchful eyes of others—touches forbidden. 'Twas for the best, she supposed, to placate and silence a rumor-filled court. Still, she missed Corwin more than she could bear.

And Corwin missed her, too. She could see his growing impatience, hear it in his voice. If she didn't do something, and soon, Corwin would take action. He would confront the king and demand his due, and that could be disastrous.

This eve, with the aid of the queen, if all went well, the waiting would be over—with Corwin safe. Judith would finally be free to love him as she wished to—forever and without restraint.

"As prepared as I can be with shaking hands," she confessed.

"Understandable. 'Tis rare for you to perform for so lofty and large an audience." Matilda brushed a wisp of stray hair back into Judith's braid. "You must only remember to sing with your heart, and you will do well. Is all arranged with Lady Bronwyn?"

Judith smiled, thinking of Bronwyn's overjoyed eagerness to conspire with Judith and Matilda. "Aye. She is most willing to help and knows her part. She cannot wait to give Corwin his gift."

Matilda laughed lightly. "I imagine. She has been angry about Henry's stalling. We now know King Alexander will abide by Henry's decision. All of the lords who are suspected of being involved in the rebellion are locked in the White Tower. There is no longer a need for secrecy except in Henry's concern for his nobles' reaction. Between you and Bronwyn, by the end of the night, only the most petty will dare voice an objection."

"Bronwyn will not get into any trouble, will she?"

Matilda shook her head. "Nay. Henry will know who to blame, and the worst he can do to me is send me back to Romsey Abbey. A punishment I shall gladly undertake."

The nobles knew of Corwin's rescue of Judith Canmore, but nothing of the rebellion—by strict order of the king. Tonight, they would know all.

"I just hope Henry does not send *me* back to the abbey."

Matilda smiled. "Have faith, my dear. Remember that all of the men who have shared your trencher lately are prospective husbands. That should both set your resolve and calm your shaking hands."

'Twould help.

Judith grabbed the harp Matilda had gifted her with and followed the queen out of the palace and across the yard to Westminster Hall.

She made straight for the dais, bowed to King Henry, then took her chair. After giving a brief greeting to the man seated next to her, a baron, or so she thought, Judith sought out Corwin.

Near midhall, looking more handsome than ever, he hovered about the seat he would take at the trestle table that stretched down the length of the room. Upon his recovery, Corwin had trimmed his hair and shaved his beard, to better fit in with the Normans. This eve he wore a rich dalmatic of scarlet and gold. With his confident bearing and knowledge of court manners, Corwin looked more like a Norman baron than a Saxon knight.

Bronwyn was nowhere to be seen. Her husband, Kester, sitting high near the dais, knew of their plans and didn't look worried. A good sign.

Servants began streaming into the hall, bearing platters of food and flagons of wine and ale.

Her stomach churning with nervousness, Judith ate little, and did her best to converse with her supper companion. All the while, a song ran through her head—the tale of a hero of the realm that only she could tell.

When at long last the platters had been cleared from the king's table, when only flagons and goblets of wine remained, Queen Matilda leaned over to whisper to her husband. Judith reached down for her harp.

Smiling broadly, Henry stood and held his hands up for silence. ''Ladies and lords,'' Henry said in the booming voice that belied his size. ''Lady Judith has agreed to grace us with a tale.''

Sounds of approval rippled through the hall. Judith rose and moved to a chair at the side of the dais, praying her tale pleased more than the king. She must convince the nobles of the court that her knight was worthy of an heiress.

Lovely as ever. The thought flitted through Corwin's head as he watched Judith adjust the harp in her lap.

The man who'd shared her trencher this eve, the fifth man in as many days, thought so, too. His eyes had devoured Judith even as he'd eaten his meal. Corwin's fist yearned to connect with the man's leering gaze, but flattening a baron in full view of everyone would only get him arrested and tossed in a Tower cell.

Tonight, after the evening meal, his suffering would end. At Corwin's insistence, Kester had arranged an audience with King Henry. Purposely, he'd put on a dalmatic of scarlet and gold, Wilmont's colors, to remind Henry of the powerful baron Corwin served, and had prepared a retort for every objection Henry might voice.

And if Henry denied him, both his and Judith's horses were well rested and waiting in the stables. He knew of a remote manor where they could hide until Henry came around. And if Henry didn't, well, he hoped Judith didn't object to an extended visit to Italy.

Either way, from this day forward Judith would share a trencher only with him.

Every eye in the hall gazed at Judith. Silence reigned but for the sweet strains of the harp. Then Judith's voice rang out, clear and strong.

"'Tis a new tale I give you, of a hero, and a villain, and the struggle between them. A tale of honor, of duty, of love."

Judith looked at him then, gazed straight into his eyes—and smiled.

A cold shiver ran up his spine. *She wouldn't.*

Every fear Corwin had ever known paled beside the terror clenching his heart as she began her tale. Of a lady kidnapped from an abbey and the rough men who held her captive. Of the daring knight who rode to her rescue.

Corwin prayed as he'd never prayed before that she would stop there. But she went on, putting herself squarely between him and the king and the court. He didn't want to think about what punishment she might suffer for so boldly defying the king's wish for silence on the rebellion.

Corwin knew what she was doing, and he couldn't allow her to take the risk. If the silence was to be broken, then he would do it. If there was a punishment to be handed down, he would take it. But as he put his goblet aside, intending to interrupt Judith's tale, Corwin looked at the king's face and didn't move. Never had Corwin seen Henry quite so enthralled, as was the rest of the court.

With an expression of voice that was Judith's alone, she wove the threads of the tale into a beautiful tapestry—a tale of betrayal and rebellion against the crown. Of Corwin's decision not to rescue Judith, but to risk his life to save a kingdom, to protect a king.

As Judith moved through the days of the ordeal, Corwin once again stood before her and told her of his plan, and heard once more her words of trust. He relived the hard days and uneasy nights of their journey, heard his vow to keep Judith safe—and of his promise of escape, to take her to safety, to warn his king of the danger to the throne.

Once more he fought Duncan, refusing to enter the rebel stronghold blinded, yet went in without his sword, risking certain death if unmasked by the rebel leader—Ruford Clark.

She told all—of how Ruford recognized Corwin's courage and so admired his skill with a sword he agreed to grant a large reward if he'd train the rebel soldiers. Of the rebel captain who offered Corwin the rebel army, and the throne, if only he would take it. And Corwin refused, for he loved his king.

Of the night of the escape, of how he'd taken Judith from the stronghold to a place of safety. Of how he'd loved her all the night long, giving her comfort and relinquishing his heart.

Of the brief stop at Wilmont, and then the ride to London.

Of the attack on Wilmont's troops, of Corwin's wounding and yet bringing Ruford into the hall to toss at the king's feet. Of Corwin refusing the king's reward, asking instead for a desire of the heart, and collapsing into fever.

'Twas their tale she told, and yet, if he separated himself from it, 'twas also a tale for the ages.

Judith hit a resounding chord, and let it fade away.

While all around him began to stir, coming out of the enchantment Judith had cast on them, Corwin stared at Henry. The king glanced at his queen, a wry smile upon his face. Matilda merely lifted a shoulder and smiled back.

From the far reaches of the hall came a man's voice. "Lady Judith, you must finish!"

Judith smiled indulgently. "I am not at liberty to divulge the rest without the king's consent."

"You could, at the very least, add that Corwin survives!"

To the laughter of the court, Judith said, "Aye, he does survive, much to my relief and joy."

"The reward!" called another. "Surely you can tell us of the reward."

And yet another chimed, "Aye, the reward! Majesty, the man deserves his reward!"

A clamor rose, from cups banging on tables. Nobles and servants alike demanded a reward for the hero of the realm.

King Henry rose slowly from his chair, bringing an end to the noise. Corwin held his breath.

"'Tis true, Corwin of Lenvil deserves a reward, and a rich one, for no one else in this hall or without has, with only his wits and the edge of his sword, ended a bloody war before it could begin. Every one of us owes him a debt of gratitude."

Henry paused and with narrowed eyes, waved a hand at Corwin. "But as Lady Judith told you, this man, whose devotion to duty and love of his king we celebrate this eve, has spurned the land and coin offered and asked for another prize. 'Tis unusual, and rich, and within my power to grant. Shall I give it to him? Shall I give Corwin of Lenvil his heart's desire?"

The court's frenzied agreement was both immediate and ear shattering.

King Henry raised his hands for silence. "Lady Judith, finish your tale," he commanded.

Judith picked up her harp. "All of it, sire?"

"Aye. 'Tis time the court knew who among them sought to betray them."

Judith tilted her head. "And the reward?"

"'Tis also your tale, Judith. Give it the ending you wish."

Corwin closed his eyes, hardly daring to believe his ordeal had come to an end. Judith had done it—brought a court to its knees, all with a harp and a song.

He wasn't naive. He knew that on the morrow, or even later this eve, some of those nobles who'd gotten caught up in the tale and resulting frenzy would come to their senses and complain to Henry. Henry would, however, simply remind them that any objection should have been voiced earlier.

When again Corwin looked at the woman he loved beyond his own life, she'd begun to strum at the harp strings. Again she sang, of Ruford's cowardly suicide, of the seven lords now locked in the tower for aiding the ignoble Ruford's quest to wear the crown of England.

Then tears welled in the silver eyes that gazed deep into his, but her voice never faltered as, in her song, King Henry granted Corwin the desire of his heart—the hand of Lady Judith Canmore.

In the shocked silence, Corwin heard from far back in the hall the unmistakable whoosh of wings and the tinkle of bells. A peregrine falcon glided through the hall, its wingspan wider than the trestle table, trailing scarlet ribbons and golden bells. Corwin recognized it as one of Wilmont's. He'd taken a swan with it not a month ago.

The magnificent bird swooped along the length of the table. As it approached the dais, it screeched and flew sharply upward to the vaulted rafters high above, there to circle.

Before Corwin had even wondered how the bird came to be in Westminster Hall, King Henry stood up and shouted with ire. "Lady Bronwyn, what is the meaning of this?"

Corwin's head snapped to where his sister, smiling hugely, flounced forward from the far end of the hall, in one of her highly decorated gowns, a leather glove on her hand.

"A gift, sire," Bronwyn called, "from Gerard of Wilmont to Corwin of Lenvil on the occasion of his worthy vassal's betrothal to Lady Judith Canmore. Her new master has but to call the falcon to claim her."

His heart so full of joy he could hardly contain it, Corwin snatched a tidbit of venison from his trencher, then leaped up on the trestle table, thrust his arm in the air and whistled thrice.

The falcon made a steep dive for his arm. Corwin tensed for the landing, giving a brief thought to sharp talons, then decided he didn't give a damn for his garment or arm. She landed as she always did, with force and a cry of triumph. Corwin gave the falcon her tidbit and wrapped the ribbons loosely about his arm.

He leaped down, only to be hit with force again, this time from Judith. Corwin wrapped his free arm around his heart's true desire, nuzzled the silky strands of her hair and whispered in her ear.

"My dearest, sweetest love, you and I must have a talk about these tales you tell. First, however, we must thank the king."

She sighed and looked up at him. "I gather I am in for a lecture. But I cannot care, for now we *can* talk—and more."

Corwin wanted nothing more than to take Judith and the falcon and run from the hall with both. But he couldn't, not without a word to Henry. The king may have been pressed into a decision, but he didn't look unhappy about it. Indeed, Henry looked with open admiration at the falcon.

Corwin then realized why Gerard had sent the bird. Not for him, but for the king—an appeasement. Though Corwin coveted the falcon, Henry had given him Judith, and Corwin certainly didn't mind giving up one to have the other.

Besides, he knew who he could talk out of another one.

"Magnificent," Henry said.

Corwin completed a low bow, then let go of Judith and slowly unwrapped the jesses. "Magnificent, indeed," he agreed, running the back of his forefinger along the peregrine's downy chest as he had several weeks ago, pondering the unfairness of the king's Forest Laws. He still thought the law unfair, and suddenly chafed at the idea of

Henry hunting with this particular falcon. He didn't have
to give the falcon to Henry.

"Think her worthy of a perch in the royal mews, sire?"

Henry smiled. "Most worthy."

"Then I should like to make a gift of this falcon to Her
Majesty, Queen Matilda, if she will accept."

Matilda instantly rose from her chair. "Oh, certes, we
would be most pleased to accept! Bronwyn, the glove, if
you please."

Judith giggled at her aunt's delighted expression as Corwin handed over the falcon, and he knew he'd done the
right thing.

After giving Bronwyn a quick hug, Corwin led his be-
trothed—he liked the sound of the word and all it in-
ferred—out of the hall.

Judith almost had to run to keep up with him, but she
didn't care. Tonight she had wings, could fly with falcons.

Once outside, Corwin picked her up and spun her
around. She tilted her head back and laughed, so full of joy
it bubbled forth without constraint. She was both dizzy and
giddy by the time he put her down.

He held her close and asked earnestly, "By the saints,
Judith, what were you thinking? Do you know what Henry
could have done to you for such a display?"

"Aye. Matilda and I discussed it thoroughly beforehand.
As you can see, Matilda had the right of it, and you now
belong to me." She ran a hand through his already mussed
hair. "All mine, and I can hardly believe it. Tell me 'tis
true, Corwin, for I fear my head and heart deceive me."

Corwin cupped her face in his strong, gentle hands.
"'Tis true. You are all mine and I can hardly believe it."

Then he kissed her hard and long, with promise of more
to come deeply imbued within his kiss. She clutched his

dalmatic within tight fists, holding on through the storm for all she was worth.

"Judith," he whispered, "you must never, ever, take such a risk again, especially for me."

She'd expected Corwin to object, to play the protector. Truly, she didn't mind, for no one else had ever loved her enough to try before. She wouldn't let him take things too far, however.

"If not for you, then who? I love you, Corwin. No power on earth could keep me from coming to your aid if needed. Is that not what people in love do—stand by each other in times of both good and bad?"

"Aye, but—"

"Nay, no exceptions, Corwin. We are in this together, you and I. I shall make you a bargain. I will relinquish my harp when you relinquish your sword."

Corwin stared at her for a moment, then gave a long, resigned sigh. "Well, when put that way, how can I argue?"

"You cannot. Now, if we could but marry tonight, I would be the kingdom's happiest woman."

He smiled. "Now that I know we have the rest of our lives, I am willing to wait until tomorrow, or the next day."

"'Twill more likely be several days. There are invitations to be sent, oaths to be given, alliances made, papers to be signed."

"For what?"

"Our wedding, and the bestowal of my dowry."

"'Twill be interesting to see who Henry gives it to. Mayhap he can quiet some of the nobles with it."

Corwin, apparently, thought he'd received only the prize he'd asked for.

"Sorry, Corwin, but I fear your life is about to change more than you wanted it to. You see, I am an heiress, and

you are about to become a very rich man, well on your
way to owning enough land to be named a tenant-in-chief.
A baron.'' She smiled at his shock. "Would that not be
grand, a Saxon baron within England's court? The poor
Normans will not know what to do with you, especially if
you regrow your beard, which I hope you do because I
rather miss it.''

"The poor Normans? Judith, *I* will not know what to do
with me!''

Judith took Corwin's hand and led her stunned hero of
the realm across the yard toward the palace, toward an el-
egantly appointed chamber with a bolt on the door and a
soft bed.

"'Twill be alright, Corwin. I know what to do with
you.''

"I love you, Judith Canmore.''

She'd waited what seemed a lifetime to hear those words,
from the man who walked at her side—the answer to a
maiden's dream. Miracles *could* happen.

"I love you, too, Corwin of Lenvil. Do you think we
might walk a bit faster?''

* * * * *

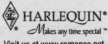

3 Stories of Holiday Romance from three bestselling Harlequin® authors

Valentine Babies

by

ANNE STUART

TARA TAYLOR QUINN

JULE McBRIDE

Goddess in Waiting by Anne Stuart
Edward walks into Marika's funky maternity shop to pick up some things for his sister. He doesn't expect to assist in the delivery of a baby and fall for outrageous Marika.

Gabe's Special Delivery by Tara Taylor Quinn
On February 14, Gabe Stone finds a living, breathing valentine on his doorstep—his daughter. Her mother has given Gabe four hours to adjust to fatherhood, resolve custody and win back his ex-wife?

My Man Valentine by Jule McBride
Everyone knows Eloise Hunter and C. D. Valentine are in love. Except Eloise and C. D. Then, one of Eloise's baby-sitting clients leaves her with a baby to mind, and C. D. swings into protector mode.

VALENTINE BABIES

On sale January 2000 at your favorite retail outlet.

HARLEQUIN®
Makes any time special ™

Visit us at www.romance.net

PHVALB

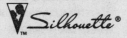

Come escape with Harlequin's new

Series Sampler

Four great full-length Harlequin novels bound together in one fabulous volume and at an unbelievable price.

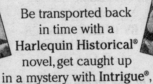

Be transported back in time with a Harlequin Historical® novel, get caught up in a mystery with Intrigue®, be tempted by a hot, sizzling romance with Harlequin Temptation®, or just enjoy a down-home all-American read with American Romance®.

You won't be able to put this collection down!

On sale February 2000 at your favorite retail outlet.

This season, make your destination
England with four exciting stories from
Harlequin Historicals

On sale in December 1999,
THE CHAMPION,
The first book of *KNIGHTS OF THE BLACK ROSE*
by **Suzanne Barclay**
(England, 1222)

BY QUEEN'S GRACE
by **Shari Anton**
(England, 1109)

On sale in January 2000,
THE GENTLEMAN THIEF
by **Deborah Simmons**
(England, 1818)

MY LADY RELUCTANT
by **Laurie Grant**
(England, 1141)

Harlequin Historicals
Have a blast in the past!

Available at your favorite retail outlet.

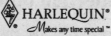

HARLEQUIN®
Makes any time special ™

Visit us at www.romance.net   HHMED10